SUZIE LOCKHART-SMITH

After spending most of her childhood in Kenya, Suzie Lockhart-Smith moved to England but still considers Africa home. She has a passion for painting and worked as an art teacher for many years. This combines with her love of the natural world to infuse her writing with colour, light and movement. She is a graduate of Bath Spa University's MA in Creative Writing, has two daughters and lives in Bristol.

The Hyenas Are Silent

Suzie Lockhart-Smith

First published in the UK by Rusty Latch, 2021

Copyright © Suzie Lockhart-Smith 2021

The right of Suzie Lockhart-Smith to be identified as the author of this work has been asserted in accordance with the Copyright, Designs and Patents Act 1988.

All rights reserved. No part of this book may be reproduced in any form without permission from the publisher, except for the quotation of brief passages in reviews.

While the author has on occasion drawn upon real places, people and events, the result is a work of fiction.

ISBN 979-8-7372-8044-4

*Dedicated to
Caroline Anne and Vik
and in memory of Tim*

Contents

Like Mother, Like Daughter *1*

Cobwebs and Kitchen Soot *10*

The Hyenas Are Silent *18*

Produce of Scotland *26*

How Long Is a Fortnight? *37*

Near the Edge *48*

Strange Things Happen in Stories *55*

Blue Toes, Sulphur Hair, Red Freckles *63*

No Colour I've Ever Seen *81*

I Am on Saturn *95*

A Chameleon Can Swallow a Person Whole *101*

Purple Rain *111*

Four Husbands *119*

An Aeroplane Screams into a Dive *135*

Rosette for a War Horse *145*

Lots of Love, Leo *153*

Stain *164*

Sister Gabriel *173*

Cologne and Stale Cigarettes *181*

Sunset in a Wristwatch *191*

Shoulder to Shoulder *205*

Lilac-Tinted Love Affair *212*

Part of the Eagle *221*

Running Dreams *230*

Alice in Gold and Light *235*

Casting Away *240*

Dappled Things *244*

Like Mother, Like Daughter

I was born drunk. The final seconds of 1947 were counting down as I entered the world in a hospital on the side of a mountain in Zomba, Nyasaland. I was an African child of midnight, perfect, pink and pickled in alcohol.

The hospital overlooked the town, which hugged the shore of the vast Lake Nyasa as though keeping watch over its fishermen who made their living there. All day the town sizzled in the sun and at night the water glittered with silver points of starlight. We didn't stay in Nyasaland long, just long enough for Edith, my mother, to sink a quantity of gin and tonic, lose a husband, and give birth to me.

Whether the mountain is as steep as I remember, or whether the town hugs the lake, is not important. I am not telling the real story of Zomba; I am telling the one that dwells in my mind, where the hospital is as white as bleached bone on a verdant mountain, the air shimmers pure and blue above it and the town crowds the lakeside and smells of charred fish. And since Nyasaland became Malawi, it is lost somewhere between dream, memory and forgotten history.

Edith was attending a party next to the lake when her labour pains started. Everybody was in various stages of inebriation. She was swaying as she looked for Wilfred, my father, among the guests, but he was nowhere to be found.

Walls of pain hit my mother on three sides, corralling me in one direction and forcing her to make a decision. Gathering up her floaty evening dress that was the colour of bronze chrysanthemums, and slipping off her sequinned shoes, she wedged herself behind the wheel of her Morris Oxford and drove to the hospital. A nurse was the only member of staff on duty. She put Edith to bed alongside a window overlooking a spread of lights like strings and clusters of strewn jewellery.

My mother's last contraction spilled me onto the bed as midnight struck and the window flared with fireworks from the town. I lay on the white sheet, my face screwed up and my eyes tight shut. Behind my eyelids I witnessed the luminous greens of the Northern Lights; I knew the whiteness of equatorial midday, the blue of cloudless afternoons, the scarlet of fresh blood and the yellow of Van Gogh's cornfields. All colours flared against a black that was as wide and deep and featureless as the void before creation.

The beginning of my world spun and whirled like a catherine wheel. I was too drunk to take my mother's breast. Edith rapidly developed an infection and a bad temper, and the pretty plump nurse, fresh from England and as sweet and green as willow fronds, was tearful. All New Year's Day she struggled to get Edith to yield milk. The two women were abandoned. The partying masses were silent and absent, lying low in a misery of hangovers. The nurse was without doctor or midwife, Edith without husband or friend. They were locked in a fractious struggle – one to do her duty and keep mother and child alive, the other protecting her septic breasts, seismic with resentment.

One day I learn that Zomba is situated on a plateau as flat and even as a cow pat. From my point of view, that's a different town. I have assembled the events of that day from bits and pieces of conversation, and the rest I have made up. I have imagined, exaggerated, omitted and lied.

It's possible that my mother had been maternal and sweet tempered after all. She had a reputation for magnetic charm but was peppery and uncooperative when frightened or among unfriendly people or circumstances. Perhaps Edith was afraid in that hospital on the mountainside – I mean, the plateau – no, it's *my* story; I'm grafted to the steepness of my early being.

It is seventeen years later. The fluorescent light hums quietly above the rows of silent pupils in the study hall. The sound of pens sliding across paper, pages turning, feet shifting under desks and throat clearing is muffled in the stuffy air. I am Tanzie, child of midnight and head prefect at a convent boarding school in Shropshire, which I have attended for the last four years. I have learned very little here except how to be a good Catholic wife and mother, how to play tennis and how to appreciate Shakespeare. Edith and my stepfather Ken have left Africa and bought a farm in north Devon. I feel settled and calm at last.

I am at the front of the class, supervising the other girls, but my nose is in a copy of *Samson Agonistes*. I am trying to memorise sections of the text for no reason other than I like it. 'O dark, dark, dark, amid the blaze of noon…' I feel an affinity with the words; I feel the darkness in the bleakness of motherless days, damp English winters, unclean menstrual blood and Catholic sin. 'A little onward lend thy guiding hand to these dark steps…' Like Samson, I have felt rage enough to bring the pillars of the portico down upon convent heads, but everything is better now that Edith is in the same country and I can phone her in the evenings.

There is shuffling and whispering at the back of the study hall. A plump girl festooned with flaxen curls is giggling and nudging her neighbour. I catch her eye and she looks down at her books. A couple of minutes later, the snickering starts up again. I am needled that she has so quickly forgotten being the recipient of one of my famous disapproving looks. I watch her. She is fluffy, pink, and luminous under the fluorescent light. She notices my eyes on her but just giggles again. Her neighbour though is trying to ignore her, now that I am focussing the full weight of my authority on that area of the hall. The others look up from their desks, waiting, interested. I descend from the platform and stride between the rows of desks. I stare down at the pale yellow coils of hair. The girl tries to hold my gaze but soon drops her head, a smile still tugging nervously at her mouth. The name on her exercise book is Vanessa Painter. She is reaching with her foot to cover a piece of paper on the floor. I pick it up.

'*Look at that Tanzie Kent, fat cow.*'

I throw the note on her desk. 'Write two hundred times, *I mustn't call Tanzie Kent*…what you called me.'

'A fat cow.'

Shocked laughter stutters round the room.

I grit my teeth. 'Yes, a fat cow.'

'But I'm going home for the weekend.'

'So?'

Next Monday morning Vanessa waylays me in the top corridor of the main building and presents me with her lines.

'Where were you born?' she says.

'None of your business.'

'Well, you don't have to tell me 'cos I already know.'

I walk off. She follows me.

'My mother says your mother was a bitch.'

I turn and look at her. She fidgets.

'You were born in Zomba, Nyasaland,' she says, nodding her head and pursing her lips as though she has just spat out something offensive.

I hate the names of my homeland in the mouth of this pink and white strawberry meringue. I maintain what I hope is a pitiless silence. Her ears, nestled in the platinum profusion of curls, turn scarlet.

'I think you're just like your mother. A bitch.' She turns and moves away quickly.

'Would you like to repeat that?' I say.

She affects not to hear me. I notice her uniform is too tight across her rump where her flesh rolls under the grey flannel of her gymslip. When my mother sent me to England I was tanned and slender but I soon grew fat too. Although I am losing weight, now that my mother has moved from Africa and I'm no longer overeating in an attempt to forget how much I miss her, I am still large and white. A stab of compassion for us both makes me blink, but I quickly adjust my attitude.

I raise my voice at the retreating figure. 'I think you said something unpleasant about my mother?'

She stops and half turns toward me.

'Yeah, I did. My mum said she was a horrible, difficult woman. My mum was the nurse when you were born.' Vanessa raises her chin at me. 'It was New Year's Eve.'

She is bold. I am silent. I am always confused when Edith is described as difficult; it's not something I experienced growing up. But perhaps I haven't noticed how contrary she can be because I've surpassed her. She has been eclipsed; she pales like the shadows falling around someone under a street light.

'How do you know that your mother was my mother's nurse?' I say.

'Because of those lines' – she indicates the paper in my hands. 'She recognised your name. She thought you were unreasonable to give me lines at the weekend. She said you must be just like your mother.'

'A bitch?'

'It was me who called her that.'

'How could you? You don't even know her. I can't believe you're so hell bent on getting more lines.'

'Anyone who upsets my mother upsets me.' Vanessa hesitates. Then she shrugs and, putting her arms behind her back, pushes her chest out, daring me.

We stand face to face in the top corridor, two big girls, one heavy and square like a bag of wet clay, the other round and light as air. I could blow her away or pop her but she sticks to me as if by static. My dark and brooding inner world needs order; she needs to provoke, and she is succeeding.

'I don't believe you about my mother.' My face is hot.

Vanessa makes a small challenging shuffle towards me. I grab a fistful of her angel curls and twist, taking care to keep my own head out of reach of her flailing arms.

'Keep still!' I hiss between clenched teeth.

She stops struggling and I hold her head back and slightly down.

'Get off me!' she says, breathing heavily. 'Wait till I tell the nuns you attacked me. You'll be in such trouble.'

'Wait till I tell the nuns you called me a bitch. You'll be on your knees with your rosary for hours.'

There is silence while I think I'm no better than the bullies I despise, but I don't know how to release the girl's hair without losing face. I notice a tear trickle down her cheek. My fingers feel stiff with the tension of my grip. Then she twists round and grabs a fistful of my hair, a movement that enables me to slew her sideways to the floor. She sits with one leg bent at the knee, flat to the ground in front of her, while the other is bent the opposite way behind her. By yanking upwards I cause her to scrabble her legs but prevent her regaining her feet by manoeuvring her from side to side.

'Pax!' she shouts.

I hesitate.

'Pax!'

She has given in first.

I let go of her hair, slowly as it's hard to uncurl my hand. She stays on the floor and a hurt sound grazes her throat.

I step back with my arm trembling and my fingers like a claw. She shows me that she has a thin tress of my hair caught in the sweat of her palm. I show her the blond curl lying in the damp creases of my fingers.

'Bloody hell!' she says, rubbing her head.

I touch my head. 'I've got a lump the size of Kilimanjaro.'

'Feel mine,' she says.

I don't want to, but I do. I pat gently. 'It's not as large as mine,' I say, though I can tell hers is much larger.

She reaches for my head and searches for the lump. 'Bloody hell,' she says.

She has no further lines to write and no rosary to say.

I go home to Devon for half term.

'Tell me about my birth, Ma.'

Edith looks up from the *Farmers Weekly* she is reading at the kitchen table. 'Your birth? It was painful. Why do you ask?'

'You had a nurse?'

'A nurse? Of course.' She frowns slightly, concentrating. 'Hard to think of her as a nurse though, she was so young.' She returns her attention to her magazine.

'You had sore tits, maybe?'

She winces and places the *Farmers Weekly* protectively on her chest, as if to ward off a hardened, swollen memory.

'What's this, Tanzie? Why does your birth and the state of my body interest you all of a sudden?'

I tell her about Vanessa Painter and her mother, now a matron at Shrewsbury Hospital.

'I was difficult, yes, but I was in pain,' Edith says. 'The nurse was *very* young, blond, pretty – and plump. She was supposed to take milk from me. It was excruciating and she was out of her depth, but I suppose my temper didn't make it easy for her. She was quite tearful, poor girl.' She pauses and unconsciously rubs her chest, crumpling the *Farmers Weekly*. 'You were born at midnight, you know?'

I pull my lips into a smile and let it widen.

Cobwebs and Kitchen Soot

Edith puts down her gin and tonic, places both hands on her chest and makes strangled sobbing noises. There are tears spreading through the creases of her face.

'You couldn't breathe,' she gasps. 'You were so badly winded.'

She has just told me the story of when I was a small child and had the breath knocked out of me.

'Hey, Ma,' I say, falling to my knees by her chair. 'It's alright! I'm here. I survived.'

She looks at me as if she were a small child. Then she gawps like the very old woman she is quickly becoming. Finally, she climbs back into the present, smiling and reaching for her drink. I return to the sofa.

The emotion has tired her out. She takes a large swig of her gin and closes her eyes. Soon, her head falls back and a small snore dovetails with the cat's purring on the padded footstool beside her. Now I could reach for my book, but I don't. Instead I rest my arm along the back of the sofa, look out at the River Wye flowing through the valley below, and think about the time I was winded.

She is like a ripe aubergine. Her skin is dark and smooth, stretched over plump flesh. She is Myayah.

We are on the top step of the veranda. She has chewed a twig and is using its splayed end to clean her teeth; I notice the inside of her mouth is raspberry pink. I attempt to climb into her lap but she blocks me with her arm. Her flesh is resistant as I try to pinch it, so I have to grip hard. Too hard. She swings round on her rump and slaps me. For a shocked moment I hold my breath, then I lean my head into her armpit and bawl until she relents. She places the twig in the corner of her mouth and uses both arms to haul me onto her knee.

'You're too big for babying!' she says, trying to squeeze her arm between us to resume her teeth cleaning.

'I want to see!' I put my hands on her mouth to lift her lip and admire her bright gums and white smile. 'Keep still! I want to see.' When I've finished looking, I wriggle until I'm leaning back against her shoulder. She holds me loosely with one arm, rocking me from side to side, while I watch a puffball cloud in the soft blue sky as it swings in and out of the veranda roof. Myayah grows tired. She pushes me off her lap and I lie on my back on the stone floor. She holds one of my bare feet absently and resumes her twig chewing.

'Hey, Ayah, time to feed the child.'

Happy has appeared at the door, flapping a tea towel. She is wearing the same outfit as Myayah – royal blue dress with white cotton scarf stretched low over the brow and tied at the nape of the neck. She is thin and tough, not loose limbed and easy going like Myayah.

'C'mon, quick, quick,' she barks as Myayah takes no notice. 'Hey, Ayah, the *bwana* will be home soon and the *toto* must be fed and bathed.'

I don't move, enjoying the feeling of my foot being held in Myayah's hand. Myayah doesn't move either. Happy looks cross and stands with her hands on her hips, the tea towel hanging at her side. Eventually Myayah removes the twig from her mouth, pockets it, spits, and gets to her feet. She gathers a fistful of my dress at the back and lifts me up like a bag, holding me away from her so I don't bump into her legs. She struggles towards the kitchen, ignoring Happy, who flicks her tea towel in irritation.

'Make the child walk,' Happy says.

Myayah ignores her again, plumps up the cushions on my chair and lifts me into it. Happy dumps in front of me a plate of two boiled eggs and soldiers with a small mound of salt and a dab of pepper on the rim. I start licking the butter off a piece of toast while Happy continues to look annoyed and Myayah stares up at the sooty cobwebs on the ceiling. Then Happy sighs and storms off back to the kitchen. Myayah smiles lazily and knocks the top off my eggs.

Afterwards I wait with Myayah in the library for Daddy to come home and I play with the little red book I have found there. It fits neatly into my hand. Pretending it's a Dinky car, I zigzag it along the parquet flooring, making *vrum vrum* noises. Myayah is looking out of the window in the same way she is always looking into the far distance or up at the cobwebs on the kitchen ceiling.

Edith comes in. 'Thank you,' she says, touching Myayah's arm. 'You may go now; the *bwana* is home. Goodnight. See you in the morning.'

Myayah smiles, strokes my head briefly and leaves. Edith lifts me up. I have my arms round her neck and a fistful of her hair in one hand while the other still clutches the little book.

Edith carries me into the hall, puts me down on the floor and exhales with a great rush of air. 'Ooof,' she says, 'you're getting too big to carry!'

Daddy comes in holding a pink gin. A few strands of my mother's hair are threaded through my fingers as I run towards him, holding out my arms. 'Daddy, Daddy!'

But he doesn't drop to his haunches with his arms spread to receive me as he usually does. Instead he sips his drink and pulls his forearm across his forehead, darkening his pale hair with sweat. He frowns. I can't see his eyes because light is glinting off his specs but I can see that his mouth is bunched up. I hold up my arms to him. I have the book in one hand while the other still trails dark strands of Edith's hair. Daddy stays standing above me; his unseen eyes make me anxious. I lower my arms.

He raises his head. 'Edith, what does the child have in her hand?'

Edith looks surprised. I hold the book towards her and she kneels and cups my hand in hers.

'Oh, it's your Masonic book. She must have found it in the library.' My mother leans close to rub noses. 'It's Daddy's book, yes, it is…' she says with a smile, expecting me to giggle, but I step away.

I hold my hands open, the book cradled like a precious offering for my father. He snatches it violently, and I move backwards, flinching as he hurls it at the library door. His pink gin follows, spiralling liquid through the air, shattering glass on the marble floor, splintering the book with crystal.

I stand as still as held breath. Daddy reaches for me. He grabs me by the back of my dress and throws me against the newel post of the staircase. I fall forwards. Edith screams. The pain spreads out with my limbs, flayed, solid, heavy and far away. I can't find any muscles to breathe. I hold my face square to the floor while broken noises of air squeezing through a tight space hum in my ears and darkness gathers before my eyes.

Gradually the thin squealing fades as my lungs suck in more air and the blackness clouding my head lightens. Edith kneels in front of me. Daddy is hanging over the newel post. Myayah comes skidding round the corner. 'Aiyeee!' she screams, sliding to her knees beside me.

Happy follows her. She hesitates a moment, trying to understand the scene, then she attacks Daddy. 'Bad man,' she breathes between punches, 'bad man!'

'Happy! Stop that silliness. Help me with the child,' Myayah tells her.

Happy drops down beside Edith. She strokes my forearm while Myayah pats my back softly and strings of my dribble pool onto the marble floor.

When I recover Myayah carries me up the stairs. Happy follows. Over Myayah's shoulder I see the little book splayed against the library door, and the image of spiralling liquid and flashing glass repeats itself in my mind and feels blinding to my eyes. I close them into the aubergine darkness of Myayah's neck.

*

Edith opens bleary eyes. She sees I'm looking at her from the sofa, where I have been watching the river flow by. 'I must have dropped off for a moment,' she says, reaching for her gin. 'How's your drink? D'you need a refill?' She drains her glass. Then she turns her head towards the pearly green of the valley, inhales and gathers her energy and concentration. 'So, I left him,' she said. 'After what he did to you.' She slams her glass down. It makes me jump, and the cat flattens her ears. Edith's fury folds into the ensuing silence and dies, and the cat resumes purring. I look out at the silver thread of river winding into the distance.

'Mama, why?'

'Why what?'

'Why did he hit me?'

The cat's purr strings moments together like the wire tracing the telegraph poles alongside the river to Ross-on-Wye. Edith lets out a great sigh and it is as though her voice has broken loose from a taut mooring. 'He was a brilliant man, but he was difficult, angry. He didn't sleep much, pacing the floor night after night.' She raises her eyes to heaven and shakes her head. 'He paced and paced, working his court cases out in his head. Then a colleague claimed he was accepting bribes to represent black people. He was under enormous pressure.'

'Do you think he was accepting bribes?'

'Ridiculous idea!' – she flaps it away. 'Wilfred wouldn't do that. Anyway, you need money to bribe a lawyer, and only white people had money. But his representing Africans brought trouble, and the stress was dreadful. The same night he hurt you and we left, he was placed under house arrest for his supposed political activities.'

'That was some night!'

'It was.' Edith inspects the bottom of her glass.

My eyes follow the river. 'What happened to Myayah?'

'Which one? You called them all "my Ayah". But I don't know what happened to any of them.'

I feel sad. I long for sanity, which is female, blue-black and plump and defiantly slow to move. I don't even know her name. She may be just someone I have imagined. Perhaps I have created her out of shadows and coloured her in with the soot from the kitchen ceiling.

'What about Happy, who used to supervise the kitchen?'

'I don't recall anybody called Happy; it sounds like an improbable name. Do you remember Government House itself?'

'My memories are of the veranda being dark stone and shabby, in contrast to the very grand front with its balustrades and white façade. The library floor was parquet. The hall had a marble floor and a grand stairwell.'

'You've remembered it pretty well. It's such a shame though that all the photographs from Nyasaland were burned when I left them too near the fire.'

'Pity.'

'Pity.'

Edith struggles to get up. She shuffles and grunts and heaves herself to her feet. The cat uncurls itself, yawns, stretches and drops off the stool to accompany her.

'Will you have another drink?'

I watch my mother rocking her bulky body side to side on slender legs, making small increments of forward movement. She is stiff. Her thick white hair, set once a week in the village, has flattened at the back where her head has rested on the chair. I listen to her. 'Now don't be a silly cat, get your head out of the fridge. Here – what's this? You'd like some liver pâté? Alright. Now be a good cat and don't get in the way.'

I look out again at the river, snaking its journey to the sea. As it meanders out of sight, I imagine that a thin rope of it disperses into the Bristol Channel and continues like an optic fibre nosing out towards the ocean. It sinks under the storm waters of the Bay of Biscay, idles through the Mediterranean, weaves in and out of the ships in the Suez Canal and the Red Sea, and races down the East coast of Africa. It surfaces at Malindi. It becomes a thought carried on the winds far away to the shores of Lake Nyasa, where it lingers alongside an old black lady cooling her feet in the shallows, holding her skirt above her knees. After a while, the woman lifts her head and faces north. A slight nod shifts her shadow on the shore. She hears a child whisper 'Myayah', and I hear it too.

The Hyenas Are Silent

Somewhere beyond the forest, hyenas laugh. I hold my breath as the sound yips and gurgles and soon my arm begins to ache from suspending my toothbrush in front of my face. I decide not to finish brushing my teeth. My mouth in the mirror is white with froth, and the low sun flooding the window fills my reflection with blood and citrus streaks. I look fearfully out at the road then snatch a flannel to wipe my mouth. The road runs along the edge of the forest and darkens with the sun sinking to the west of it, and as I look back at the mirror it drains of colour like the face of someone who is about to faint. I quickly switch on the light, and the window glass turns black. The sun has gone. I climb onto the chest of drawers to close the curtains and shut out the laughter and the darkness.

Fear makes me rush to our bedroom door, but I don't want Edith to know I'm frightened so I slow down, pretending to be calm. The lamp is on and she is sitting at the dressing table brushing her hair. I move towards her, sliding my socked feet along the polished tile floor like a slow-motion skater. I pick up her lipstick.

'Turn round, Mama. I'll do your lips.'

She shunts her chair around to face me and holds her mouth ready. I reach up to apply the bright red colour. I'm careful but I try to be quick so she doesn't tire of my attention. I fetch a tissue from the Kleenex box and hand it to her. She blots her lips, pressing the tissue between them, making a lovely kiss shape. She transfers the image of her lips often – onto my forehead, people's cheeks, and her gin and tonic glass, the lip imprint dancing with the lemon slices. I have tried to draw this fluttering dance in my sketchbook and colour it in.

I pick up the hairbrush, gather Edith's dark, heavy curls, and begin to brush with slow strokes, starting from half way down her head, which is as far as I can reach.

'Cora isn't back yet, Mama.'

'She'll be here soon, don't worry.'

'What if she isn't though?'

Edith retrieves the hairbrush and taps me lightly on the nose with it. 'She'll come,' she says, turning back to the mirror to rearrange her hair more to her liking, which is with a side parting that accentuates her cow's lick. I always want her to wear a middle parting. How the hair goes up, before it curls over, is not as pretty as it is falling closely round her face. It would be hard to object to a real lick though – if a cow happened along and slurped its tongue to create that shape in my hair, I would be thrilled.

Edith goes to my bed and unties the mosquito net. I try not to feel panicky because she hates it when I let my distress show. Since she left my father, she doesn't have any choice but to go to work. We are staying in a tiny chalet that is part of the Banda Hotel complex owned by her friend Eleanor, whom everyone refers to as just 'Memsahib', and although the rent is cheap, it still needs to be paid. Edith is employed as a flight controller, and the airport is not far from here. She says I shouldn't make a fuss when she goes on shift, but I can't understand why I'm not allowed to accompany her, and bring Cora too. We could sleep in the doorway of the air control tower. Or we could sleep in the car. Or we could all go back home and live with Daddy again, and then she wouldn't have to go to work. Because she has left Daddy, I have too, although I didn't mean to.

'Hop in,' Edith says, holding up the net. I climb in, trying not to cry as I open my arms for her embrace. Leaning in, she kisses me, leaving her lipstick thick on my face. She takes a handkerchief from her sleeve, which like all her hankies is dainty white cotton with a curly letter 'E' embroidered in the corner. She moistens a patch with spittle and begins to wipe my face. I hate it when she does this so I start to squirm and wriggle away, but I also crave her attention so I giggle while she holds me down. She laughs. Her laughter and mine blot out the sound of the hyenas in the forest. She tucks the blanket round me, and I feel secure for a moment as she folds the net under the mattress. Then she gets some hairgrips from my bedside table and pins together the large hole in the net.

'Memsahib will check on you soon, and Cora will be back in a while.' Edith switches the lamp on next to my bed, and the other one off. She checks the contents of her handbag, her car keys jangling in her hand. Then she hesitates, but I'm not sure if I should take advantage of this to try to make her stay. If I fuss, she'll probably go. I don't fuss, but she goes anyway, leaving the top half of the room's stable door slightly ajar. I hear her footsteps crunch on the gravel and fade, then the sound of the car being driven away.

The night is thick with insect noise. The hyenas are silent, and they are stalking. I can feel them close, slinking low on their bellies towards the door. Each mouth is drawn back in a red grin, glistening with silvered moonlit saliva. There's a scrabbling sound as they reach the chalet. But as the top half of the door opens outwards, maybe they won't manage a smooth leap into the room? Maybe I have time to race for the bathroom and wedge the chest of drawers against the door? But I can't move. I can't even scream. There is a scratching sound as the first one makes an assault. Two paws hook themselves over the bottom half of the door, and a black nose nudges aside the top. The paws are pale yellow! My fear turns to relief as a golden retriever struggles to haul herself up and into the room.

'Cora,' I whisper. She makes straight for my bed, claws the hairgrips away from the hole in the net and climbs through. She wriggles in greeting and pants into my face, her breath a stink of rotting carcass. I settle her under the blanket and turn my back on her. She has her nose under my hair and her breath is warm and rhythmical against my neck, which is lovely, but the smell is still disgusting. After a while I get used to it. I concentrate on watching the door every few minutes, needing to know that Memsahib will be coming to check on me, but I've never yet stayed awake long enough.

*

I know it is morning by the underwater blur of pale green that washes beneath my eyelids before I open them. The sun is just beginning to rise and its rays seep under the leafy foliage outside, staining the curtains and infusing the room with a luminous lime-green glow. The stable door is closed and my bedside light is off. Dead insects sprinkle the bedside cabinet like black pepper. Edith is asleep in her bed, and Cora is wheezing softly in her sleep.

As I slowly rouse myself, I feel delight. I lift my head and look through the dog-sized hole in the net towards Edith. Her hair, coiled in loose whirlpools, is like diesel oil lit with a phosphorous radiance.

I need a pee.

When I've finished, I glance down at the toilet bowl and see a trick of the early light has made my pee look like Rose's lime cordial. If this is the colour of my waking happiness, then pulling the chain is like flushing away morning sunlight and gladness.

I climb onto the chest of drawers to open the curtains. The eucalyptus trees of the forest, dotted with egrets as white as snow, rustle their silvery green leaves. Then I get back into bed. It's not long before Edith wakes up. The first thing she does is fetch the ashtray and pair of tweezers from the dressing table and hand them to me through the hole in the net. She then untucks the net and twists it into a knot above my head. I take off my pyjama top and turn my back to her, shunting Cora out of the way for more space.

'Here's a fat one,' she says. She applies the tweezers to the tick she has found on my back and then places the bloated grey body, gorged on my blood, in the ashtray.

'Let me see!' I plead, although I can see it already.

'That's all I can find,' she says, running her hands over my skin. My bruises aren't tender anymore so the feel of her hands is lovely.

'I'll get the ticks off Cora, Mama.' She offers me the tweezers but I shake my head, preferring to use my fingers. 'Here's one! Look, Mama, it's even bigger and fatter,' I say, holding it up.

Edith screws up her face in mock disgust and points towards the ashtray. I hold the tick above my head. 'I'll squash it,' I threaten, but Edith is already moving off to the bathroom. I show the tick to Cora, who just sniffs it politely, without enthusiasm. I throw the two ticks, fat with blood, out of the door before Edith has time to light a cigarette and burn them.

We go to the main building of the Banda Hotel for breakfast, where Cora spreads herself out under the table. There is a chair for me with cushions on it. Mwangi – tall, lean, very black, and wearing a crisp blue kanzu – approaches us. His teeth are as white as polar ice, and dimples like craters indent the sides of his startling smile.

'*Habari yako, Mwangi?*' I say, feeling the enthusiasm of greeting ripple under my skin like a remnant of early morning happiness, of sunshine not yet flushed away.

'*Mzuri, toto,*' he says. '*Na wewe?*'

'*Mzuri, asante sana,*' I grin. 'I'm fine.'

Mwangi is nice to me but is alert for instructions from my mother, who is looking away, preoccupied. She just asks for coffee; she has cigarettes and coffee for breakfast every morning. I order toast and Marmite and fruit juice.

Memsahib comes into the dining room and moves quickly to Edith's side. She plants a peck on her cheek before looking around. We are the only customers in her hotel having an early breakfast. She smiles at Mwangi, then more broadly at me. She is thin, smart and pale and smells of lavender and furniture polish.

In the corner of the room, there is a tall, bare pine tree standing in a bucket that has been covered with red crepe paper. Beside it is a large cardboard box overflowing with decorations. Edith and Memsahib are talking about Daddy, and I try to understand what they're saying. He's been arrested and sent to London for trial. He's accused of accepting a bribe to get a black person off murder.

Eventually I lose track of the content of the conversation, but if the tone of Memsahib's voice is anything to go by, she sounds fond of Daddy. 'But, Edith, you must remember he was under a lot of stress,' she says with a pleading half-cry.

Edith gazes somewhere distant, and it's as if her eyes are looking straight through everything. Her mouth goes thin as she folds her lips in and holds them between her teeth. 'You should have seen the bruises on the child's back,' she says. 'You should have seen how she was winded and couldn't breathe.' She turns to look in Memsahib's face. 'She couldn't *breathe*!'

Memsahib pours herself a coffee from the jug that Mwangi has put on the table. I use tongs to lift two lumps of sugar into her cup and pick up a teaspoon to stir it for her. I enjoy this ritual, especially tapping the spoon twice on the rim before clattering it into the saucer. I put my arms on the table and rest my chin on them, looking up into Memsahib's face. I wait for her to notice me. She smiles and then gives me some bright-green plastic scissors as a present.

'Can Mwangi and me decorate the tree?'

Memsahib and Mwangi exchange a glance. Mwangi looks around the empty dining room, shrugs, and nods. Memsahib says we may.

I like the red baubles. Mwangi likes the silver tinsel. It glistens against the high sheen of his skin as I drape it playfully around his neck. His eyes swim, reflecting the shine of the glassy decorations beginning to weigh the branches down.

My world is coloured in. Mwangi is spangled with tinsel and glitter. Edith and Memsahib drink coffee in a smoky light that is almost the faded gold of Cora's coat.

This Christmas is the red of lipstick and baubles and mirrored sunsets and a hyena's blood-soaked grin. It is the green of sunrise and eucalyptus trees and plastic scissors and the trick-of-light of my early morning pee. White gleams freshly in my toothpaste froth and in Mwangi's smile, and its brilliance flickers off the wings of egrets and glints in the sugar lumps I put in Memsahib's coffee. I see the black of night glass when I close my eyes, and the darkness of Marmite and dead insects.

Blue is Mwangi's kanzu.

Blue is a battery of yellow-rimmed bruises.

Produce of Scotland

There were two things I wanted when I was a child. One was to go to Scotland, the other was no more nights.

I was living on a farm in Kenya with Edith and my stepfather Ken. The farm was at the edge of the Rift Valley where the Kinangop Plateau stretches to the Aberdare Mountains. There was a large framed painting in our lounge of a red stag on a Scottish mountainside. It was thrilling and I used to stare at it for ages, admiring the stag's magnificent body and proud stance. When I learned to read, the writing on the bottom told me the picture was *Monarch of the Glen*, by Edwin Landseer. Another painting on the wall was of a pheasant, as proud as the stag, standing in a sea of purple heather. It wasn't signed – Edith had just taken a fancy to it in a shop in Nairobi.

We had no books in our house, but when I went to school I read stories about the clans and glens of Scotland, and they fed my imagination about that purple and green country with the spangles of light dancing on its lochs. The Scott's Porage Oats packet on the kitchen sideboard at home had a picture of a sturdy, kilt-swinging Scot with oak-solid calves supporting a torso built to inspire trust. He was the promise of health and strength. Oats were food for heroes, the sustenance of strong men who could defend us from the dark.

Nights were frightening, whether they were black, under a canopy of tiny scattered points of white light, or starless – or even moonlit. A moon deepened shadows and hid dangers, even those in my imagination, making my skin prickle with tension and my breath shudder. A Mau Mau terrorist often lurked under my window, beneath the honeysuckle bush, waiting for everyone to fall asleep before rising up to kill me, a white enemy child. I listened for their breathing, for a rustle of movement as their muscles ached and forced them to shift position. One day, I scooped out earth underneath the foliage – 'Look, Cora, I've made a lovely bed for you! This is where you will be sleeping from now on!' I tried to sound authoritative. Cora sniffed the ground and wagged her tail, and I'm sure she promised to do what I asked, but when night fell she just joined the other dogs to sleep by the kitchen door.

When I wasn't too frightened, I was cross with God. I prayed and prayed for no night time, only daylight. Even when I was old enough to know the Earth moved around the sun, I still thought that if God could command 'Let there be light' then he could let there be no darkness ever.

Although I was sure that the Mau Mau pursued their fight for freedom during the day as well as the night, I wasn't afraid during daylight hours. The Mau Mau might move with stealth, glisteningly dark behind gold walls of wheat, and fresh blood might glaze the stems of barley crimson, but this blood could easily have come from a jackal's rabbit kill. By day I was invulnerable – confident – empowered by the revealing brightness of the sun.

We had Scottish neighbours on the Kinangop. The nearest, as the egrets flew, was Angus Ferguson, but we couldn't see his house because it was two miles away on the southern boundary of our farm, behind a copse of eucalyptus trees. His home was small, round, whitewashed with distemper and had pansies nodding in the breeze or dozing in the sun outside the front door. He lived there alone.

I was nearly five when we moved to the farm, and I spoke to Angus before Edith and Ken had the chance to introduce themselves. 'I like your pansies!' I said, peering up at him when he answered the door to us.

'Then you must nod to them,' he said, bending his knees and touching a flower. 'See their funny faces? See how they bow in the wind? They'll like it if you nod back to them and say hello.'

The idea of pansies with funny faces responding to a nodded greeting appealed to me. Pansies became a favourite flower, and Angus became a favourite neighbour.

The house consisted of just one room and a separate bathroom. The kitchen area was a blackened cast iron stove to the side of the room, with a table next to it and a shelving unit covered with floral curtains. Other shelves with pots, pans and tins, and a few whisky bottles and glasses, were curved round the walls to the side of one of the two windows. A couple of old but clean armchairs covered in a William Morris fabric stood either side of a faded Persian rug. A large radio resided on an upturned crate with 'Produce of Scotland' stamped on it. There were a few wooden steps leading to a mezzanine platform with a mattress on the floor. Angus must have treated this like a fortress because three rifles were lined up along the retaining rail and boxes of bullets were placed on the stairs. He shared his home with a large lion-coloured mongrel that looked more Alsatian than anything else. The dog had run a long way to meet us on the farm boundary and chased our Studebaker down the dust track, but he couldn't keep up. When he eventually got back home, Edith was sitting in one of the armchairs, which judging by his pacing and huffing was also his bed. It must have been a tight fit because he was a big dog. When Angus told him to behave, he lay down facing Edith with his head on his paws, his eyes fixed on her reproachfully, and ignored my overtures of friendship. His name was Bod.

Angus farmed vast acres of Africa and was beautiful, with thick honey-blond hair and golden skin. His build was manly. I had no difficulty imagining him swimming in the green waters of Highland lochs, rivulets of silver water streaming down his chest as he emerged from the shallows. If he lived in Scotland, he would fight alongside his clansmen. He was fearless and heroic, I was sure.

My mother saw him differently.

'He's frightened,' she said.

She said she felt a maternal tug of anxiety whenever she thought about him, because he lived alone in a dangerous part of the country.

'But he's not alone, Ma. He lives with Bod, and Bod's even allowed inside the house!'

'He's only twenty-two,' she said.

Twenty-two seemed a mature and fearless age to me. But Edith saying that he was afraid of the Mau Mau unnerved me, and my fear of the night deepened.

One day, not long after we'd arrived in the area, I was colouring in a paper kilt for my cut-out doll when I heard a vehicle coming down the road. I got up from the table and went to the kitchen stable door, in time to see a large woman stepping from a Holden estate. The dogs surrounded her joyfully and she had to struggle towards me, the bottom half of her body hidden from view. When I remembered the scene later I saw her as a clan warrior cutting a swathe through a sea of hounds.

She reached over, a strong square hand outstretched. 'I've come to welcome you to South Kinangop,' she said. 'Your mother is Edith and your stepfather is Ken, I'm told, but I don't know your name, sorry. I'm Mrs Lennox and I live on the edge of the escarpment.'

'I'm Tanzie Kent,' I said, fitting my hand into hers. 'Do please come in. Would you like a whisky and soda or a gin and tonic?'

She didn't flinch. 'It's too early for me to drink, thank you, wee Tanzie. Are your Mummy and Ken out in the farm buildings?'

'They've gone to Naivasha to see about the Studebaker and to fetch groceries.'

'Are you alone?'

'No, Mzee's here. Would you like to see my colouring?' I led her to the kitchen table, and she sat beside me on the bench.

'Who's Mzee? Is he the man in the herbaceous border? The gardener?'

I nodded and held up the paper kilt. 'The tartan's too difficult.'

'Very nice, wee Tanzie – a pink kilt! I'm a Scot, you know.' She ruffled my hair. 'Are you on your own?'

'I just told you I was with Mzee! He's black as night time. I like Mzee, but I don't like night time.'

'Not unusual for someone your age. I expect you imagine things too?'

I nodded and picked up my pink colouring pencil.

'What time are your Mummy and Ken coming back?' She smoothed a tress of my hair behind my ear.

'Lunch time, twelve o'clock.'

Mrs Lennox looked at her watch. I reached across and turned her wrist towards me. Only one hand was on the twelve.

'Not time yet. I've prayed to God – prayed and prayed and prayed.' I squeezed my eyes shut as though I was fervently pleading. 'I've really, really, prayed…'

I saw she was peering at me with deep lake-blue eyes. 'About the time? You prayed about the time, wee child? Prayed for Mummy and Ken to come back?'

'No!' I sighed and rolled my eyes. 'About night! I want God to stop the sun going away, but He doesn't listen.'

'Good job too,' she said. 'All sorts of things would go wrong if we didn't have days followed by nights. When would we ever rest? And all the nocturnal animals would starve…'

I wasn't convinced and nibbled my pencil; then I chewed it fiercely until I had splintery bits of wood in my mouth. Then I scribbled all over the kilt.

Mrs Lennox took the pencil from me and stood up, pulling me with her. She enfolded me in her swathes of silk and fine cotton in the middle of the kitchen. She was enormous and formless. She seemed to float and undulate as she moved her body from side to side, cradling me. She smelt of a dust storm blowing through eucalyptus trees, and faintly of kitchen soot. When I wriggled free of her embrace we went to lean on the kitchen stable door, she resting on her elbows and me standing on tiptoe with my chin on my hands. We could see Mzee weeding in the flowerbed by the far fence. Mrs Lennox told me about her dairy farm and the milk yields, and I felt very grown up. I also liked that her conversation was peppered with the endearment 'wee child'. She was kind but later I suspected that this quality was probably reserved for children. I didn't see her often, but when I did, we were affectionate with one another, like old friends.

Nobody knew much about Mrs Lennox. As time went by there didn't appear to be any Mr Lennox, and rumour had it there never had been. She was heir to the fortune of Lennox's steelworks, it was said, and came from the Firth of Forth. She had valuable silverware, especially tableware, as Angus Ferguson, who was often a guest at formal dinner parties, would confirm with awe. He said she was a good cook when she could be bothered. But he also said that outside of a dinner party, she used to eat off a spread newspaper in her kitchen, where the walls were charcoaled with soot.

When I tried to picture her in Scotland, as I had Angus, it was more difficult. She didn't quite fit the woman who stayed at home cooking porridge and looking after her lusty menfolk. But I could see her on a big stout horse, brandishing a weapon alongside the men, or I could imagine her at the front of a wild clan like a Scottish Boadicea, a girded, outward-bound warrior queen. The idea of Mrs Lennox like this could slightly calm my horror of the night. If I visualised Angus riding in her slipstream, I fancied he grew less afraid of the dark too. It became a comfort to imagine her and Angus riding out on an African plateau, through barley fields and pyrethrum flowers to the edge of the forest. I thought I could hear a thin wail of bagpipes slide over the mountains. The sound wound through the trees like tendrils threading Africa and Scotland together, entwining them in my mind.

The Starling family who lived on our most eastern border was also Scottish. I didn't take much notice of them until I was about ten years old, but then they were in my thoughts a lot, especially the sons. Their big stone house was imposing. It had rich wooden floors and staircases, terraced gardens surrounded by clustered pine trees, and cedars that spread their branches like welcoming arms. The family held Scottish music evenings, where we danced to 78s. When they celebrated the New Year, they also had pipers, whose sound made tiny insects with frayed feet whisper along my spine. Outside, a bonfire flared like a tangerine flower in the black night. Children sang 'She'll Be Coming Round the Mountain' and in my mind Mrs Lennox came, varnished orange, weaving through the fire's flame and smoke 'with her knapsack on her back.' Even now, if I hear bagpipes, the air might swirl with the smell of burning pine logs and the panting whisky breath of an elderly dancer puffing gamely through the Gay Gordons.

I fell in love with four of the Starling sons. There were five, but the youngest, Humphrey, who was my age and in my class at school, held little attraction next to his mature and sophisticated brothers. Bliss for me was dancing the Gay Gordons with any of his brothers. My prayer to God began to offer compromise.

'Please God, if there has to be night, let it always be filled with bagpipes and bonfires and the Gay Gordons, and at least one of the Starling boys, but not Humphrey.'

We were hectic – Angus Ferguson, a Starling boy, and me – as we strained to keep up with Mrs Lennox's furious pace through the Scottish glens and African plains. Mostly I imagined myself clinging to a Starling on his fleet and elegant thoroughbred. When I felt very frightened I held tightly to Angus, needing his strength and the muscular broadness of his horse. Sometimes Bod joined us, weaving between hooves or racing ahead. We drove the night in front of us and chased my fear away.

Africa and its terrifying nights gave way to moist English twilights, when I was sent, at twelve years old, to boarding school in Shropshire. My fear of the dark vanished instantly. English nights were not black and thick with insect clamour or human threat but were fluffy and layered with cloud and mist. Sound was recognisably unremarkable. A church spire might shimmer through the mist, amethyst and gossamer, like a dream, but there was nothing to cause alarm. My fantasies of Scotland became a weapon against backward thoughts of home, now that night struck me not with fear but with heart-sickness.

In Shropshire, I had access to a wider range of books, including romantic novels, where Gretna Green seemed to be a recurring feature. I don't think any of the books I read described Gretna Green itself, but as it was usually the destination of lovers in a desperate flight from England, I thought it had to be romantic. I imagined horses' flanks trembling, mouths foaming, rib cages heaving. Soaring above flying manes and hooves and carriages, I saw dark mountains stippled with purple heather. Granite castles brooded amidst black clouds. Carriage wheels hurtled over the border and eloping couples were safe from pursuing hordes of outraged relatives. Reconciliation between families was achieved beside the deep, still waters of a nearby loch.

When I finally went to Scotland, I was a young woman. My first stop was Gretna Green.

It was a disappointment.

I was glad that distressed parents weren't pursuing me. It was a relief that my love of a Starling son had not resulted in an elopement, but the landscape surrounding me was unimposing, banal. The smithy was not the romantic place I had imagined. I felt depressed. The reality of Scotland was not even a pale shadow of my imagination. It was as dull as – I suddenly saw – cold porridge, as flavourless as Scott's Porage Oats without salt or sugar and cream. To save myself even more disappointment, I considered going no further. But perhaps it was the smell of clean air or of sweet cool water that decided me to continue with my journey? Did I catch a purple glimpse of heather in my memory, or jagged antlers and flared nostrils in the periphery of my vision?

So, in a spirit of vague hope, I travelled deeper into Scotland. My heart sang as I found the country beyond Gretna Green worthy of romance, of clan warfare and of the man on the Scott's Porage Oats packet on the sideboard at home on the Kinangop. My senses were full of pleasure as I stood among heather, high up in thin, still air and thought I heard, very far, and very faint, the sound of bagpipes. Closing my eyes I felt a swirl of tartan brush my legs and I caught the aroma of whisky as a kiss grazed my cheek. Churning the ground, wild horses came out of the glen, Mrs Lennox leaning low over the neck of one, her elbows out, her clothes flying, her blue eyes smiling under ferocious brows. Angus Ferguson was close behind, his mount's mane indistinguishable from his own streaming honey locks. And was that Bod bringing up the rear, glimpsed in a blur of movement?

'Hi, Mrs Lennox,' I yelled as horses' hooves flung clods of earth past my head. 'It's me, your wee child…' But as I always suspected, Mrs Lennox reserved her kindness for children. She could see I wasn't wee anymore, so she didn't respond.

How Long Is a Fortnight?

With the dust swirling in through the open window and the bitter smell of vomit, I can't wait to get out. I'm always sick on car journeys, but this time was worse than usual. I wasn't able to warn Edith in time for her to stop and let me out, and then we didn't have anything to clean up my mess. So now the well under my feet is spread thick with a half-digested breakfast of toast and marmalade.

As I spill out of the passenger door, wanting to inhale fresh air but having to cover my mouth with both hands while the swirling dust subsides, Edith fetches my suitcase from the back seat. She puts it down, places the flat of her hand on the small of her back and stretches. She grimaces as though in pain and scans the ground. I look down as well but see nothing for her to worry about.

Edith has pulled the car up on a circular track that runs round a high bamboo-fenced garden. Banana fronds hang over the fence, creating a small shade for weeds to escape the noonday heat. On the other side of the track the ground falls away steadily and is covered by dense entwined foliage. A lane, shadowed by a canopy of bougainvillea, runs down the side of the slope. I can see the roof of what I think must be the school just visible above the tangle of greenery at the bottom of the incline. I point and look expectantly at Edith. She nods; she's been here before.

She is hesitating. I draw heart shapes in the dust on the back windscreen while I wait to see what she is going to do. She leans into the car and presses the horn lightly, then waits a moment before repeating the action. But the sound might have been smothered by the heat and dust because nobody comes up from the building. So we walk to the top of the sloping lane and peer under the trees and bougainvillea. Edith frowns and fidgets and then sighs.

She puts a hand under my chin, tipping my face up to look at her. 'I'm sorry, Tanzie, but I'm too scared to come with you,' she says. 'They've got rats.' She touches my arm. 'At the bottom of the lane, go through the door at the end of the courtyard on your right. The lady who runs the school is called Mrs Hale. She's expecting you.' Edith moves her hand to stroke my hair but I move away, angry that she is making me go on my own. She hands me my suitcase, which I have to take in both hands because although it's not heavy, it is bulky. Turning me around to face the lane, she nudges my back, applying pressure to move me forward. I resist and drop the suitcase then stand awkwardly, hanging my head, scraping my sandaled foot to and fro in the dust.

Edith is still and quiet. I look up and see her running trembling fingers through the back of her hair. Of course she could also be upset about leaving me, but the real problem is the rats.

I make up my mind, heave the suitcase against my chest, and hold up my head to receive my mother's sticky lipstick kiss. As I struggle down the slope I feel the imprint of her lips like a red jewel. It is a jewel cold with impotence and despair, brilliant with rage, hot with umbilical blood.

'I'll see you in a fortnight,' she calls.

I have to put the case down several times before I reach the bottom, from where I can hear a piano being played. I look back and have to bend down to see Edith. She is at the top of the slope under the bougainvillea, also squatting to see me. She blows a kiss, which I catch easily with one hand close to the ground, then waves and disappears. I hear the car engine and see a cloud of orangey brown dust billow into the lane as she drives away with my congealed vomit. I close my eyes and see the shape she made at the top of the slope, squatting, gathering her full skirt round her knees, her sunglasses masking her expression. Her shape becomes white against black, then red, then just a shape. I fall into nothingness, like sand dissolving through an ebbing tide, until I am only a red kiss shape in the cinnamon air of piano tunes.

I feel dizzy. Suddenly a dog pants in my face. I open my eyes and fall onto the neck of an old sandy mongrel. His tail wags stiffly and his breath is as hot and putrid as mine is cold and bitter. I hug him hard. As I resume my struggle with the suitcase, the dog limps into the shade of the foliage and lies down with a grunt. The door off the courtyard is glass paned and slightly ajar, and I heave the case through it.

The piano falls silent. I'm in a large sparsely furnished stone room and I'm sure the people in there are all the same family as their heads are similar shades of white, blond and pale gold, and they are mostly stocky or sturdy, if not plump. A lady who stands out because she is thin leaves the piano stool and comes towards me. She is old; she must be Mrs Hale.

I feel a bit panicky and hurry to say something. I want to be the first to speak. I want to feel like myself. 'My name is Tanzie Kent and I live on the Kinangop and we have a green Studebaker,' I announce.

Mrs Hale puts a hand on my shoulder, and she is smiling through a frown.

'Tanzie, we have been expecting you.' She looks at the door I have come through. 'Where's your mother, dear? Is she following you?'

'She's gone. She's afraid of rats.'

'I don't understand. We don't have any rats here…oh…perhaps she's thinking of the mongooses…?'

The family exchange glances and a girl of about fifteen – she has a lumpy chest – goes to the door. She is pink and plump and gold like an angel. A movement by her feet alerts me to a family of mongooses flowing through the door, undulating like a ribbon in the wind. I drop into a crouch and put my hand on the floor. The mother mongoose comes to see what I'm offering, and the rest of the ribbon follows her. Then all the babies are running over me; they vanish under my gingham dress and emerge at my collar and their feet and whiskers tickle. I am instantly and perfectly happy. Until I remember that my mother isn't with me. Memory cancels happiness.

'How long is a fortnight?' I ask Mrs Hale.

'It's not long at all,' she says. She turns to a girl around my age who is standing pigeon-toed and sullen by the piano. 'Come and meet Tanzie. Tanzie, this is Belinda. She is nearly five years old, like you, and she is the youngest of my children.'

Belinda hunkers down beside me on the stone floor and begins to name the mongooses for my information. I think she is naming them according to whim but I pay close attention and notice that she gives the same one two different names. It has slightly paler fur than the others and more of its pink skin shows through.

'No,' I say. 'This mongoose is called Sidney, not Hilary. You told me its name was Sidney.'

'No! It's called Hilary.'

'You said it was Sidney.'

'How can it be called Sidney when it's a girl?'

Belinda holds the creature upside down and we put our heads close together to examine its underside. I don't really know what to look for, so I pick up the mongoose recently dubbed Molly and upend it, hoping for enlightenment. It looks like Sidney.

'Well, you told me its name was Sidney,' I say, putting Molly down, along with the argument.

'They're *my* mongooses – I should know what they're called!' Belinda is upset and lies on her back, kicking her feet and slewing her body around. Sidney/Hilary skids across the smooth stone like an ice-cube on a glacier, ending up under the piano, and the other small creatures skitter and scatter around the room. I stand up in a blaze of hatred. I'm considering throwing myself on top of Belinda to trap her flailing limbs when I see a tall lady come in from the door opposite the courtyard. I know she is not a Hale because she is dark and sleek and fine featured. She hauls Belinda to her feet, holds on to her with one hand and puts her other hand in mine.

'Hello, Tanzie. I'll be looking after you; my name's Sheila. Do you want to meet the other children? We've been playing outside. You can come too, Belinda.'

I struggle out of Sheila's hold to retrieve Sidney/Hilary, who seems to be unhurt, and put it in my pocket, covering it protectively with my hand. I then return to Sheila and place my other hand back in hers. Belinda wrenches herself free, making it look as though Sheila has been holding her tight. She goes to the piano where her mother is sitting down again. For a moment, I worry about abandoning my suitcase, but I'm happy to be with Sheila and quickly forget about it.

Outside some children are sitting on their heels or kneeling under the pepperberry trees, making mud huts. A stone wall surrounds the garden and now I understand why the Hales have mongooses as a wall with gaps makes a perfect habitat for snakes. I can see that the children are building a village with roads that connect to each hut. They are using torn-up clumps of grass for the roofs. None of the children look up from their play. Sheila gives me a bucket of water, shows me a space to make a hut and scrapes up some earth into a pile for me. As I squat, Sidney/Hilary climbs out of my pocket and runs off to find its family. I begin to make the mud and mould it into a hut shape while Sheila collects blades of grass to make the roof. One of the boys notices Sheila helping me.

'Who's she?' he asks, and I think he sounds as if he's accusing her of wrong doing, or is hostile to me – maybe both.

'Duncan,' Sheila says, smiling. 'Let me introduce you to Tanzie. She's new to the school.'

'Oh!' Duncan inspects me, while I inspect him. I notice that he has a crop of dark brown freckles.

'What's that on your face?' he says, gesturing with his muddy spade towards my forehead.

I reach up and touch where he is pointing. 'Lipstick.'

'Yuck! That's a funny place to have lipstick.'

'It's better than having brown marks on your face!'

I'm envious of his freckles, and I don't know why I'm being so nasty about them. Duncan turns away, his ears reddening, and gets back to what he was doing.

A bell sounds from the house.

'It's time for afternoon tea,' Sheila tells me. She calls to the others, 'Come on everybody, let's go and wash our hands. You can leave the buckets and spades here until tomorrow.'

I hurry to finish my hut, but Sheila says, 'Would you like to stay until it's all built, Tanzie? You may, if you like.' While I am trying to make up my mind, the old dog that I met on my way in limps towards us.

'Here's Mustard,' says Sheila. 'He'll keep you company, won't you, boy? I'll come back for you in a little while.' Mustard wags his tail a few times then lies in the dust nearby.

I use the strands of grass to make the roof of my hut and then stand up to admire my work. I notice that it's set quite a distance from the other huts and suddenly it feels like me in a way that I don't really understand. The sun vanishes behind a cloud, darkening the dappled shade, and I feel my heart fall into shadow. I place my foot on one of the grouped huts and feel the thick mud ooze out from the sides of my sandals. I step on another and the mud bulges outwards like pain seeping away. It makes me feel easier, like when Edith rubs me better after I have knocked myself against something hard. I begin to stamp and dance and mash my feet, and when the sun comes out again, the trampled mud glistens red and glutinous and the grass lies mangled, pink and wet. Only the hut I made still stands.

I'm frightened. I start to run towards the house, just as Sheila is coming to fetch me. She catches my hand and hurries me off to wash. I'm too upset to resist when she cleans Edith's lipstick off my forehead. She leads me to the dining room. My brow feels as shiny as the polished table where the other children are already eating.

Tea is ham and radishes. The children are complaining.

'Ugh! I hate radishes!'

'Yuck, they're horrible.'

'Oh no, not radishes.'

'I like them,' I say, and immediately they all pass their radishes down the table to me until the pile on my plate obscures the ham. There are too many and I soon feel sick. Belinda, sitting on my right, says, 'You have to eat them all, you'll get into trouble if you don't. You have to leave your plate empty.'

I am eating them long after the other children are wolfing down strawberry trifle.

I fall asleep in the dormitory that night thinking about a fortnight and wondering what Mrs Hale's words 'it's not long at all' mean. When I wake up, the same thoughts are with me, lurking, clogging my chest with worry. Morning lessons pass with me still feeling tight and anxious, although I do enjoy making figure-of-eight patterns fit between two lines, which Mrs Hale shows us how to do. We have a mid-morning break sitting at the small tables lining the veranda and drink a glass of milk before we are released to play. As the others swarm into the garden, to their mud village, I hold back. I see them standing still amongst the trees, looking down, searching for sense. I walk towards them as slowly as possible.

'It was you!' Duncan jabs my chest hard with his finger. The pain is sharp but numbing. It feels like a rod of ice driven into my heart and I step back and cover my injury with both hands.

'You horrid nasty horrible nasty horrible girl!' he shouts. 'Look! Look what you've done!'

I look at what I've done. I want to shrink from it, shrivel up like I'd seen sea anemones in the coral reef near Mombasa do when threatened. The pain in my chest still aches and I rub it hard.

'You've ruined our village,' wails Duncan, his face reddening. He comes close and his breath lifts the hair on my forehead. I step away but he stands over me closer than before. I try to shrink into myself again, turning my head, half shutting my eyes. When he finally turns away from me it is to jump high in the air on the only undamaged hut – my hut. He treads the dried mud in a frenzy. It's a war dance and dust rises like ashes.

Belinda appears beside me, too close. She leans into me, calm and superior. 'We don't like you,' she says, speaking for everybody. 'We hate you.' I drag my eyes away from Duncan's fury and stare at her, shocked at her cold hostility.

There is a pause while the others appreciate the destruction of my hut. My worry about Edith's leaving me returns. In this moment I understand that even if a fortnight doesn't mean forever, it is still far, far too long. The numb stab in my chest begins to spread and tighten in my throat and I can't release the sob that aches along my jaw.

Footsteps are closing behind me. It's Sheila, and she scans the flattened village. Gathering me to her side, she instructs the others to return to the classroom and get out their colouring books. 'I will be with you in a minute,' she says.

'But she destroyed our village. It was her! Her hut wasn't smashed. I smashed it to pay her back. Everything is her fault. She's ruined everything!' Duncan screws his fists into his eyes as he moves off towards the schoolhouse. The other children complain or whimper as they go. Belinda trails them, walking backwards, watching Sheila.

Sheila has gathered us on the veranda. 'This afternoon, when it's playtime again, we're going to make a new village,' she says. Her arms hold me in front of her and I'm wrapped in the folds of her skirt. It is white with huge red poppy swirls and lime-green leaves. She wears a petticoat with white lace that you can see when she lifts her knees. She's very pretty.

'Why should we be bothered to build it again?' says Duncan. 'I don't want to play anymore.'

'What's her punishment going to be?' asks Belinda.

'The new village will be more splendid than the last one; we can use real raffia for the roofs. And we can make some stables for the farm animals from the play chest.' Sheila smiles round at the children, but they are not responsive. 'Now Tanzie has something she wants to say.' She nudges me forward, but her skirt is my sanctuary and I am reluctant to move towards the wall of upset children.

'I'm sorry for ruining the village.'

The children watch me but they're still not ready to accept the idea of the improved village, or my apology.

'You'll forgive Tanzie won't you, Duncan?' Sheila says, inclining her head and looking at him. He puts his hands over his eyes and his brow creases like rumpled silk. Freckles become half freckles on his forehead. I think he loves Sheila but hates her too for asking him to forgive me.

'I'm sorry, Duncan. I'll build you another hut if you like,' I say.

I've made it worse. Duncan's face loses even the half freckles, his rage obliterating them with a red heat. My heart feels like it's been punched. Clutching the hem of Sheila's skirt with one hand, I reach out to him with the other. His frown deepens. I'm about to let my hand drop when he grasps it and, like a sea mist clearing, his face lights up. He grins. I know his smile is for Sheila, but my heart lurches anyway. He doesn't see how relieved I am because his smile is enormous, squeezing his eyes shut.

At that moment Sheila's floral skirt, Duncan's vanished eyes, Sidney/Hilary, and the promise of raffia and play animals make me feel that, as long as there aren't radishes for tea, a fortnight might not be unbearable after all.

Near the Edge

Mr Hale, who runs the kindergarten boarding school along with his wife, spreads the *East African Standard* on my bed. He rests his blunt finger on a picture of a woman with dark hair.

'She's my mummy.' I push my bedclothes aside and lean forward to see more clearly.

'She *is* your mummy,' he says.

The other children in the dormitory clamber onto my bed, expecting the usual bedtime story. Duncan squeezes himself between Mr Hale and me, crumpling the paper as he settles.

'Why's her mummy in the paper?' He places his index finger next to Mr Hale's. His hand is small and freckled like his face and his breath smells of dry hay.

'Tanzie's mother has been very brave and captured four dangerous Mau Mau terrorists,' says Mr Hale.

'How? Did she have a gun?'

'She was warned by her gardener, Mzee, about some armed Africans hiding in the wheat. They jumped in the Land Rover and drove to where Mzee had seen them, realised they were Mau Mau terrorists and rounded them up.'

The electric light is too white and bright. The small panes of glass in the metal windows that line one side of the dormitory are as black as onyx. White and black hurt my eyes and become distilled in the image of my mother in the newsprint.

Duncan peers into Mr Hale's face. 'Why?'

Mr Hale looks confused. The question seems unanswerable. He says, 'Tanzie's mother was very brave.'

'She's not brave. She's frightened of rats,' I say, shielding my eyes from the glare of pain in my mind.

Duncan turns to look at me. 'Why?'

Duncan's questions are too difficult. I shrug. Mr Hale shrugs. 'Time to close the curtains,' he says, causing a scramble of children off my bed.

When Mr Hale turns the lights off, the bullfrogs' calls bulge out into the night against the background throb of the generator. The pond where they gather after the rains is outside the windowless end of the house, under dense foliage that leans its weight like a closing parenthesis, marking the end of the house, the country, the world. I know nothing beyond it. I imagine the frogs pulsating, booming their sound, belching and burping, sliding fat limbs over each other in a glistening slime of greenish darkness. They inhabit the edge of everything. There is cataclysmic emptiness beyond them.

When the noise of the generator dies and the bullfrogs are quiet, I can hear another rhythmic sound far away along the escarpment. It stops and starts. The soldiers of the British Army must be at the top of the valley, shelling the papyrus that edges the lake below. They shell it because the Mau Mau hide under the water, breathing through papyrus stalks, ready to attack in the deep of night. I imagine their dark shapes sliding into the thick lucerne plantations, creeping to the foot of the hill, ready to climb. The guns sound soft in the distance, popping – *putt*, *putt*, *putt* – like a motorbike. As I drift with tiredness I feel the sound is in my bloodstream too, a tiny motorbike travelling with my circulation in a red stream of fluid. I let my mind track the position of the soldiers. They must be beyond the burial place of the Hales' firstborn child.

The grave is a mound inside a small walled enclosure. It stands alone on a rise at the edge of the steep stony descent to the farm. A little girl, five years old, is buried in the ground, which is piled with stones grey in the starlight. She is the same age as me. I see myself in her place under the cold boulders where snakes slither from the enclosing walls. I summon the Hales' tame mongooses in my imagination and I hear them scuttling through the dry grass. They haven't come to save me. I am the dead child in the grave. I am beyond saving. But they have come to do battle, like Rikki Tikki Tavi against Nag. They have come to fight in the arena of the small child's last resting place, keeping it free of serpents. There are no flowers, just grey dust and stones, and mongooses keeping away the small movement of dislodged rubble and the long slide of belly-crawling fear.

My fear of snakes helps me understand my mother's terror of rodents, but the thing I worry about even more than snakes is being without her. When I think of the Mau Mau attacking, my heart slides sickeningly, my blood slithers, my mind side winds. If Edith is killed, I want to die too. Before I came to this school with soldiers on the hill protecting us, we were attacked at home. I was frightened, but I was with Edith. My anxiety about her now, after Mr Hale has read us the newspaper story, is more intense than when experiencing the horror first hand.

It is a late Sunday afternoon after a large lunch. My grown-up half-brother Michael, Edith's son, is home for the weekend. He and my stepfather Ken are overfed and slightly drunk. Michael is playing 'Happy Families' with me. Edith has cleared the lunch debris and I can see her through the lounge window picking flowers in the front garden. The dogs are milling around her.

A shot rings out, stunning the afternoon. The dogs crash through the stillness and rush around the back of the house. Another shot, a yelp and the dogs increase their alarm. Ken and Michael run to the hall chest for the guns and arrange themselves at the rear windows. Edith flies in from the garden. She catches my arm, scattering my hand of 'Happy Families', and drags me towards the bathroom. 'Lie on the floor on your tummy with your arms over your head,' she says. She leaves the bathroom door open. The windows in here are high, so I'm safe from low-skimming shots. I watch Edith take flares from the chest. The cardinal-coloured tiles are cool under my body. The sun pours in from the veranda, flooding the hall tiles, bleaching them. Edith walks into the dazzle of outside light, out of my sight. The dogs keep up a ferocious noise round the other side of the house, and I worry about the dog that yelped. There are shouts – 'Aiyeee! Aiyeee!' Has a dog caught hold of an attacker?

A flare that Edith attempts to launch misfires, enters the hall, and is whizzing around the floor, creating an orange track of fiery heat. I can hear her laughing. What's so funny? My ribs hurt, pressing on the floor. I listen for my mother outside in the sunlight with shouts and shots and dogs clamouring. My body convulses, my lungs fill and a sound echoing my mother's laughter escapes my mouth. When the flare is spent I want to crawl towards the charred pool of sunlight on the floor, like a cat searching for the warmest place. I could lie there and bask. Sunshine makes me feel secure, giving horror daylight ordinariness.

Edith comes back indoors. She picks up the walkie-talkie from the hall table. Her voice is shaky.

'We're under attack, Angus. I've put up flares. Did you see the flares? Come quickly! Over.'

Night falls and Angus and the other neighbours are shakily accepting a whisky and I am crying over the dead dog. The police have taken away several wounded Africans. I look out onto the lawn. It is pale and dewy in the moonlight, and the flowers that Edith had been gathering are strewn like slain warriors after a battle.

My fear at that time is not like this fear now. Then my feelings had shadowed my mother's. I was part of her. My fear was hers. Now I'm as alone as the Hales' firstborn child in the stonewalled grave on the rise of the hill.

The boy in the furthest bed of the dormitory, next to the end of everything, stirs. The wall near his head is smeared and streaked with congealed snot he has picked from his nose. I can't see it in the dark but I know it's there. Robbie has catarrh, which smells bad.

He breathes loudly through his mouth but I can't hear him tonight. I sniff to see if I can catch his yeasty smell but I can only pick up the metallic odour from the iron beds.

'Robbie – are you awake?'

He doesn't answer. I'm relieved. I don't want to risk my feet on the floor as it might hiss and slither. Even if I get into bed with him and turn my back, taking comfort from his nearness but avoiding his breath, I'll still be too near the edge of things, too near the bogies and the bullfrogs and the dark and tangled foliage marking the beginning of the void.

Duncan sleeps in the bed nearest the door to the veranda. Although Duncan and I are friends, he complains if I get into bed with him. When I've done it before he's thrown an arm over me in his sleep but in the morning has turned so red with fury that his freckles have vanished like blood spots in a furnace.

I make up my mind to risk the floor and I run to Duncan's bed. He moves over and I burrow into the warm space. His breath is sweet. I think of Edith rounding up the African terrorists and worry if Mzee will be in danger because he warned her about them. I think of his gappy grin, his gluey eye, and I hear his chuckle. When he laughs he tucks his chin into his chest and shakes his hands like maracas and his fingers click and clack.

I think of Edith and Mzee in the Land Rover. I imagine Mzee jumping out and approaching the bodies hidden in the wheat. He points at the surprised Mau Mau, then starts shaking the fingers on one hand and holding his stomach with the other as though Edith has just told him the finest joke. Listening to Mzee chortling, snorting and clattering his fingers, I feel as if daylight has broken over me. I feel it in the warmth of Duncan's body as I begin to enjoy the events developing in my imagination. I drift towards sleep, and distant gunfire clicks and clacks to the rhythm of Mzee's amusement.

A vision of the terrorists standing in the golden fields, rocking on their heels, guns lowered, sharing Mzee's hilarity, folds itself into my dreams. Edith holds her gun slung backwards over her shoulder and grins, and Mr Hale stands by holding a newspaper and smiling approval. My breathing deepens. Sheets of the *East African Standard* fly like birds, casting flickering wing-beat shadows above the plateau before sinking over the edge into the Rift Valley.

Strange Things Happen in Stories

A pea-green boat is re-coloured in the flood of a crimson sunset. It bobs alarmingly in the disturbance created by the dhows crowding into the shore from Zanzibar. I screw up my eyes to see better against the glare of the red water. The owl and the pussycat are beginning their journey 'for a year and a day'. The cat's eyes are as translucent as my daddy's pink gin that he holds against plump pink knees.

Daddy and I share a chalet for a season overlooking the Indian Ocean. He tells me stories on the veranda every evening before putting me to bed. Strange things happen in stories. A cat and an owl go away together on a long adventure. There's a lady who swallows a horse; Daddy says she'll die, of course. I have seen a Sumatran tiger stroll off a dhow arriving from India, and on its back is an old lady from Riga. The tiger flows up the beach like a smooth incoming tide and slinks across the huge sun that rolls behind the palm trees along the coast. The silhouettes of a tiger and an old lady slide out of the sun circle and disappear behind the chalets.

After Daddy puts me to bed he walks along the beach to the inn to drink with his friends. When I am certain he is out of sight I reach under my pillow for my torch. It has a button that changes the lens in an instant to either a berry juice red, citric lemon yellow or underwater turquoise. I scramble out from under my mosquito net and walk along the beach away from the inn, using the yellow light. I meet Peter coming towards me, as usual. He shares the end chalet with his father, who has also gone to the bar. Perhaps his parents are divorced too. We never talk about that sort of thing.

Peter is the type of boy who is at ease being friends with a girl. He happily sees the pussycat's great blood-orange eyes and smiles about the tiger and the lady from Riga, asleep now under the palm trees.

The night is black. I switch the torch to red and the sea turns cochineal. Peter, in his pyjama bottoms and with his hair sticking up in tufts, looks coated in thin beetroot juice. He has a coconut in his hands. On our way to smash it against a veranda wall we catch a slithering movement in the torchlight and a sea snake slides in the redness of the world.

We jump back. I drop the torch, Peter lets the coconut fall, and we run.

The next morning, after Daddy has left to catch a flight to Bombay, maybe for a year and a day, I scramble into my swimsuit and hurry to find my torch, but there is only the coconut half buried in the sand. Peter is on the veranda of his chalet, eating cereal. I fling myself on the bottom step.

'My torch, Peter,' I wail, nursing the coconut against my chest and scrunching a fist into my eyes to stop the tears stinging. 'My magic torch!'

He listens to me sob and complain as he spoons his breakfast into his mouth, pausing from time to time to hear me more clearly. At first his face is soft with sympathy, but when I get up and hurl the coconut against the veranda wall he frowns and clatters his spoon in his dish.

'Damn,' he says, 'can't you shut up about the bloody torch? Stop whining. C'mon, let's bring in the sea. Let's turn the tide.'

He gets to his feet, scans the horizon, runs his hands through his hair and thumps his chest. He leaps off the top step and makes for the sea, which from here is just a sliver of silver along the skyline.

How can he understand about the tiger but not about my magic torch? I scream into the sun and shatter the sky. He keeps running.

Sobbing, I follow him and plead with him to wait, but he is not listening. I can hardly breathe from the tears running down my cheeks and into my mouth, the fist of pain in my chest and the mucous drizzling down the back of my throat. I have to stop and gasp for air and try to let go of the despair weighing me down. But I can't bear Peter getting so far ahead. I can't endure him ignoring me; it's the worst shock. Can't he hear the hurt in my voice?

I plough through the loose sand, slide down into it, crawl forward, and stagger up again. When the sand gets firmer, it is easier to move. My feet begin to fly, which lifts my sorrow, and I enjoy the light, swift feeling in my limbs. When we reach the ocean we have to outrun it back to the shore. I catch excitement from

Peter's shouts as he dances backwards, turns, and flies before the water. There is a diving platform anchored in front of us. Peter runs past it. I climb it, misjudging the speed of the ocean, and the sea overtakes it. But Peter is flowing ahead of the waves. He is like a wildebeest surging through a raging river, racing to avoid crocodiles.

'Peter, save me! I'm going to drown – save me!' I shriek, balancing on the edge of the platform.

'Hang on, I'm coming!' he yells. He splashes back through the waves.

'Hurry up! I'm stranded. Be quick, I'm going to drown!' I shout with glee.

'Don't worry, I'll save you from a watery grave.' Peter splashes to the side of the platform. The water swirls around his waist. 'Climb onto my back.'

'I'm too scared.'

'Trust me, I'm your hero.'

I clamber onto his back. The sea is churning, but I am safe against Peter's smooth seal skin.

We are dumped on the shore by the waves. Peter is indented in the sand, pressed down by my body. Pushing me off, he staggers up the beach, salted like the rim of a glass of Margarita. My hair and skin are sticky with seawater, and my mood is spoiling fast. What's the point of turning the tide when all my torch magic has gone? A heavy feeling sinks through my heart, and the sting of Peter's lack of understanding salts my wounded thoughts. There is a sob swelling in my chest, but I don't want to risk Peter's irritation again so I stifle it, closing my eyes tight. Colours of red and orange and darkness are behind my eyelids, forming tiger stripes.

I hear a low rumble like a cat's purr. It's very close; it's in my head. When I open my eyes there is a tiger coming out of the sea, water streaming off its coat. It shakes itself and some of the drops fly into my eyes. I watch it flump onto the sand, growling softly, and then stretch out to bask. We must have brought it in with the tide. My heart lurches with delight as I look round to see if Peter has noticed. He is smiling, and I don't know if it's the iridescence of tears and water droplets, but I'm sure I catch a glimpse of tiger stripes in the blue of his eyes.

I get sunstroke. Daddy is worried because he has to fly to Bombay again for a couple of days and doesn't want to leave me alone. He fetches the innkeeper, Mr Henderson, and asks if he will please call a doctor, and Mr Henderson says he will. Peter arrives at the same time the innkeeper returns with a doctor. Daddy has gone, but I don't mind if Peter is nearby. The doctor pricks my ear and puts blood on a slide to take away to test, 'just in case'. I can hear Peter's bare feet slapping on the stone floor of the veranda as he walks up and down, waiting while the doctor and Mr Henderson confer.

The doctor hurries away and Mr Henderson stands at the foot of my bed, scratching his ear and sighing softly through his nose. He calls Peter to come into the room, then appears to be at a loss as to what to do next, frowning down at his shoes.

Peter relieves him of his indecision. 'I'll stay, Mr Henderson, make sure she's alright, if you think I should?'

'That's very good of you.' Mr Henderson puts a hand on his shoulder. 'Peter, isn't it? Arthur Eliot's son? I'll be in the lounge bar if you need me. Make sure she drinks plenty of water, but no gulping, just sipping.' He pats Peter awkwardly as though he isn't used to young people. 'I'll come back soon to check how she is.'

I'm wet with sweat and not really interested in anything, but sometimes I am aware of Peter sitting on the chair beside me, reading comics or drawing in his sketchbook. I'm restless and uncomfortable and very hot and shivery. I don't know how much time passes – it may be a year and a day – but it's at least two days because Daddy is back. I wake up in the dark to find my mosquito net tucked into my mattress. I can hear Daddy snoring next door. My mouth is dry and I whimper as I try to cry. Daddy appears in shorts and bare feet, pours a glass of water from a jug at my bedside, untucks the net, and leans in to lift my shoulders from the pillow. He gives me two pills and holds the water for me to swallow them, then takes a corner of the sheet to mop the sweat from my face. 'There, there, Tanzie. You'll feel more comfortable soon. Shall I tell you a story? Will it help?'

I don't remember the story and when I wake again Peter is peering at me. 'You look loads better! You've stopped sweating. Your skin is still red though.'

'I need a pee.'

'Can't help you with that! I could help you out of bed though. You could lean on me. I could be your hero.'

I feel weak so I let Peter help me to the bathroom door. 'Wash your face while you're there,' he says. 'And clean your teeth – your breath is disgusting.'

When I'm back in bed Peter finds my hairbrush and untangles my hair, tying it back with a shoelace from one of Daddy's shoes.

Peter and I draw pictures together. His are cowboys and pirates, while I favour princesses, mermaids, horses and dragons. We have even more fun when we mix up our characters. The cowboys are pretty, festooned with pink ribbons and jewelled tiaras. The horses are ornate with green scales and eye patches, and the dragons wear Texan hats and silver slippers. I really like the princesses in stylish cowboy boots with glistening spurs, gun-slinging their spangled bodies across the page.

'Drink some water,' Peter tells me.

'I'm bored with water.'

'You need to drink it, the doctor said.'

'No!'

'I could go to the bar and get some lemonade.'

'That would be lovely.'

'I haven't got any money though.' Peter pats the pockets of his shorts and shrugs.

'Charge it to my daddy's account,' I tell him. 'And get lots – some for you as well.'

When Peter returns, he is carrying an enormous jug of lemonade with ice. He pours us each a tumbler full, and I feel thirsty as I anticipate the coolness, loving the sound of ice tinkling against the glass and the smell of lemons. When I drink, bubbles tickle the back of my throat and prickle my nose. I hold the glass up to the sunlight and watch the ice glisten, the bubbles fizz, and the condensation glitter. Soon the jug is empty.

'Peter, I feel sick,' I gasp as saliva swamps my mouth. I climb out of bed and lurch outside to the veranda. My stomach rises at the same time as I lean over the veranda wall and, too late, a clear liquid pours out of my mouth and onto an anthill.

I feel instantly better. Peter leans over the wall beside me. We stare down at the swarming ants.

'Good shot,' Peter applauds.

'But it's sick, Peter. Yuck! Poor ants.' I sigh tragically and feel a bit tearful.

'They like it. Pure sugar, very delicious.'

'They'll drown.'

'No, they won't. Look, the earth is already absorbing the sick; it'll be dry as a bone in no time. And I expect the ants think they're in heaven, with all that sweetness falling out of the sky.'

'That's bees!' I try to remember about vomit. 'Isn't the bile too acid?'

'I don't know. They look happy enough.'

We lean shoulder-to-shoulder, peering down at the busy ants. I try to spot any that are drowning, but as Peter said, they seem happy enough.

Blue Toes, Sulphur Hair, Red Freckles

She moved on giant legs. Her sandals squeaked and slapped as she strode down the middle of the dormitory, checking our beds for neat hospital corners and our hands for clean nails. Our hair had to be neat and off our collars, and our ties straight.

I didn't know how to knot a tie. I tried to get the girl who occupied the bed opposite mine, Nell, to assist me, but she was too frightened of Matron herself to help. So I just twisted my tie into some semblance of a knot and tucked it into my jumper. My hands shook as I prepared them for inspection, securing a clean handkerchief under my palms with my thumbs while displaying my nails in front of me. Matron was near. I closed my eyes but the slap, squeal and pause of her shoes magnified my panic. When the sound stopped altogether my eyes flew open. Her irises were dark grey, flecked with silvery splinters, beautiful and cold.

'Why haven't you knotted your tie?' she said with a strong Afrikaans accent.

'I don't know how to.' My answer hung in the air between us and I wondered if I'd spoken at all. Straining to hear an echo of my voice, to believe in it, made the silence sing in my ears and, feeling faint, I leaned against the bed to support myself.

'Stand straight.'

I stiffened my limbs.

'Didn't your mother show you how to do your tie?' Matron folded her arms across her chest and settled her weight on her hip. In no hurry to finish her early morning inspection, she was like a great sailing ship in a lull between steady winds, relaxing her bulk on the waves as the sails slackened and sound stilled.

'I think she forgot,' I stammered.

'You think she forgot?'

I couldn't work out who Matron thought was at fault – my mother for not showing me how to knot my tie, or myself for thinking she had forgotten.

'I'm not sure if she forgot.'

Matron looked as if she was trying to find a satisfactory response to my – or my mother's – unpreparedness for the tying of my tie. I dropped my head and concentrated on the large toenails that protruded, bluish and deeply ridged, from her sandals.

Eventually she said, 'Who would like to teach this child how to do her tie?' She loosened her arms and swung away on one foot as though a sudden gust of wind had slewed her around. Children surged forward but Nell was the first to lay hands on me. The others fell back to stand at the end of their beds, while Nell complacently tied the knot and patted it into place before resuming her position. If there was any instruction, or demonstration, I missed it.

Fear confused me, but the savage thought 'Goody Two Shoes' came through clearly as my eyes slid over Nell's careful presentation of handkerchief and nails for inspection. The tie remained just as Goody Two Shoes had fixed it, for the whole term. I loosened it over my head morning and evening, until I could see Edith again and she could teach me how to do it properly.

I always made a great effort not to attract Matron's attention. I watched carefully and tried to stay in the shadow of my peers, moving as one with them, keeping perfectly in line, in step, not daring to twitch unless in unison. But one night I suffered a sore throat and toothache. Although I tried to stifle my whimpers, my mouth was crammed with pain.

In the morning Matron singled me out again. 'What have you got in your mouth?'

I felt my face and discovered it was swollen, as though I had a gobstopper stuffed in my cheek.

Matron's hands suddenly clutched my arms, bringing me close to her face. 'Open your mouth.'

I opened it stiffly, letting the pain yawn out on my hot, stale breath. Matron dropped me roughly, making me stagger; soreness jarred and a sound grazed out of me like a rusty door hinge in a strong wind.

'Nell,' she said, 'collect this child's pyjamas and accompany her to the sanatorium. Be as quick as you can and don't be late for breakfast.'

The sanatorium Sister put me to bed in clean, starched sheets. She took my temperature and gave me painkillers, and I drifted into the safe, peaceful world of that white envelope of sheets. I liked the sound of Sister moving briskly along the corridor. She was efficient and impersonal, which made the world seem fair and unthreatening. The occasional distant ringing of a telephone reminded me of home, which edged my feelings with sadness, but mostly I was just relieved to be safe and free of the main school.

I was sick a lot that first year, with mysterious high temperatures. This, along with the permanently knotted tie, helped me survive. I was frequently admitted to the sanatorium and endeavoured to stay there as long as possible, enjoying the cool detachment of Sister and the hygienic whiteness of the wards and bathrooms. It was a sanctuary. I escaped old Blue Toes and Goody Two Shoes, and I avoided the agonising daily arithmetic lessons.

When my fever came down the first time, I had mixed feelings. I was glad to be well but reluctant to return to the world. On subsequent occasions, I managed to stay in sickbay by deception. It was part of Sister's efficiency to distribute thermometers throughout the wards rather than wait by each bedside in turn for the time it took a fever to register. She would then return with a pad to record the patients' details and remove and check the instruments. As soon as she had put the thermometer in my mouth and left the room, I would hurry to place it in the pool of sunshine that invariably lay across my bedside locker or the windowsill. By the time Sister came back to collect the thermometers the magic would usually have happened.

Being in sickbay was the nearest thing to bliss I knew, with the exception of being with Edith. Daylight hours were idled away doing jigsaw puzzles or reading, every now and then reminding myself to pretend to feel unwell. At night when the lights were put out, Anglican hymns were played on the gramophone. They echoed down the corridor, spilling into the wards, sounding distant and ethereal. I developed a lifelong fondness for these hymns. Although I never found a lasting attachment to religion, I felt a spiritual uplift from the romance of a valiant pilgrim relentlessly following the path of goodness. Once I even tried to draw with my pencils a God 'in light inaccessible, hid from our eyes'. Kneeling on my bed I could watch the night train thread its way along the floor of the valley below, like a string of glittering stars that had fallen from the night sky.

During a spell where I'd failed to manage my temperature with sunlight and was back in the main school, I had an unexpected visitor. Nell and I were playing marbles with some other children during break time when Blue Toes strode into our group and hauled me out. 'You are needed in reception,' she said, with no explanation. I didn't want to trust my marbles to anyone else so I twisted away from Blue Toes and squatted quickly to retrieve them, which ruined the game. As I hurried off, the marbles rattling in my pocket, I could hear the grumbling behind me and worried about a confrontation later.

Waiting in reception for me was Iris Constantine. Iris was my mother's friend and lived a few miles from our house on the Kinangop. My heart leapt with pleasure at seeing her, but immediately sank as I wondered why she was here and not Edith.

'Hello, Tanzie! I've come to take you to hospital. Edith couldn't make it,' Iris said. She tried to gather me to her, but I wasn't responsive. Hospital! And why couldn't Edith make it? Too busy as usual, I supposed. I crumpled with fear and distress.

The sobs were deep and ached in my chest at first but soon they were flowing freely enough for me to speak through them. 'Why? I don't want to go to hospital!'

'Don't worry, Tanzie. Don't cry. It's nothing to worry about. Dr Craddock is just going to take your tonsils out. You've been ill so often this last year that the sickbay Sister thought it would be a good idea.'

I knew immediately that I had overdone it with the sunlight.

My second year at school had the potential to be far worse than the first since, with my tonsils removed, I wouldn't get to enjoy the blessed peace of the sanatorium. But the year saw a new dormitory and with it a new matron, Miss Simpson. When talking amongst ourselves, we referred to her as Old Ma Simpson. She was untidy, and her large bosom was squeezed into a grubby overall that was already tight with cigarettes and matches. The colour of her unruly hair was the same as the ash that powdered her chest and shoulders, except for a sulphur stripe that swept up from her brow and arrived smoothly, but less yellowed, at the nape of her neck. Like Edith, she could hang a cigarette from the corner of her mouth without any discomfort; unlike Edith, though, she didn't look in the least glamorous in the process. Her mouth drooped at the side and gathered spit, which glinted in the bright light of morning when she did her inspection. Although I was impressed by her smoking ability, Nell – who still occupied the bed opposite mine – showed signs of disgust; gone was the complacent tilt of her nose and the pert flounce of her ponytail. But I liked Old Ma Simpson.

During one morning inspection a few weeks into the term, Old Ma Simpson shambled to a stop in front of me and caught my hands, bringing them up to her face short-sightedly to inspect my nails. When she had finished, she nodded towards the pale-blue knitted dog with long ears and button eyes that was reclining on my pillow. 'What's that?' she said.

Perhaps I'd misjudged this shabby woman. Edith had knitted Blue for me with leftover wool. He usually lived crammed in the back of my locker, only to be sneaked out after dark – I couldn't believe I'd forgotten to put him back.

'I'm sorry, Miss Simpson.' I snatched my hands away and scrambled to remove Blue before he could be confiscated.

'Just a minute!'

I stood still, my heart sinking. Blue hung from my hand.

'Let me see, dear,' said Old Ma Simpson.

I gave her the dog and waited while she turned him over, examining him more closely than she had my nails.

'Quite an interesting pattern,' she said. She handed him back and I quickly moved to put him in my locker.

'Don't do that, dear,' she said. 'You can keep him on your bed. Of course you can. Whoever heard of a child without a favourite toy on their bed?'

The next Saturday saw the writing of letters home requesting favourite toys, and soon the beds in the dormitory began to pile up with them. Even Nell had two dolls. 'What are they called?' I asked.

She held up a smartly dressed doll with bright nylon hair. 'This is Goldie.'

'So this must be Baldy,' I said, picking up the smooth-headed doll.

She hesitated a moment before deciding not to take offence. 'It's Emily.' Her smile was a bit tight, but it wasn't hostile.

'Now, what's the matter?' Old Ma Simpson tucked her chin into her chest and looked at me from under the brim of her frowning brow, her mouth exaggerating despair. 'You look as though the weight of the universe is on your head.'

I was silent, not knowing where to start. I'd come to her door in a panic, to escape the bullying of Liesbeth and her cronies. Old Ma Simpson had pulled me into her over-furnished sitting room and sat me down in a soft chair, but I wasn't relaxed enough to sink into it. I sat stiffly, trying to think of an excuse for being there.

Old Ma Simpson took up her knitting. Her breathing was nasal and heavy as she clicked away with her needles. Through the half-open window, I could hear pupils playing tennis on the courts. There was no sound of the Afrikaner bullies' feet thudding, or their calls to each other as they tried to work out where I'd gone. The room smelt of stale smoke in spite of the faint stirring of warm air from the window.

'Who are you hiding from?'

'I'm not hiding.'

Old Ma Simpson nodded without looking at me, chewing her lower lip as she knitted. She coughed, setting off a loose rattle in her chest. 'Do you know the best way to deal with bullies?'

I shook my head. 'No, not really.'

'It's simple – very, very simple. But it takes courage, at first.'

My heart sank. She was going to tell me to stand up to them, but their voices were louder than mine, their manner boisterously confident, their physicality overwhelming. They were bigger and stronger and more developed, like older pupils.

'If a bully attacks you verbally – if they use words to upset you – don't show that you are hurt, that they have succeeded. Instead, agree with them enthusiastically.' She held her needles still and smiled at me. 'If they shove you, pretend you think it was your own clumsy mistake. Apologise in earnest. It won't be easy, but it's worth a try.'

This shabby old woman's advice, just because it was she who had given it, was certainly worth a try. From then on, whenever I was called wet, or stupid, or whenever chicken clucking noises were made as I stalled trying to jump the wooden gym horse, I smiled as if amazed and grateful to be so kindly enlightened. Then, after a moment of apparent deep thought, I agreed that I was wet or stupid or chicken. In the case of my failure to leap over the horse, I even made a pantomime of despair, putting my hands over my face, then tearing my hair out and grimacing, then smiling and bowing with contrition.

It worked. I even enjoyed it at times and was almost disappointed when the bullies eventually left me alone. My newfound tactic made me less intimidated, and it may even have given me the confidence to make a new friend.

Her name was Joy. She had red-ginger hair cut off unbecomingly at chin length and standing out from her head like a triangular Egyptian headdress. Small red freckles stippled the whole surface of her skin but were especially intense across her nose. Her body temperature was hot to the touch. She was a heated kind of person with her flame colouring and hot skin, and when she whispered in my ear I used to lean away, imagining her breath was a searing desert wind. Her secrets could burn my ear canal, and singe my brain. I encouraged her to speak these secrets boldly at arm's length. She was not bold though, and she didn't have to tell me she was being bullied; I'd seen her surrounded by Liesbeth's gang. She'd hung her head and stood as though she badly needed a wee, her hands bunching her gymslip in front of her, legs clamped at the knees, and one foot placed on the other. I knew how she felt.

If she and I were to be friends, I needed her to be able to deflect bullying; otherwise I'd draw attention to myself if I tried to protect her. So I told her my secret. I instructed her in the mysteries of my technique and encouraged her to put it into practice.

One day as we rounded the corner of the high white main building, which stood above the playground terraces and overlooked the flamingo lake, we bumped into Liesbeth and her bunch. Liesbeth wasted no time in insulting Joy.

I could tell Joy was nervous, but she faced Liesbeth. 'Yes, I know I'm a bitch,' she said.

'I said "*ginger* bitch", bitch.'

'Yes, I mean ginger bitch.'

I felt fearful. Her voice was small and trembly, and her head was dipping forward, against my advice. I moved and stood close behind her, placing my hand on the small of her back. She lifted her head.

I coughed and cleared my throat casually. 'Of course she's a ginger bitch. That's clever, Liesbeth! To notice that she's ginger, and a bitch,' I said, my heart thumping. I took a breath and feigned interest in the swallows swooping in and out of their nests under the roof of the central building.

I must have sounded stronger than I felt because Joy seemed to take courage.

'I'm pigeon-toed as well!' Joy looked down at her feet, exaggerating their position to display turned-in toes.

'Bloody hell – yes – look at her feet!' I said. 'They're silly, aren't they?' I aimed my question to the gang in general.

'And I'm a real yellow belly and I'm frightened of you,' said Joy, getting into her stride. She looked through her ginger-gold eyelashes at Liesbeth and blinked.

Liesbeth, swarthy and relaxed, shifted her position to rest on her hip, and curled her lip. 'You are admitting that you are a coward and that you are frightened of me?' She turned to her followers, her eyes wide and mocking, then let her jaw drop in astonishment. For this, she received a smattering of laughter from the girls crowding close to her. Those at the back were hidden enough to look away, bored.

She turned back to spill more scorn on Joy. 'You're a fool,' she said.

'I'm a fool,' agreed Joy with enthusiasm.

Liesbeth blinked. I could feel Joy's response was too swift.

I kept my voice steady, matter of fact. 'Yeah, she *is* a fool.'

Liesbeth swept her dark hair aside from her face and looked at me. 'Why don't you mind your own business? I wasn't talking to you.'

'I was only really, really agreeing with you.'

'Just shut up! Shut up!'

'Okay.' I covered my mouth with my hands and peered at the girls at the back of the group. They wouldn't look at me.

Liesbeth leaned forward, narrowed her eyes and hissed through her teeth into Joy's face. 'You are so stupid!'

Joy leaned forward. She squeezed her eyes into slits and with her mouth close to Liesbeth's, as though to kiss her, said, 'I am *s…s…so…s…stupid*.'

'No, no, Joy!' I screeched in my head. 'Don't mimic her – just agree with her!' I felt sick. I wished the hot desert sands would breathe through Joy's lips and blast Liesbeth's face. The whole point of this game was to avoid violence by countering threat with indifference or eager agreement, but now Joy was going to unleash Liesbeth's fury. Liesbeth's eyes flickered, her breath was held, her shoulders were bunched. Somehow I must distract her. I pretended to sneeze the most enormous sneeze and then coughed, again and again. Liesbeth turned her head towards me. The relief was sweet and I brought my shoulders up to my ears in a shrug.

'She's such an idiot.' I shook my head in disbelief.

'I don't know why I'm wasting time with you,' said Liesbeth.

'That makes two of us,' said Joy.

'More like three of us…well, maybe all of us?' I looked hopefully at the gang behind their leader.

A moment or two passed, with Joy poised, waiting to agree with the next insult. I sensed that the confrontation was almost over.

'Oh, get lost, will you,' snarled Liesbeth. She strode off, followed by her gang. A few stragglers, the girls that reluctantly occupied the fringes of the group, threw us a smile or two.

We stood watching them until they were out of sight among the pepperberry trees, then we turned to each other, wide eyed.

'See! It works,' I said, and assumed an attitude of calm superiority as if there'd been no doubt it would. Then I pretended to buckle at the knees with relief, and Joy laughed.

Being friends with Joy made school much better. It was fun to join in games. We would shout 'salt, mustard, vinegar, pepper' as we jumped in and out of a skipping rope, or we would join a ribbon of roller-skaters weaving along the tarmac on the top terrace, holding the shirt of the person in front.

Liesbeth began to smile and wave from the terraces whenever she saw me, and pick me for her side during sports lessons. But I felt tense being in her team. I was a slow runner and only average at most games, and it was hard work trying to keep up the pretence that I wasn't afraid of her. Then she asked me to go home with her on one of the 'long Sundays' that straddled half term. 'Think of the poor girls whose families live too far away, or who are too busy,' the headmaster had said at assembly the day before, so Liesbeth must have thought about them.

'I didn't have the courage to say no!' I told Joy. 'I didn't manage to think up an excuse fast enough. What am I going to do?'

'It might be alright. At least you'll be away from school, and you might even have a nice time,' said Joy, frowning. Her frown was more believable than her words.

Liesbeth's mother was a coarser version of Liesbeth. Alma had a deep voice and chewed the inside of her cheek as though it was the remains of a meal that had been hard to swallow. She greeted her daughter by shoving her shoulder hard and saying, 'So there you are!' Her driving was fast and careless. Liesbeth and I were thrown against each other every time a corner was negotiated. I think she found that as uncomfortable as I did. Fortunately, although the road was rough and pitted where the tarmac had worn, there weren't many corners. Alma didn't have much to say. Liesbeth seemed a bit subdued. I felt awkward and shy. I watched the landscape for wildlife. Herds of buffalo grazed in dark clumps under distant trees; I could almost hear the flies buzzing round their ears and feel the tick birds pecking their rumps.

When the car turned off the main road the dust began to obscure the view. Alma rolled the windows up, which didn't help my habitual carsickness. Even hot air blowing dust into a car was preferable to closed windows. I shut my eyes. 'It's because I'm feeling sick,' I told Liesbeth when she nudged me.

As the car pulled up in front of a house, an Alsatian dog rose out of the dust on the end of a chain, barking fiercely.

'Shut up, Caesar,' said Alma, getting out and leaving the driver's door open. It stayed open until the return journey.

Caesar wagged his tail and slunk back into the dust and shade near the house. Liesbeth made no attempt to greet him, but I held out my hand. 'Hello, boy!'

'Don't talk to him. He's a guard dog. He's untrustworthy. He only likes Mum. Follow me, I'll show you round the house. D'you want a Coke?'

The house was a ramshackle barn-like wooden building with a dirty-looking Makuti roof. Inside, some of the floorboards were missing and the rugs that were spread at regular intervals were mostly threadbare. It would have been okay if the place looked lived in, but it had an air of abandonment, as if nobody ever gathered there to enjoy one another's company. Chairs weren't grouped together, there were no half-open magazines or books or cups and saucers left lying around, and no ashtrays. Considering we were in the blaze of day, the rooms were dark.

Liesbeth went through to the kitchen and came back with two cold Cokes. We sat on a window seat. Through the film of dust on the outside of the window I could see farm buildings. In contrast to the house, they looked sturdy and well maintained. There were three Massey Ferguson tractors and a trailer neatly parked in a partitioned shed.

'What animals do you have here?'

'None, it's a sisal farm.'

'Oh!' I couldn't believe there was only Caesar. 'No cats, mongooses, parrots?'

'No.'

The day passed slowly. My fear of Liesbeth, combined with the alien atmosphere I felt there, didn't help me relax, and we found little to talk about. There were patches of the day that were fine though. It was fun making our own sandwiches, slapping butter on the bread and mixing Marmite with peanut butter. We also mashed up bananas with plenty of demerara sugar and poured cream on top.

'Where do you buy your cream?' I asked, spooning the mixture into my mouth with relish. It was thick and yellow and the brown sugar dissolved into it like caramel.

Liesbeth wasn't interested. 'I dunno. I think Mum just gets it from the *duka* down the road.' She yawned. I thought it was strange not to know where your food came from. That was the trouble – because Liesbeth didn't seem interested in things, it was hard to talk to her. Even when we played a game she just seemed to dominate rather than share.

We played Cowboys and Indians in the sisal plantations, kicking up dust and shooting each other from behind the plants. This was fun for a while; I loved being shot and leaping backwards with a bullet in my chest, screaming wildly as I fell into the dirt. But soon Liesbeth began competing with my dying antics and the game became more about trying to get shot than about avoiding death. We went through quite a few reincarnations before we got too hot. Our clothes and skin were dirt streaked and untidy when we headed back for another Coke.

The return journey with Liesbeth's mother was as awkward as the outward one had been. When we arrived back at the school, I thanked Alma for having me.

She nodded and started the car up. 'There you go!' she said to Liesbeth.

'There you go, Mum,' Liesbeth replied, waving goodbye as the car leapt forward.

'Did you enjoy the day?' asked Liesbeth as we walked to the dormitory.

'Yes, thank you,' I said.

But it seemed that Liesbeth wanted more than politeness because she responded with, 'You had better promise to tell everybody that you had a good time, or you'll be sorry.'

'Okay, I promise.' My words squeezed themselves through clenched teeth.

'Tell them that we drove the tractor and helped load the trailer.'

'Yes, Liesbeth, I will, Liesbeth, of course Liesbeth.'

Her tone became more of an enquiry 'And you'll say it was good fun?'

'I will,' I answered wearily.

Joy was the only girl I told about how little I'd enjoyed the day. I gained status among the other girls for going home with Liesbeth, but perhaps I hadn't shown the required level of enthusiasm about it all because Liesbeth avoided me for a while after, as if my neutral attitude might be noticed. I was relieved. The girls who kowtowed to Liesbeth still saw me as worthy of respect, but now I didn't have to pretend to like her.

For long Sundays after this one, Joy persuaded her parents to take me to their house on the fringes of Naivasha. Each time was great. We only had Joy's grown-up brother's old bicycle but we could imagine it into any form of transport, from ship to aircraft to horse. Being a boy's bike and a bit big for us, we kept hurting our pubic bones on the crossbar and hopped round clutching our private parts through our shorts, saying 'Owie, man!' and laughing. There was a tree in the middle of the circular driveway outside the house, which was like a magnet. We kept losing control and riding into it. Under the dappled shade, when the sun was bright, Joy's hair flickered like flames as she crashed into the trunk.

No Colour I've Ever Seen

Iris is a strider, an arm swinger. Her smile is ready and wide. She holds her head high and is confident, jolly and wholesome, and big. She is English. Arlo is short and stocky with a thick dark pelt of hair. He is half Italian, half French. They live in a wooden house on stilts on the farm beyond Angus Ferguson's place. To me they seem rather old, but Edith says they are not much older than Angus, who is in his twenties.

One day when Edith and I are making the farm butter into blocks and wrapping it in greaseproof paper, the dogs start barking. We hear a Land Rover engine. We hear Mzee and the dogs being greeted, and then Iris appears at the open top half of the kitchen stable door.

'Don't let me disturb you, Edith,' she says, leaning in to unbolt the bottom half. 'I was just popping by to see if you need anything from Naivasha? That butter looks good. Hello, Tanzie – helping your Ma? Such a trouper.'

'No, thanks, Iris; I've already fetched the post and been to the *duka*. But come in, come in…' Edith lifts the Aga lid and moves the heavy kettle across.

I know Iris and Edith are all set for a long chat in spite of Iris's 'just popping by'. After Edith has made the tea they sit at the kitchen table. I continue working with the butter while they talk and Edith smokes.

After some time the conversation turns to the Dawson family on our northern border. 'Peggy is expecting again. Neville is very pleased. I think they're hoping for a boy this time, after the two girls.' Edith refills Iris's cup.

Iris sighs. 'The thought of having children appals me,' she says. 'I'm actually getting sterilised on Thursday at Nakuru Hospital – did I tell you? Dr Craddock has arranged it.'

'I suppose you know what you're doing. How does Arlo feel about it?'

'He says if we are happy as we are, why change things?'

'But children can change things for the better.'

'Not for me they wouldn't, I'm sure! To be honest, I'm scared of being pregnant, and as for giving birth, no thanks. And then all that business of changing nappies and feeding. No, I don't want kids.'

'Well, I know what you mean, Iris. It can be a bit thankless, child rearing. What made it acceptable to me was the army of ayahs, and after that boarding school…' Edith smiles ruefully. 'And good neighbours.'

I'm bruised by Edith's thinking child rearing is thankless, and anger and confusion somersault over each other in my heart.

Then Iris looks at me and ruffles my hair. 'Of course, if I could guarantee having a child like this one, I'd have a whole tribe of them.'

I watch Edith with my chest clogged. She is busy unwrapping a new packet of Players and doesn't notice my need to bring her joy. I sneak away outside to find Cora.

'It would serve her right if I went to live with Iris and Arlo. You could come too,' I tell the dog. But I don't feel much better for this meanness because I have a suspicion that my defection wouldn't really dent Edith's equilibrium.

Iris likes me and often offers to take me to school and bring me back. I have mixed feelings about this, much preferring Edith to accompany me. But Iris's sturdy confidence does have its upsides.

Unlike Edith, when Iris takes me to school, she carries my suitcase, striding straight into the dormitory. I follow, half pleased and half embarrassed. Although Edith would never bother settling me, I would be proud of her well-dressed, well-heeled good looks and easy grace. Iris's unselfconscious clumsiness and vigorous support make me feel uncomfortable as well as secure.

Iris sits on my allocated bed and smiles at the girl sitting on the next one. My heart sinks as I see that it's Liesbeth. Liesbeth does not return Iris's smile but just nods in acknowledgement.

Iris leans across and extends her hand. 'Iris Constantine,' she says. 'Pleased to meet you.'

Liesbeth may be top dog in a narrow world, but she has few social skills and holds out her hand hesitatingly.

'This is Liesbeth,' I say flatly.

*

The time Iris turns up to take me to have my tonsils out I cry and make a fuss in a way I wouldn't have done if it had been Edith collecting me. Iris drives me to the hospital and after I've been admitted and am propped up with pillows, she sits on my bed. I'm feeling ill already, just from crying and being in this strange place. Opposite me, in the four-bed ward, a girl is sleeping. I'm glad she's not awake to see me snivelling.

Iris places her huge hands, with severely cut nails, either side of my head and plants her lips on my forehead. Then she draws back and cuffs me playfully on the arm. 'Gosh, I've missed you, my lambkin,' she says. 'And now I've got to leave you again. But I'll be back in a few days.'

I submit to her leaving with no comment. I didn't enjoy the possessiveness of 'my' lambkin. But as soon as she leaves the ward I wish she would come back. I jump out of bed and follow her. She strides, arms swinging, down the corridor towards the exit, her big sandaled feet slapping the floor. She easily outstrips me and I return to the ward disconsolate.

I wake up gradually, trying to come to terms with my surroundings. Slowly, I recognise the pastel blue-green paint of the hospital ward and the smell of surgical spirit, hot dust, stale catarrh and, faintly, roses. I turn my head away from the wall.

'They've put your bed sides up because you thrashed about and pushed it away from the wall and fell under it while you were unconscious, and you fought demons.'

The girl has spoken to me from the opposite bed. Her tone is slightly accusing. She has been here seven months, so the nurses told me when they came with a syringe. She can't walk and is near the door for the nurses' convenience. Her hair is no colour I've ever seen on a human head. It's the palest lime, with fine gossamer strands straying out over her pillow. She has the assurance of a favoured pet, and is a little smug, it seems to me. I'd be wary and hostile if I weren't so in awe of her lime-coloured head.

'You've got blood on your face,' she says.

I touch my face and then hold my fingers in front of my eyes. I can smell the blood, it's like rust. I can smell the roses on her bedside locker. There's a faint clean soapy smell from my sheets. The blood seems to be coming from one of my nostrils.

The girl picks up a little silver bell from her locker and rings it until a nurse hurries in.

'What is it, dear?'

'It's her. She's awake, and she's bleeding.'

I live in a world of disgusting catarrh, ice cream, pleasant nurses, bad dreams and a fluctuating temperature. During the day, the lime girl tries to engage me in conversation but even though I'm fascinated by her, I'm too comfortable in my own world of sunshine penetrating deep into the ward and roses releasing their scent to respond. And in the evenings, after the sun has gone down, I'm too uncomfortable with soreness and flushed skin to pay her any attention.

After a few days, Iris breezes in. She's rude and energetic. She brings the whole world of the city and the wide rural smells of Africa in her wake. It's as though her body punches a hole through the sick world of tonsils and polio.

She throws a suitcase on my bed, smiles across at my pale companion, then turns to me. 'Dr Craddock said you could go back to school, but there's not much term time left, so I thought I'd take you home to the Kinangop. We'll call in to school for your clothes and then you can stay with me while we get you fit, feed you up. Edith has already agreed to it. C'mon, get cracking.'

But I'm not used to standing up and Iris has to half carry me. As we leave the ward my eyes meet the lime girl's, and I smile my regret at heading off before I've had chance to make proper friends with her.

Iris and Arlo's house is made completely of wood. Daylight shines through the floorboards, defining the striped alignment of planks. In some places the gaps are wide enough for snakes and scorpions, so I'm glad we are at an altitude where such creatures aren't found. I'm frightened at night though. The Mau Mau could easily crawl under the house and set fire to it.

Iris looks after me. Each night before bed she bathes me, as if cleaning away weakness and sickness. My skin glows with warmth from the scrubbing. I enjoy the dark rooms with up-lit streams of sun streaking through the floorboards and I drift about contentedly. Iris brings me comics from the *duka* and books from the library in Njabini.

Edith comes to see me. I'm sitting on the veranda as the Ford Zephyr pulls up. She's in her afternoon visiting dress, sunglasses pushed up on her head. She hooks her handbag over her left arm, like royalty who carry gloves in that hand to free up their right one for greeting people. I put down my comic and run down the steps. I feel warm and happy as I take her free hand

and we go to find Iris, who is making marmalade in the kitchen. As usual I cherish the lipstick imprint Edith has planted on my forehead.

We all settle round the tea tray in the lounge. Although the excitement of Princess Margaret's visit to the Highlands has eased off a little now, everyone is still keen to talk about it. The suit that Arlo wore to be presented to her is still gracing a hanger on the door. I have no idea what services he rendered to the country, but I do know that Edith was commended for bravery.

Edith is laughing as she recounts her meeting with the princess. 'I thought I was going to buckle at the knees.' She surveys her audience, while Arlo, next to her on the sofa, smiles broadly. 'I could feel Arlo trembling alongside me as she got nearer and nearer. He was so nervous he was clutching a fistful of my dress. It was making my nerves worse.' Edith turns her head and looks at Arlo. He smiles in confirmation.

'I thought I'd never be able to drop my curtsey. It would all go wrong, what with Arlo hanging on to me. I thought I might lurch forward, crash into her and drag him with me, and we'd all collapse in a tangle. Then she was there in front of me and I was being presented and somehow I managed to bend my knees and mumble some response. What did she say to me, Arlo? It's such a blur, I can't remember.'

Arlo spreads his hands, raises his shoulders and shakes his head, smiling at us. He can't remember either.

'Well, anyway, I managed the curtsey and then she moved on to Arlo. I was relieved my turn was over but then I saw Arlo drop into the deepest curtsey imaginable.'

Iris gasps. 'No! I don't believe it. After all that rehearsal of the shallow bow.' Iris begins to laugh and is soon fishing in her handbag for a hanky to mop her eyes.

Edith adds, 'But the most embarrassing part was that I couldn't stifle my laughter. I snorted. It was painful. And then I noticed that Arlo was inspecting the floor and his shoulders were shaking like a jelly on a steam train. Well, we just lost control. Poor Princess Margaret walked on to the next person as though she hadn't noticed a thing.'

Iris throws her head back and raises her arms to the ceiling, still clutching her hanky. I adore it when somebody laughs so hugely. I fall sideways into her lap and my ribs begin to ache, even though it's not *that* funny. The amusement is infectious, and we hold our sides and struggle for breath between fresh bursts of explosive sound.

Iris hands me a glass of milk and a scone. Talk is general and light and the mood is mid-afternoon delicious. I compare the white of my ankle socks with the white of the milk. I look at the few drifting clouds to assess their whiteness. My ears begin to tune into the adult chatter again.

'Well, Arlo has been looking into it for a long time, Edith. This country is going to the dogs. It's all a bit unstable, and the Africans are restless. I'm frightened at night, I don't mind admitting it.' Iris smoothes her dress, dusting off the crumbs from her scone as though clearing her lap of Africa.

'I'm not surprised you're frightened. Heavens above, I'd be afraid living here.' Edith glances at the floorboards. 'You don't even have a high fence round the place or guard dogs; I'm sure you'd feel safer with them.'

'In Australia you don't have to think about things like that, Edith. We think we'd have a better future in a country with a decent outlook.'

'They don't have very good quality farm land.'

'Arlo has looked into Merino sheep ranching. He's negotiating about some land at the moment.'

I'm suddenly in turmoil. Perhaps Iris and Arlo will take me with them to rear sheep in Australia. Edith might be pleased because a child can get in her way. But unexpectedly, in a slow realisation of something true, I know Edith would not let me go, and I feel safe. I don't want Iris to go either. She'll miss me too I think and my sadness is laced with gladness. As usual I'm mixed up and my chest hurts. But organising a move to Australia takes time and I soon forget about it.

When the first circus to visit Kenya arrives in Nairobi, Iris offers to take me. As it's quite a distance away, she arranges for us to stay with some friends who live close by. We set out early in the morning, and after a long drive, we arrive at the Sheppards' house. It seems huge, built round a quadrangle, with an inner veranda lining a courtyard. There are several doors each side of the square. We are shown to a room that is surprisingly small, with a double bed pushed sideways against the wall under a window.

The family has a pack of Alsatians. When I get bored being with Iris and the Sheppards in their lounge, I leave them to go and have a look around. The dogs find me. My feet must have echoed on the stone under the veranda roof. They crowd me, their noses very close to my face. Their tails are not wagging and their inspection of me is humourless. I've not met unfriendly dogs before, and a wave of fear causes me to step back and feel the wall behind me. The move is a mistake and one of them growls. I realise I have to be calm. The wooden rafters above me are thick with spider webs, and I examine them with feigned casualness. After a while I squat down and attend to a buckle on my shoe, and try not to pull away as I feel the breath of muzzles creating a draught in my ears. The dogs widen their circle, mill around more, then hear something the other side of the quadrangle and slope off like wolves scenting a kill. I feel weak; the hem of my skirt is trembling.

I decide to go back to the lounge to ask Iris what time the circus is.

She excuses herself from the family and joins me in the quadrangle, checking her wristwatch. 'We should leave in about an hour. You can have a shower first, if you like.' She points towards the bathroom. 'And if you're hungry I'm sure the Sheppards won't mind if you go and ask for a sandwich in the kitchen. It's that outbuilding through that gap over there.'

'What about the dogs? What if they follow me?'

'They are a bit frightening, aren't they? You're used to dogs though, and they're only doing their job. Don't you let them worry you.'

'But they shove their noses at me and don't seem to smile. They're like bullies at school.'

'No, they're not, and anyway if you treat them like you do the bullies at school they'll be much less frightening.'

'So I have to convince them that I don't really care if they tear me up and splatter me all over the walls, turning everything red?'

Iris laughs. 'Go and get us both a sandwich and I'll meet you back in our room.'

'Okay, but if the dogs surround me, I'm going to give them our food.'

The circus is exciting. I love the clowns and the acrobats on horseback. The ringmaster is splendid with his theatrical stage presence and strutting postures. But the trapeze artists really enthral me. They fly above us, strong and graceful as though the air is as buoyant as water, trailing silver and blue ribbons that are sewn to their costumes to look like tail feathers.

My cheeks are hot and I'm very tired when we return to the Sheppards'. Iris helps me to bed and says goodnight. 'I won't be too long; I'm just going to chat for a bit. Don't hog the bed, and sweet dreams.' She leaves, switching off the light and closing the door. As I drift off to sleep I hear the snuffling of Alsatian noses under the door.

I sleep on my stomach. I've heard it said that if you do that you're fearful. I'm fearful – of the night, of strange people, of strange places and of dogs. Earlier, being surrounded by the pack had made me put my back to the wall, but in some ways I'd be more comfortable keeping my face to the wall. Hiding, shutting out, shielding myself, protecting my eyes, my thoughts and my heart help me feel secure. So I sleep flat to the mattress, shoving the pillows aside. As I warm up I spread star-shaped across the bed.

Tonight my head is full of lights and flashes of colour and movement. Dazzlingly costumed trapeze artists fly behind my eyelids, but even so my recent persistent worry breaks through. Iris likes me, and would have a tribe of me. Edith may not mind if Iris adopts me. I hate Edith for her tepid motherhood; I hate Iris for her reluctance to have her own child.

Am I sleeping or am I awake in a thick atmosphere of loathing, where my knees are hooked back over a trapeze rung and I'm swinging Edith at the end of my arms, my hands rigid so she doesn't fall into the sawdust far below? I can't release her. The trapeze swings back and back and suddenly I seem to be trapped behind a bulk of resistance. I can't swing forward. So I turn onto my side, draw up my knees, place my back to the wall and shove with all my strength – to create space and find release, and to keep dogs at bay, bullies subdued and life at arm's length. I wake up as I push. Iris's great body moves forward easily as though the bed surface is oiled metal, and crashes off the bed.

I pretend I'm still asleep. I'm appalled. But I'm also pleased and excited, potent and powerful. Finally, I'm too tired. I think I'm already asleep before Iris climbs back between the sheets.

I miss Iris when she and Arlo leave for Australia so, as many times before, I use my imagination to help cope with the loss. Iris is amongst a flock of plump Merino sheep, looking happy, smelling of the lanolin from their wool. But as I don't really know what Merinos look like, the sheep I imagine are Romney Marsh.

Edith and Iris mean to stay in touch but as time passes strings loosen. Macmillan's 'winds of change' speech causes upheavals amongst the white and Asian populations and people lose each other across continents.

Many years later, I'm visiting Edith, as I do most weekends. She's in her eighties now and lives above the

Wye Valley. I call up the stairs to her flat from the front door, scooping up her mail from the rush matting.

Edith appears at the top of the landing, arms akimbo, feet planted squarely. 'Come up on the chairlift,' she says. Her thick white hair is lit up like a gauzy halo from the window behind her, where a bright sun is just holding its own against twilight. Her specs are clamped down on her head as if to stop her hair taking flight.

I walk up the stairs, and as I reach the top, Edith steps into my arms. I hug her hard and briefly, inhaling her smell of soap, cooking fat, humbugs and Olbas oil. She takes the letters from me and we move into the kitchen.

'Put the kettle on. How are you?' She settles stiffly on a chair. 'Ginger, move off there.' She flaps the envelopes at the marmalade cat sleeping on the seat next to her.

'Don't worry, Ginger,' I say. 'I'll sit on the other one.'

The cat continues dozing peacefully.

'Are you staying the night?'

'I've brought my toothbrush.'

'Lovely. In that case, forget the kettle; let's have a tipple.'

We settle down with a whisky and soda, but Edith's post remains unopened on the table.

'You've got an airmail,' I say, pointing to a flash of blue and red border.

Edith picks up the envelope. 'I'm sure I recognise that handwriting.' She begins to look around. 'Now, what have I done with my specs?'

'They're on your head!'

'Oh yes.' She plants them on her nose and opens the airmail, from which a photograph falls. I pick it up while she begins reading the letter. 'It's from Iris Constantine!' she says. 'How lovely. It's years and years since we were last in contact.'

I examine the snapshot. 'Look, Ma, it's a photo of her and Arlo. But I don't know who all these big blokes are with them?'

Edith looks across briefly before returning to her letter. 'Nor me.'

After a while she says, 'Those big blokes? They're Iris and Arlo's sons. All five of them.'

'That can't be right! I thought she didn't want children. I thought she was sterilised?'

'So did I. I'm sure she was. In Nakuru Hospital.'

We inspect the five sons closely. Standing on Iris's right, they are tall and muscular. Their father is to her left. There is something charmingly ridiculous about the grouping and we laugh.

'Well,' I say, reaching for my glass, 'those guys look mighty handy – dead useful for running a sheep ranch. Here's to Iris and Arlo and their big boys.'

'Cheers!'

As I lean over to switch on a lamp in the dying light, I consider how my imagination had failed to gift Iris such a marvellous reality. I wonder why she had five children, when at one time she hadn't wanted any. Was she trying to have a girl? Was she trying to reproduce me?

I Am on Saturn

Mr Blakey, or Snakey as I call him, stands at the front of the classroom with his back to us. Today I watch him especially closely. I absorb the athleticism in his stillness, the deep luxury of his hair, and the smooth silky tan showing through his white shirt.

He makes us wait.

The desk I am standing on is not level, and I stiffen my leg muscles on one side to stop my shaking from being audible and drawing attention to me.

I know Snakey is poised to enjoy himself, but today I am just as prepared as he is for what is going to happen. He is steady and firm and full of grace, and he has power, but despite my trembling, I now have power too. I can leave him. I can fly over his head, through the window and over the pepperberry trees on the playground terrace towards the flamingo-fringed lake, the soft moss hills, lavender mountains and beyond – well beyond, to the edge of space or to the heart of a jacaranda flower.

How it works with Snakey is that as soon as he enters the classroom, we must climb onto our desks and stand to attention. He then marches up and down the aisles between each row of desks, firing mental arithmetic questions at each child in turn. We call out our answers and he responds with either a nod or a shake of his head. If our answer is correct, we are allowed to stand on our chair; an incorrect answer means we must stay on our desk as Snakey completes his circuit of the room and starts again. After two correct answers, we can sit down, breathe easy and watch the entertainment. But my answers are either always wrong or I am too slow in responding, so I am the last child standing on their desk, every time.

At first, I tried hard to respond correctly to Snakey's quick-fire questions. Seduced by his rich beauty, I wanted to shine for him, but I am not mentally agile enough. The more I feared him making me a public failure just with a maths question, the further I retreated from him. But I don't want to feel shaken and impotent and stupid anymore, don't want to have everyone witness the tears and snot glazing my face. So today, as I stand above Snakey, I have made my mind as vacant as Oliver's scoured porridge bowl.

'Are you deaf? Or are you stupid? The class is waiting for you to answer. You are wasting their time…are you crying? I'm not surprised – I would cry too if I didn't even have the brains of a kindergarten child.' Snakey speaks very slowly: 'You can't answer even *one*' – he holds up his index finger – '*small*' – his voice is squeaky as he presses his thumb and forefinger together and screws up his eyes to convey the struggle to see such a tiny thing – '*simple*' – he takes a deep breath, opens his eyes wide, brings his shoulders up and holds his hands high, shaking his head from side to side – '*easy*' – he whispers, knitting his brows and pulling his lips away from his teeth in a grimace, collapsing his face into a broken cry-baby sob – '*question*.' Everybody enjoys this performance and laughter punctuates each dramatic emphasis. Snakey is right about me on all counts. Then he picks up a ruler from the desk of the pupil behind me and uses it to smack the back of my legs.

It had taken me a long time to recognise how much Snakey relishes my discomfort, how he exploits it for fun. But once I understood my role as Snakey's sport, I couldn't stay in the room and be the centre of humiliation any longer. So now I practise being somewhere else, through my imagination. I daydream right in the middle of all that horrible misery. But I'm not simply absent; something hard and careless is gestating inside me.

My face is devoid of tears, my reaction to the ruler smacking the back of my calves unflinching. Snakey's voice is rising, but I can't hear him because I am on Saturn, gliding through rings of colour. Then his voice falls, murmuring sarcasms so delicately that the others strain to hear. Harsh and loud, or threateningly soft, he provides pauses for everybody to fill with laughter. But ridicule is wasted when the target is a butterfly flying close to the ground in Madagascar, tasting the dust in a swirl of wind, or drinking the sweat from the hide of a grazing beast. After a while, I suspect that Snakey is beginning to feel stupid shouting at someone who is too far away to hear him, and embarrassed that the laughter in the room is now sounding rather nervous and forced.

It can't be long until break time. Snakey is below me, tapping his left hand with the ruler. There is an impatient quality to the rhythm and out of the slant of my vision I get the impression he is frowning. I let my eyes slide over him briefly. He is almost ugly with his eyebrows drawn tight into the middle of his forehead. Suddenly I am filled with cold hatred. I look down at him and hold my gaze, steadily and icily. My limbs stop trembling, and my desk is still. Our eyes remain locked. It's an impasse. Some of the children fidget. A small flutter of laughter ripples across the room, but I think it makes Snakey more uncomfortable than it does me, because I no longer care.

When breaktime comes at last, the others get up and leave, while I am made to stay on my desk. I stare into the sky through the window; it is colourless, bleached and sucked free of blueness by the sun. Snakey lingers, and sighs. Then, because his audience has gone, he walks with irritated energy straight out of the door. Only when I hear his footsteps ringing on the concrete walkway do I climb down from the desk.

Joy, my best friend, is waiting for me on the terrace steps. She already knows what has happened because my classmates have been talking about it. Joy is in the B stream, and I'm in the A stream – on account of my being good at English and subjects that need writing about, such as history and geography. But my mental arithmetic is bad even when I don't have a frightening teacher because I can't carry remainder numbers in my head. I'm glad Joy and I aren't in the same class; I don't want her to feel she has to join the others laughing because I can't add, subtract, divide or multiply or work out how many potatoes Farmer Joe will plant in five hours if he takes two hours to plant 500 potatoes and takes a four-minute tea break every hour.

Joy hands me my milk that she has queued for. As I sip it, still shaky and weak with relief, she puts her hand on the small of my back to comfort me.

'I'm alright, hey!' I say, trying to reassure her.

'Man, you ought to make an effort. It's easy. Why don't you just answer that bloody fool teacher?'

She pats my back a couple of times. She thinks that I won't, rather than can't, answer that bloody fool teacher.

As the bell screeches through the heat haze on the terraces, we get up and return our empty milk bottles to the crate.

'See you after English,' Joy says.

'Yeah, man, see you then.'

I touch her hair briefly, returning the comfort she has just shown me. She loathes English lessons, but because she is nowhere near as bad at English as I am at arithmetic, a quick stroke of her hair is all the sympathy necessary. Her class will probably just be left to read *Jock of the Bushveld* anyway while Miss Perry smokes cigarettes in the staff room and tries to seduce Snakey. Everybody knows she fancies Snakey. Everybody fancies Snakey. And Joy may even find pleasure in a book about a yellow dog adventuring in the wilds of Southern Africa. She's fond of dogs.

The next Monday morning, we hear Snakey's footsteps approach. They are more rapid than usual. We scramble to climb onto our desks, but Snakey's voice cuts into the noise.

'Sit down, everybody.'

We are surprised and settle quickly. We sit perfectly still and are so quiet that my eardrums seem to burst with the beat of my heart.

Snakey goes to the front of the classroom, leans against his desk and folds his arms. 'Eleven multiplied by eight, divided by four?'

The question explodes from his mouth, sharp and clipped. After a moment of confusion, because this isn't the usual start to mental arithmetic lessons, several hands are raised in the air. Snakey quickly nods at a pupil, accepts their answer, and just as quickly fires another question. He never looks at me. I never put up my hand. Never again are we required to stand on our desks.

Years later, I learn that Snakey drowned on a fishing trip off the North Wales coast. The old sourness seeps through my veins. His beauty swims before my eyes, before deforming slowly into a blue bloated corpse.

A Chameleon Can Swallow a Person Whole

I grow moss.

Looking for it under the coolness of the trees that mark the school boundary, I follow the stream. Although I had been too timid to compete for one of the school's larger recreational gardening plots, I'm happy with this small one right by the stream, which no one else wanted. Unlike all the other children's gardens, mine is under a tree with prominent roots and is almost always in shadow. Moss thrives here, and there is no room for flowers.

It is a green velvet place, cool and sweet. The quiet trickle of clear water mingles with the rustle of gold grasses beyond – beyond in what might, for all I know, be wilderness. The whine of a zillion insects lends distance and dimension to the hum of nature's music, though all sound is muted now due to the wad of cotton wool stuffed in my right ear.

Today is a hot Saturday afternoon. My friend Joy has one knee under her chin and the other in the dirt as she attends to her patch. It is next to mine but is in full sunlight for most of the day. Joy is busy rearranging the stones that she used to define her area. Her curls glisten against the blue sky as though varnished with a marmalade glaze, and her orange and gold marigolds look like fallen clumps of her hair. She makes me feel hot, and I'm thankful for the shade of my own moss coolness.

'Where's the watering can?' Joy runs her hands through her flowers like a comb, as if letting them know she cares for them. She stands up. 'Where is it, Nell? The watering can?'

Nell, busy in her own plot beyond Joy's, sighs and straightens up, inspects her surroundings and then points with her trowel to a battered old watering can upturned among her pansies.

After a moment, Joy obviously realises that Nell is not going to bring the can to her, so she fetches it herself. 'Thanks for nothing!' she says, wiping her forehead with her free arm, streaking her hair with sweat.

Nell bobs and dips, bending and planting, her ponytail bouncing and swinging. She is neat and precise. I am watching her beyond Joy, who is now on her haunches with her arms round her knees, assessing her decisions. But Joy's position seems difficult to maintain and she spreads a leg out to the side and then reaches around her other knee to move another stone. Nell though would never rest on her haunches; she keeps her feet together, bends at the knees, and works the ground directly beside her. Nothing about her is splayed. She is like a ballet dancer who knows all the moves but interprets them stiffly. Only her hair is expressive, inclined to be wild if the wind is strong or if she is running or skipping.

Joy comes to the stream with the watering can, removes her plimsoles and stands in the water, throwing her head back in an expression of bliss. Then there is a sudden distant eruption of splashing and shouting from the swimming pool beyond the kai apple hedge bordering the garden plots. Practice for the swimming competition must have begun. Nell and Joy are not competing because they aren't strong swimmers, and I am exempt due to my ear infection.

Looking towards the hedge, I forget the noise for a moment while I wonder, as I often do, if there might be a chameleon lurking in its dense greenery. I've never found one in Nakuru though; it must be too hot for them down here on the Rift Valley floor. But at home on the highland plateau, where we have kai apple hedges on two sides of the lawn, sap-green chameleons might right now be shivering among the foliage, pretending to be leaves trembling in the breeze.

I drift into memory, to a time at home. I am a magician and my wand is a beautiful chameleon, clinging to my forefinger as I strut around. I point it at a fly, which is magicked out of existence with a flash of the creature's tongue. Emerging from behind the disused hen house, I point my wand at Mzee, who is cutting flowers to take indoors. 'Abracadabra,' I shout. Mzee's eyes lock onto my hand and are wide with fright. It's real; he's not just humouring me. A tremor of excitement prickles my skin at this new power to instil fear, and I approach Mzee like an evil magician.

He shakes his head and whimpers. '*Hapana, hapana* – no, no.' His lips tremble and his gluey eye weeps tears that roll down his cheek.

I lower my arm, and the chameleon reverses itself and climbs towards my shoulder. I reach out my other arm to reassure Mzee, but he shudders away from me.

My mother comes out of the house, carrying her knitting. She must have witnessed my role of wicked magician from the divan in the lounge window. She drops her knitting on the veranda wall and hurries towards Mzee. As soon as he sees Edith, Mzee rushes to her, full of fear and complaint.

Taking the flowers from him, Edith shepherds Mzee round the back of the house, towards the kitchen. 'Come and have some chai and rest a while.'

I go to the knitting, thinking to return it to Edith. The wool is bright red and cheery, and I place the chameleon on it, hoping for a spectacular colour change. But my companion remains muted orange-brown.

When I ask Edith later why Mzee had behaved so strangely, she says, 'He believes chameleons can swallow a person whole.' I'm stunned at the kind of magic that can not only change colour but can also make Mzee think he will be eaten by a creature that fits on the back of my hand.

The clamour from the swimming pool returns me to the present. Both Joy and Nell are listening intently. We walk quickly to the hedge, but then we are undecided. The small building that stores our garden tools, amongst other things, blocks our view of the pool.

'Doesn't sound like practising for the swimming races to me,' Nell says.

'Something's wrong,' Joy says.

'We must find out,' I say.

We race down the steps leading to the road past the store, and head for the pool. Suddenly, girls and boys are running towards us, dodging sideways, ducking, and swiping at the air around them with their hands. Just as suddenly, Nell stops, and grabbing a fistful of Joy's shirt, brings her to a standstill. 'Wait!' she says. 'They're being stung – it's a swarm of bees! Turn back!'

As we stand still and uncertain, Nell still holding onto Joy, we see the big bully Rotuno boy from Joy's class charging towards the tennis courts down the road to our left. There is a dense black cloud on the back of his shirt, which he is trying to twist out of while running. As he arrives at the courts, the tennis players begin to flap their arms and panic too.

'What shall we do? We've got to do something. What shall we do?' says Joy, biting her lip and pulling at her hair.

'We'll just add to the panic if we get involved,' I say.

'Shouldn't we find a member of staff?' Joy pulls free of Nell's grasp and faces her.

'Perhaps Matron is in her quarters,' Nell agrees.

We turn and run again, this time to the dormitories where we lived last year, in the hope of finding dear Old Ma Simpson. Hammering on the door to her private rooms, we call out, 'Miss Simpson, are you there?' But there is no answer.

We try to think what other staff might be around. 'They're all at the pool, I expect,' says Joy.

'And any of those off duty have probably gone into town,' I say.

'Hell, man – look!' says Joy. 'There are bees everywhere!'

We hear the angry buzzing noise as small black shapes like pellets ping in the sunlight just outside the covered walkway as though flicked by naughty boys. We hang back in the shadows of the pillars.

'I've got an idea,' says Nell.

'Spit! Go on, spit it out.' I'm not confident that Nell will have a thought worth hearing, but I make myself listen.

'Let's run to the Year Two dorm – quick!' Nell shouts.

'Oh yes, what a brilliant idea!' I say, with as much sarcasm as I can summons. 'With all those open windows that we'll never be able to close in time –'

'Come on!' shrieks Nell, once again tugging on Joy's shirt.

'No!' I say.

Nell is prissy and affected. She is not someone who can be calm in a crisis. She is not a leader. She is getting on my nerves. 'There's no point going to the dorms. We need to find somewhere with no windows or where they are closed!' I'm the one shouting now. 'Will you bloody well stop! Joy, come back now!'

Joy stops and watches my face, puzzled. 'What?' she says.

'Stop and think where we can hide, where the bees can't get in.'

'Where we can hide?' Joy's frown deepens.

Is she deaf? 'Yeah, man, where we can hide.'

'But we want to do something to help, don't we?'

'How can we? Don't be stupid!'

Nell intervenes urgently. 'We can quickly grab some mozzie nets to stop us getting stung and then go to the pool.'

I don't have any time to feel embarrassed at my need to hide or my underestimation of Nell. Joy is already crashing through the door of the dormitory, leaping on the nearest bed and unhooking the net. Nell runs to the next bed. I rush to the one beyond.

'Should we take spare ones in case we can protect someone else?' I ask Nell, trying to make up for my cowardice.

'We might be hampered. Better take just one each.'

We help each other unknot the nets and get underneath.

'Gather them up and hold them in front of you so you can move,' says Nell.

'How are we going to stop bees getting in if we do that?'

'A few won't kill us.' Nell is manoeuvring herself through the doorway like a bride late for her wedding.

Almost as soon as we are out in the road again, moving with a shuffling, running gait, bees hit our nets. They cling, buzzing angrily. We are gathering black specks of enraged sound. The nearer we get to the pool, the more the darkness on our nets thickens. All the pupils seem to be screaming. Many have jumped into the water to escape, but the bees are still finding their flesh and getting lodged in their hair. Nell has caught hold of both Joy and me; she has a clutch of our clothing through the nets.

We wait for instruction from Nell. It's not long in coming. 'Let's stay close together. We'll never hear each other with all this noise if we separate.'

'What can we do though?' I ask.

'Look – there's Miss Perry. She'll know.'

We head for Miss Perry, whose wild Irish curls are littered with bees. Her usually pale skin is red with heat and stings. She is trying to mask her eyes with one hand and remove bees from the big bully Rotuno with the other. He must have doubled back and is now minus his shirt.

'Girls!' Miss Perry takes in our protective nets. 'There are children in the pool in trouble. They are in danger of panicking and drowning. See if you can get them to the edge and hold onto the rail. Tell them to keep dipping under the water and coming up for air. If you see anybody losing consciousness, stay with them and keep them afloat.'

We get into the pool and stay close to each other, as Nell suggested. Most of those in the water aren't far from the edge and we are able to reach out and pull them to the handrail. Then Joy pats my shoulder and points out Liesbeth, in the middle of the pool. She is lying backwards, half submerged. She is as red as sunrise, her hair spread out like dark molasses dancing on turquoise waves. She is not moving.

Nell tells me to go and get her. 'You're the best swimmer,' she says.

She's right, I am a strong swimmer. But the net is restrictive; my limbs are entangled in the twisted volumes of material. In the deep end, panic starts to impede my progress further.

Then I hear Joy calling to me. 'Hey, man, be calm. Just go slow.'

'Be steady. Don't flap,' shouts Nell from the pool edge, where she has just dragged somebody.

So I am calm, slow and steady, and I don't flap. But the net gets even more twisted anyway and I swallow water and struggle to breathe. When I eventually reach Liesbeth, she appears to be unconscious. I drag her with all my strength until we are close enough for Nell to haul her to the edge. I then tread water in my swirl of netting, waiting for further instructions from Nell.

But she has conceded authority to Miss Perry, who has slipped into the water to make sure Liesbeth is breathing.

As I look round the pool to see if anybody else is unconscious, I feel strange. There is a sensation of slow-motion heaviness in my limbs. Then a lump of floating cotton wool appears in front of me, attached to which is a face. It is the big bully Rotuno boy. He must have followed Miss Perry into the water. His eyes have vanished behind bloating flesh, and his mouth gapes crimson. I try to pull him in but his hands come up and push me down. I can't breathe.

When I manage to get some air again and open my eyes, there is white brightness littered with dark dots, and there are men with stretchers lifting Liesbeth out of the water. The Rotuno boy is being pulled onto the side, and despite the thundering noise all around me, I'm sure I hear his fleshy thighs slapping the stone slabs.

My limbs go slack. The net, with spent bees snagged in it, loosens around me and fans out. I spread my arms as it settles over my face. The sun burns white behind my eyelids as I close them, then crimson, then black. It seems to be my turn to drift into unconsciousness. I take the chameleon from the water, give it a shake to dispel the wetness and place it on the back of my hand, its front feet wrapped around my index finger. It is so beautiful. Its colour matches the translucent aquamarine of the water streaming from my skin. It curls its tail in a gorgeous ornamental wave down the back of my wrist. Its eyes swivel to track the bees as they buzz and dive and swerve. A long tongue like a string of mucous flashes out of its mouth and glues a bee. It snatches more out of the canopy of pepperberry trees under the deep blue sky. Joy's freckled face smiles down at me as the chameleon reaches up to her with its turquoise foot.

'It's alright now,' says Joy. Behind her, Nell's ponytail whips among the trees. Red berries and black dots and marmalade freckles rain down into my eyes.

Purple Rain

From deep within the blanket of black cloud that spanned the sky and extinguished the daylight on the plateau, thunder rumbled. It rumbled low and long. The earth was parched and I imagined it yearning upwards, willing the cloud to burst but at the same time braced against the onslaught of deluge. Tension was stored in the weight of water like held breath. I lent my will to the earth and looked up, straining towards the darkness. Then my neck got too painful and I lowered my gaze. The Rhodesian ridgeback Sputnik lifted his head and held it sideways, casting up white-edged glances and dropping and raising his ears as he tried to read my feelings about the sky. His tail hovered half-mast, ready to clamp between his legs, or swing with delight at another adventure. I patted his head. 'It's only thunder, Sputty,' I said, as much to reassure myself as him. A deep indigo curtain was already obscuring the Aberdare Mountains in the distance.

I looked up again and a drop of rain came hurtling out of the sky, barrelling downwards, and struck my forehead. The tension was broken. Large drops assaulted Sputty and pelted his hide, but he still wanted to know if we were going to run or fight; his ears and tail remained in a ready state. Then he went down on his forepaws, leaving his rear end in the air.

It was delicious to breathe through my nose, inhaling earth heat, a warm dust and dry grass smell that freshened and cleansed the air and made me tingle with oxygen. I laughed and ran as thunder wrapped all sound in its own so I couldn't hear myself shout. I couldn't hear Sputty bark either as he leapt sideways, his jaws mouthing with excitement at the rain. Then I fell over, and he was upon me, working his mouth close to my face then catching my arm playfully in his teeth.

'Get off!' I yelled, but he didn't hear me. I didn't hear myself. We were swamped in water and noise, wrapped in thunder and cloud. The earth was trying to drink the rain, but it was crashing down too fast and making the grass bounce as though it had no roots.

We played for a long time, jumping and falling and rolling, then I noticed the ground was beginning to flood. I caught Sputty's drenched coat and twisted it just enough to make him understand that we had to be serious now. He must have yelped, although I could only hear it in my imagination, as a memory of how he sounded when he was hurt or shocked. His whole body squirmed in a writhing mass of apology. He always apologised if I hurt him. And he always accused me if he was hurt through his own fault.

'We need to get home, you bloody fool dog!' I told him at the top of my voice.

We splashed and climbed into the storm. We leaned in the direction of the house. Water swept into my eyes, making the squat, single-storey stone building barely visible. Its corrugated iron roof reflected the darkness of the sky. I felt an increasing urgency to get home as the pressure of the flood built up against my shins. Sputty was jumping over the tug and pull, but with some leaps he made no ground at all.

There was a dam with a raised bank a little way off to the left of us, so I headed for that. Then Sputty turned around and bared his teeth threateningly, but the effect was lost in the noise and in his struggle to keep his feet. I looked behind to see what he was snarling at. It was Mzee, a few feet away from us, also making for the bank.

'It's Mzee!' I screamed. But my relief obviously wasn't evident in my voice because Sputty misunderstood my shouting – he leapt towards Mzee, his threat now audible above the storm. Mzee's face contorted with terror and he held his arms up and away from the impending onslaught. 'No!' I screeched, but all my voice did was communicate panic to Sputty and encourage the attack. 'No, no, no!' I cried. I tried to reach the pair but fell and swallowed water. I got up, but straightaway lost my footing again. When I was eventually able to grab Sputty's coat, I held on with both hands as tightly as I could. As we were both swept off our feet, I managed to get my mouth near his ear; it had blood on it. 'It's Mzee, Sputty. Stop! No!'

Bracing against the flood, we resumed the fight to reach the bank. Mzee got there first and reached for my hand. I grabbed Sputty's ruff and hauled him up. He shook himself violently and pointlessly. Then he looked at Mzee with seeming apology before turning to me and cringing. We crowded into each other for a moment to feel safe, Mzee's arm across my back, his ragged shirt clutched in my fist, the dog pressed between us. We calmed down and then moved apart.

Mzee stood looking towards the house. I guessed that, like me, he was hoping the African huts beyond the eucalyptus trees wouldn't get swept away; they were on slightly higher ground, so it was possible. Mzee's forearm was ripped open near his elbow and a stream of red ran down his reedy arm, thinning to watery pink. His skin was glossed and gleaming like oiled ebony. I tore the sash off my dress and tied it above his elbow. We stood, three in a row, facing the homestead, shivering while we waited for the torrent to subside.

The safety of the bank freed my imagination, released it from our frightening situation. The house was a shipwreck seen from our shore. The water running to the edge of the escarpment spilled over it like Niagara, a fall of sky filling the whole Rift Valley with purple rain. We were safer here than struggling to reach the house, which might even sweep past us and be hurled over the rim of the world.

After Edith had towelled me down and I was in dry clothes, I took my mug of hot chocolate to the window and peered through the rain-spotted glass. Although the drumming on the corrugated iron roof had stopped, the road was still a river, and the land, though visible again, glistened with wetness. Mzee stood beside me, wrapped in a blanket. His wound had been disinfected and bandaged.

'*Mingi maji*,' I said, breathing in the sweet steam from my mug. That's a lot of water.

Mzee didn't answer. I turned my head to him, and found myself considering him in a way I never had before. He usually had a lot of gunge on the eyelashes of his gluey eye, but now both eyes were clean. The force of the rain had washed him free of stickiness. His skin was normally grey and dusty as though someone had spilled talcum powder over him and discoloured his blackness, but this too was clean now. The only thing that was the same was his mouth, lips always a little compressed because he had no front teeth, even though he wasn't even middle aged. I'm not sure why we called him Mzee, which is Swahili for 'old'. I admit he seemed ancient to me but Edith said he was the same age as her; he sometimes called her 'Edith Mzee', which made them both laugh.

Edith had a few missing teeth too. But she had a very good dentist who made her false teeth that were very slightly crooked so that no one would guess they weren't her own. I knew they weren't her own though because I'd seen them soaking in Steradent – half a smile floating in a glass of water on the bathroom cabinet.

Missing teeth was about the only thing that my mother and Mzee had in common. It was obvious that Edith was well fed, while Mzee was spare and muscular, and his skin, apart from the scars and scabs, was tight. While Edith wore clean and fashionable clothes, Mzee wore tattered shorts. I knew he had another set of clothes though, for outside of work. I'd seen him once in Naivasha on his day off, sitting with a group of men on a wall under the shade of a pepperberry tree. His 'shirt' was a lady's pink gingham blouse, and with it he wore a purple tie with a picture of a yellow-haired Marilyn Monroe, curvaceous in a bikini, resting in the middle of his chest. I recognised her image from the magazines full of Hollywood stars that my mother bought at Naivasha *duka*, but Mzee probably had no idea who she was.

It was only then, standing close to Mzee and drinking my hot chocolate, that I realised with clarity that he wasn't old, and that 'Mzee' probably wasn't his birthname, in the same way that he always called me *toto* – child. Why didn't we ever call each other by our real names?

A bluebottle settled on the inside corner of Mzee's eye, catching the light from the sun that glimmered behind a cloud of a similar colour to itself. It glistened as though wet like the honeysuckle leaves brooding below the window. As there was no sticky gunge there to interest it now, I thought it would take off, but it lingered. Mzee didn't shake his head; he must have been so used to being pestered by insects that he wasn't even aware of its presence – or he was lost, as I so often was, in an imaginary world more pleasing than the current reality.

Although I didn't want to disturb Mzee if he was in a faraway dream, I reached up and flicked the fly away. Mzee's black satin frame, clothed in scavenger rags, needed ridding of carrion germs, of sewage bacteria. He was strong and beautiful on the inside, stricken and afflicted by shreds and filth on the outside – at least this was how I saw him then, as I battled to stop the bluebottle that was attempting to return to his face and pollute him.

I swiped at the air near his head. My hot chocolate spilled down my clean clothes. 'Bugger off,' I breathed heavily. 'Bloody buggerrrroffff…'

Mzee blinked and pulled back.

It took me a moment to realise that he'd understood what I'd said. His brows were gathered into deep creases above his nose and his eyes flashed before fixing on me with disapproval. I was annoyed. What right had he to be offended by my swearing? He didn't have any authority over me. But of course he did, because he was an adult, and I'd often been left in his care. He was trusted to keep me safe, but hadn't I just done the same for him, kept him safe from being savaged by Sputty?

I was tempted to swear again, this time at Mzee; to throw my hot chocolate over him; to storm off and find Sputty, or better still, Cora. Cora was used to hearing my woes, to listening with a patient attitude, soft eyes and held-back ears. Sputty lacked sympathy; not for him my complaints of unfairness and ill usage. He just wanted to be up and doing things all the time. Then I caught a glimpse of dried blood on the edge of Mzee's shorts under the blanket, and my temper softened. I thought about the three of us standing on the bank, pressed against each other as water flooded over us, Mzee's blood running thin and blueish against his skin.

Suddenly, Mzee's open hand flew towards me as he tried to swat the bluebottle, but he missed. Quick as a flash of a chameleon's tongue, I flung out my right hand and caught the fly a glancing blow, and spilled some more hot chocolate in the process. I put the mug on the windowsill.

Mzee was peering down at the insect, which was now buzzing, furious and wild, beside his cracked and leathery feet. My little sandaled feet contrasted noticeably with his large bare misshapen ones. Mzee raised a foot, a bunch of toes hovering above the stricken insect, then brought it down with a thud before twisting and lifting away.

A purple smear of death, a slime of matter, bled into the spilled chocolate. Mzee's mouth gaped, a cavern of a smile. I was horrified less by the death than by the mess.

Mzee was disgusting.

'*Eeuuurgh…*' I pulled my lips back in a grimace that hurt. How could he do that with bare feet? How could he be laughing his strange cracking sound far back in his throat like a hyena crunching splintered bone, and joyfully clacking his fingers in the air as though he had castanets on the end of his arm?

As Mzee and I stood either side of the flattened bluebottle – him amused, me revolted – the knowledge that we were worlds apart hit me with the same force that he had just used on the fly. Not because I thought Mzee was disgusting, or ragged, or didn't mind flies in his eyes, or was cross with me for swearing.

It was because, for the first time, I recognised that he was black.

Four Husbands

We were standing in a row, Edith, Mzee, and me. In front of us was a table on which sat a bowl of water, a stack of cardboard egg trays, and a few baskets full of eggs. We were preparing the eggs for sale in Nairobi. Because the sky was heavy with dark rain clouds, we were working inside the enormous hen barn; most of the hens had also chosen to be under shelter rather than out in the field. It was my job to pick out the clean eggs and place them carefully in the trays, while Mzee washed the soiled ones and Edith dried them.

We heard a Land Rover pull into the yard. Squinting through a gap in the hen house wall, I whispered a sharp warning to the others that the arrival was Mrs Marais. Although she lived on the farm next to ours, we hardly knew her, but what we did know, we didn't like. We thought she was trouble. Edith kept her eyes down, seemingly concentrating on her task, while Mzee and I watched Mrs Marais come to the door, disturbing a hen on its way out. We were silent as we worked amidst the muffled atmosphere of dust and feathers and conversational clucking.

Mrs Marais crackled with nervous energy. Her eyes darted and her tongue flickered over her lips. She waited, fidgeting. When Edith eventually looked up, Mrs Marais threw her head sideways, her lank hair sticking to the sweat on her face.

'My cows have got mixed up with yours at the new dam. I've come to report this fact to you.' Her Afrikaans accent is clipped, her voice reedy.

'You mean *our* new dam?'

'Ya.' She peered at Edith, wide eyed and innocent.

'Well, you're welcome to retrieve them, Mrs Marais. But I'm afraid I can't help you just at the moment.' She held up the egg she was drying and placed it in one of the trays.

'But, you see, your husband might have suspicions that I'm trespassing and stealing his cows.'

'Not if I tell him I've allowed you to be at the dam, and not if you don't steal any of our cows.'

'I'm not sure I know which ones are which though.'

'Ours are branded, Mrs Marais.'

Mrs Marais held still a moment longer and then began to blink rapidly. She clawed with both hands at the hair across her eyes. Before turning to go, she ducked her head in an awkward nod at Edith.

'I could get one of the men to help you,' Edith said to her back.

But Mrs Marais declined the offer. 'I've got my own *kaffirs*.'

'Just so long as you've got your own cattle too,' Edith said under her breath.

'She is bad, Memsahib,' growled Mzee, wiping his nose on the back of his arm and in the process splattering me with chicken shit water from the washing bowl.

'She scares the heck out of me,' I said, wiping my face vigorously and then flicking chicken shit water over Mzee in retaliation.

'Don't be silly. What's there to be afraid of?' said Edith.

Mrs Marais' third husband had recently died, and she was now on the lookout for another, or so Mrs Lennox told me. She also told me that the demise of successive husbands was fortunate for Mrs Marais from a financial perspective. My stepfather Ken agreed. Mrs Marais was an incompetent farmer, he said, and it was really only the legacy from each husband that enabled her to continue. Her only other income came from letting one of the habitable farm buildings.

When Ken arranged for a borehole to be drilled on our property, the engineer who came to manage the job lodged in this dwelling. It soon became clear that Mrs Marais had begun to view Mr Roseman as suitable husband material. I liked him, and I was also really interested in the whole business of boreholes, so one morning I called the dogs and went to hang around and watch the proceedings. Mr Roseman explained to me that there was water trapped underground between layers of rock, and it was his job to see that the earth and stone was drilled through correctly to reach it, and then pump it to the surface. He showed me all the equipment and I was fascinated.

I was still at the bore site at lunchtime when Mrs Marais' battered Land Rover tore along the plateau towards us, churning up dust like a stampede of cattle. As she arrived, she manoeuvred the vehicle into a sharp turn so that she faced homeward again. She disappeared into the clouds of dust, only to emerge like a Hollywood film star through stage mist. I don't mean she was beautiful. She was stringy and thin but with broad square hips, and she had annoying mannerisms. But she came through the dust as if she thought she was something worth looking at. And I suppose that if you've already attracted three husbands, you can't have too much doubt about your ability to get another.

Mrs Marais had brought lunch for Mr Roseman. Her movements were strangely slow, and she moistened her lips lingeringly with her tongue, while her eyes, though still restless, watched him from under half-mast lids. She then proceeded to find something on her skirt that needed close inspection, lifting up her hem and revealing her thighs. I was shocked. The flesh now exposed was so unexpectedly white, vulnerable, secret. Mrs Marais was offering Mr Roseman something vigorous and musky that stabbed me with jealousy. Her secret paleness made me prickle with sweat. I watched Mr Roseman intently, willing him not to be impressed with her underneathness. But his eyes shuddered over her body before looking at the ground.

Mrs Marais held out a brown paper bag. 'Beef and horseradish, Roseman,' she said. She then brushed past him, crackling, electric and abrasive once more, pretending an interest in the drilling equipment. 'Man, you need some muscle for a job like this.' She placed her tough brown hands on his forearm and pinched. 'Nice,' she said. 'Real.' Mr Roseman swallowed. I watched his throat where his collar was undone and saw his Adam's apple move. I would have liked to put my hand there and feel the graininess of his skin.

'Hey, little girl, don't you have a job to do?' Mrs Marais said. 'Don't you have to help your mother and her *kaffir*?'

I scowled, trying to find the courage to react. But all I could manage was to stick out my tongue behind her as she returned to the Land Rover. Mr Roseman watched the vehicle as it stirred up dust once more. He chewed reflectively, leaning his elbow on a nearby fence post, his eyes tracking her retreat. When he became aware that I was watching him, he smiled and winked at me. More chewing ensued, this time energetically, then he scrunched up the brown paper and handed it to me.

'Present for you!'

'Thanks a lot.'

'She likes me, don't you reckon?'

'So what? She's ugly.'

Mr Roseman shrugged, nodded, then shrugged again. 'Don't you have a job to do, little girl?'

My grown-up half-brothers from Edith's first marriage came home for the weekend. Michael, who was twenty-three, was working on neighbouring farms, picking up experience with the aim of becoming a farmer himself one day. He was a one-dog, one-horse kind of a person, with his Rhodesian ridgeback Sputnik and his stately black, eighteen-hands horse Mack.

David was a bit younger than Michael and very handsome. But I liked Michael's face just as much as David's, even though his nose drifted sideways, courtesy of David breaking it in a fight years before. Despite his film star good looks, David wasn't perfect either – under his luxurious hair was a birthmark, which you could see when the wind lifted his fringe. I felt strangely worried about this blemish, thinking it might be a sinister threat to him. Unlike Michael, David was a townie and worked in Nakuru for a seed and grain company. He often brought glamorous girlfriends home in his Volkswagen Beetle; I rarely took to them.

Edith invited Mr Roseman to join us for the evening meal; he was a similar age to my brothers and she thought he would enjoy their company. Edith was a good cook. Her lamb with mint sauce and homegrown carrots, potatoes and runner beans was always popular.

'Jees, that was good, better than I'm used to. Hell, man, it's the best tucker I can remember.'

Mr Roseman took his serviette, still neatly folded, from his lap and returned it to his side plate. Then he leaned back, smiling. As the meal had progressed, he'd relaxed more and more. At first he'd seemed unsure, watching the rest of us for clues to etiquette – not that he need have worried as Michael was renowned for strange behaviour with regard to dining. We often reminded him of the time he ordered Dover sole at the New Stanley Hotel and requested beef gravy poured over it. He often cheerfully forgot his table manners. Edith blamed this fall from grace on his having worked for a while for Mrs Lennox on her farm. They'd shared bacon and eggs as a staple diet, served on barely washed plates, or newspaper. But I think Edith secretly enjoyed Michael's carelessness, regarding it as masculine behaviour. This annoyed me, especially as I knew she was unlikely to extend the same laxity towards me. But then again, I never gave her reason to exercise either correction or forgiveness – something inside me was complicit in absolving men from the rules, in accepting that my brothers were free to be wild colonial boys, no matter how much it irritated me.

'I'm afraid we don't have dessert,' said Edith. 'Would you like cheese and biscuits instead? I've got some very nice Stilton.'

I was the only one to want Stilton, so the others left the table to sit round the fire. I brought my cheese on a side plate and sat beside Mr Roseman.

'Heck, what a stink, man!' Mr Roseman held his nose and leaned away from me.

'It's lov-er-ly. Yum. Smell!' I flew the cheese as an imaginary aeroplane close to his face. '*Vrrrm, vrrrm,*' I said, like a small child.

'Ma, isn't it the brat's bed time?' said David.

'No, Mama, no. I'll be good, I promise. Anyway, I shouldn't go to bed on a full stomach.'

'Leave her be a while,' Edith said.

Drinks were replenished. Ken knocked his pipe out on the hearthstone and settled down to refill it, while smoke from Michael's ten-cent cigarettes and Edith's Players filled the air. Conversation was about farming and the progress of the borehole. I kept a low profile.

When there was a lull in the conversation, Michael addressed Mr Roseman, chuckling. 'So, how do you get on with your landlady?'

'Ach, man, you know, she's okay. Her cooking is bad, man, but she means well. She runs round after me; it's flattering.' He gave his forehead a quick scratch. 'But there is one thing bothering me, which I'd like to ask you about – do you reckon she's a good payer? It's just that I've re-roofed her calf pens…'

Nobody jumped in with an answer, but all eyes rested on Ken, who was now paying great attention to the tamping and suction of his pipe. Eventually, he looked through the smoke at Mr Roseman. 'She's not a prompt payer. You may need to be very firm. I wouldn't vacate your room until you've secured the money either, and certainly don't pay for it. That's my advice.'

'And mine would be to get the hell out of there – fast,' said Michael.

Now everybody turned to Michael. I thought Ken and Edith might disapprove of this advice; it wasn't good manners to make guests feel uncomfortable.

'Hey?' Mr Roseman's eyebrows were steeply arched.

'I don't reckon the money or the lady's favours are worth the risk,' said Michael.

I didn't know what 'lady's favours' meant, but it was enough to make Mr Roseman's cheeks colour.

'I reckon you're jealous, man,' he said. 'She's not so much to look at but she knows how to make a bloke feel mighty good.'

Michael grinned. 'Yeah, and mighty dead!'

'Time for bed, Tanzie,' said my mother.

I felt crushed. I hated the way she could do that – pick the most interesting moment to exclude me. I was desperate to stay and hear about how a bloke could feel mighty good and mighty dead. But now Mr Roseman's eyes were on me, wide and impatient; it was obvious he really wanted me to go to bed too.

'But I haven't digested the cheese yet, Mama. I'll have nightmares. I'll be sick. I won't be able to sleep. My tummy hurts. I want to stay by the fire and keep warm.'

But I knew the moment couldn't be saved. Even if Edith allowed me to stay a bit longer, they were going to change the subject. So I tried another tack. 'I'll go without a fuss if Michael puts me to bed.'

In the bathroom, Michael put toothpaste on my brush to hurry things along, then drew the peony blossom print curtains and faced the door while I undressed. My cotton pyjamas were ironed and smelt so nice and clean; I put my nose in them and inhaled. Michael tapped a fast rhythm on the laundry basket with my toothbrush. When I'd finished sniffing my pyjamas, I noticed that the room smelt of Wright's coal tar soap, spearmint and fresh towels. My bare feet had left a sweaty imprint on the cardinal-red polished floor.

'Have you had a pee?'

'I'm just going to. Don't look.'

'Get on with it then.'

'Michael?'

'What?'

'How can a bloke feel mighty good and mighty dead?'

'Heck, girl, you ask too many questions. Well, obviously, you can't feel good if you're dead.'

'But Mr Roseman said Mrs Marais could make a bloke feel mighty good, and you said "*and* mighty dead". So what did you mean?'

'Look, you know Mrs Marais has had three husbands and all three of them have died?'

'Yeah… but…I still don't understand…'

'Three husbands is a lot of husbands to lose when you're still quite young.'

'So?' I said, even though I knew now what he meant – Mrs Marais could have murdered her husbands. Although I didn't really believe it, I felt a strange thrill thinking about the times I'd been in her presence. Her husbands appeared before me in my imagination, all looking exactly like Mr Roseman.

'Michael! That's awful. We must save him…'

Michael handed me my toothbrush. 'The deed is already done. I've planted the seed of doubt, and enlightenment will follow. He'll get the hell out, or it's his own funeral.'

I felt myself frowning, trying to understand what 'seed of doubt' and 'enlightenment' meant.

'Don't worry, kid, he'll be fine. Now, hurry up and clean your teeth and get the hell to bed.'

Mr Roseman came to live in Michael's old room, probably heeding his advice. I think he was appreciative of Edith's superior cooking, but he seemed distracted and sad. He became boring, and I went off him. By the time my next holiday from boarding school came around, he had left. But he'd left behind piped water throughout the farm, so his stay had been worth it.

On one of her visits to buy eggs, Mrs Lennox told me that Mrs Marais had married again. Husband number four!

'Not Mr Roseman?'

'No, not Mr Roseman.'

The fact that Mrs Marais' new husband wasn't Mr Roseman meant he was of little interest to me – I never even knew his name.

It was harvest time, and Michael and David were at home helping out. They were with Ken out on the plateau, each driving a hired combine harvester. Africans were assisting them with the combine work or driving tractors pulling trailers or balers. At midday, Edith and I brought them big picnic baskets full of lunch – chicken legs and sausages, hard boiled eggs, bread and fruit, as well as beer for the whites and milky sugared tea in old whisky bottles for the Africans.

We sat on straw bales. Although I knew harvest was a happy time, my temper was grazed. The sun was too strong and I was tired and hot. And I was cross because Edith wouldn't let me wear jeans and my legs were scratched from walking so far through the stubble. But underneath all the discomfort, I was content.

After we'd finished eating, I looked up and saw a dot on the horizon, dark and slightly shimmery. Packing away the picnic detritus, it soon became clear to us that the still-distant figure running in our direction was an African. We waited for him.

As he reached us, breathing heavily and with sweat streaming down his face, we saw it was Chege. We all knew him; he was a friend of Mzee's and worked for Mrs Marais.

'*Jambo*, Chege,' Michael said.

'*Jambo*, Chege,' I said.

But he ignored us and quickly handed Edith a note. As she read it, she looked perturbed.

Mzee moved to her side. '*Nini*, Memsahib?'

'What's the matter?' said Ken.

'It seems Mrs Marais needs my help...needs a *woman's* help...Chege, what does she mean?'

'Memsahib Marais is having a baby. She is screaming and clutching her stomach. Please hurry. Ladies always have trouble with birth...always make a fuss.'

Edith decided to take the summons for help seriously and hurried to her Land Rover. Mzee got in beside her and indicated to Chege to ride on the running board. I quickly shoved in the picnic baskets; there was no way I was going to carry them home.

If Mrs Marais really was having a baby – all that screaming and wailing – I didn't think Edith would be of much help. Even though she'd received a Queen's Commendation for bravery, she didn't seem very brave to me. A tiny mouse could fill her with terror. When it came to sickness or trauma, she wasn't very impressive either. As most white women did on remote farms, she ran a weekly clinic from the kitchen door. But although she fussed over the children, cleaning their cuts, applying antiseptic cream and Elastoplasts, the adults simply got handed the medication to sort out themselves. When she didn't know what to do, she prescribed a dose of Epsom Salts, in the belief that a good purge would always help.

As I walked through endless leg-scratching stubble on my way back to the bungalow, I worried about my mother with Mrs Marais. When I got close enough to home to know the dogs would hear me, I started calling and whistling for them. They came bounding to meet me, and my mood lifted.

Edith can't have been that useless though as Mrs Marais gave birth without complications to a healthy girl. Edith then drove mother and baby down the escarpment to the doctor's.

I don't know if Mrs Marais felt any obligation to my mother for her help during the birth, but she soon began to visit us, bringing her new baby with her. The baby was called Rose.

Shortly after Rose was born, Michael was at the farm on one of his weekend visits. During dinner, he mentioned the baby's name, then added that it was about nine months since Mr Roseman had left the district.

'Don't be silly,' Edith said. 'The baby must have been premature and Mrs Marais taken by surprise with the labour. Otherwise why would she have let her husband go to the coast with her other children for a week?'

'Really, Edith, anyone would think we lived in Hampstead, not darkest Africa,' said Ken. 'Having babies is different in Africa – women are tougher. They don't need menfolk in attendance.'

But I wasn't interested in women having babies in Africa rather than in Hampstead; all I could think about was what Edith had just said. 'What other children?' I asked.

'She has lots of children,' said Edith.

'How many?'

'I've never counted. Maybe seven.'

'Why doesn't she bring them all to see you when she brings Rose?'

'I suppose she thinks I have a special interest in Rose.'

'But I have a special interest in the other children, even though I didn't know there were any.'

Perhaps it was my curiosity about these mystery children that led Edith to take me on a visit to Mrs Marais' farm. Her husband was out working on the land and she led us into a dim room with a threadbare carpet in the middle and many upright, armless, paint-chipped chairs lining the walls. There was no other furniture in the room. Mrs Marais placed Rose in Edith's lap as soon as she sat down and then, putting her index and little finger in the corners of her mouth, gave a piercing whistle.

'Now the children will come,' she said.

The children came, but hung around the door. Their mother commanded them to sit down, mind their manners, and speak to the visitors. Some wore scuffed shoes but the others were barefoot, and I felt ridiculous in my polished Clarks shoes. All the children had their mother's thin lank hair, and they were all dirty. They didn't smile, and I didn't like them. I thought about the welcoming, mischievous children in the African village, where I would happily play tag or eat maize cobs straight from the fire. If these dirty sullen Afrikaner children couldn't be friendly towards to me, was it too much to want them to be hectic and wild in their strangeness?

A smell of burned wick came from the kerosene lamps on the continuous shelf that lined the room above our heads. Also on the shelf were plates, cups, mugs, ornaments, lots of bottles of home-brewed alcohol and, as Edith told Ken afterwards, 'unimaginable potions'. Rose, chubby and bright eyed, was content in Edith's arms. Edith was content too. They were a pair, wholesome and anchored in a jagged sea of awkwardness.

I swung my polished shoes to and fro over the faded carpet. My ankle socks were a white glaze of embarrassment. I hated Edith for their clean brilliance, for bringing me to see these cold ghost children, but most of all I hated her for the way she held Rose so close, as though she *loved* her.

One night, I woke to a strange noise in the distance. It was a muffled, rhythmic *doof, doof doof* sound. I imagined monstrous kangaroo-like creatures jumping and bouncing in the darkness. I screamed.

Michael opened my door, a light from the lounge across the hall cutting a yellow slice over my bed. 'What's up?'

'Listen to the *doof doofs*!' I cried.

'The dogs, you mean?'

The dogs, of course. 'What are they barking at? And why are they so far away?'

Michael drew back the curtain and opened the window. I jumped out of bed and we both looked out, the honeysuckle spilling through the window and tickling my face.

'Hmm…' he said. 'There's something going on out there.'

'Are we being attacked?'

'I don't think so.'

Soon we were all out on the lawn. Ken switched off the generator, leaving us in darkness. We could see beams of yellow light sweeping along Mrs Marais' farm road – a convoy of vehicles. Tiny bright stars spilled over the horizon behind the vehicles like silver glitter. The chill of the night made me shiver, and dread filled me, replacing my bones and organs and tissue. I was a cold body of fear.

'She's buggering off!' Michael said. 'I bet she's going south. She's moving lock, stock and barrel.'

'She's escaping,' Edith whispered.

'Where did she get those lorries?' Ken said. 'I hope she hasn't got any of our cattle in them.'

'Has she sold the farm?' Michael said.

'She hasn't had time for that,' Edith said. 'All those children…and no father.' She sighed. 'The police are going to start a search for bodies tomorrow.'

'What bodies?' I said. But I knew. Four husbands.

We stood together under the black sky, facing towards the edge of the plateau like alert meerkats, and watched the steady slide of lights getting smaller, fainter and then tailing off as they sunk over the escarpment. My teeth were chattering so much they overwhelmed the dogs' barking.

'Should we phone the police?' Edith said.

'I'm sure Angus will have seen the exodus and phoned them already,' Ken said.

We all turned in the direction of Angus Ferguson's place, screened from our farm by a thin wood of eucalyptus trees. Yes, he would have phoned the police.

No one phoned the police.

The next day, a policeman came to inform us that Mrs Marais had crossed the border into Tanganyika. He asked a lot of questions, but Edith was very quiet and non-committal in her replies. By crossing the border, Mrs Marais had changed rumour into certainty. She was a murderer. Our neighbour, Edith's visitor, was a murderer. I watched a tear fall from Edith's eye onto the dark mahogany table. Perhaps the policeman thought it was odd that she should cry over a murderess. But it was clear to me that my mother's tears were really for the chubby, bright-eyed baby she was never going to see again.

An Aeroplane Screams into a Dive

They are dead dogs. They lie on their sides, stretched out on the Persian rug. It's only when they twitch or whimper that they give themselves away, dream running through the forests that rise from the plateau and march towards the Aberdare Mountains. Or perhaps their rug is a magic carpet, slithering over the parquet, flying through the door and soaring over the forests and mountains to the sea.

I am curled up in an armchair with my watercolour box, a glass of water balanced on the wide arm, trying to paint these chocolate gun dogs. The dogs in my painting are even more dead than the three on the rug. They are dead dogs in dead colours. I can't achieve the lovely pink of their underbellies or the rich glow of their coats. I'm staying with the Coles in their farmhouse, and these are their dogs. I pause a minute to listen to the gramophone, which George and Marion allow me to use whenever I like. I'm playing 'On the Street Where You Live'; *My Fair Lady* is all the rage in

London, according to Edith's last postcard. The lyrics 'Are there lilac trees in the heart of town?' bother me a little because I don't know what lilacs look like, so I imagine them as the jacaranda trees that line the avenue near my school in Nakuru. I try to lift the flat, mud-dog shapes in my painting by giving them a vignette of the rug pattern – maybe a Middle Eastern atmosphere will bring them to life? But the scene stays disappointing. Sighing, I give the dogs garlands of lilacs (or jacarandas), in requiem.

The grandfather clock across the room tells me that it's nearly time to go to Granny Emmy's. Although I visit her often, this is the first time I've been formally invited for tea. I close my sketchbook and uncurl myself. 'Are you coming?' I say to the dogs.

Bruiser raises his head and peers at me, but the other two only open their eyes, probably worn out from running after George in the Land Rover. Bruiser heaves himself to his feet and watches me tidy up. After yawning cavernously and stretching, he shakes himself as though to dislodge an army of fleas and his ears flap like the wings of a flock of birds taking to the air.

'C'mon, Bruiser.' I turn off the gramophone and head for the stairs. 'Let's go and change for tea.'

I select a clean dress from the wardrobe, while Bruiser slumps to the floor to wait, panting gently with his tongue hanging out. I brush my hair and tie it back with a blue ribbon and then fasten a matching piece round Bruiser's neck, out of respect for the occasion. He'd suit a pink ribbon better, but I don't have any because Edith isn't fond of the colour. I take a cotton handkerchief that I've embroidered with the letter 'E', for Emmy, and put it in my pocket, making sure it's concealed. Finally, I spit on a corner of my discarded T-shirt and use it to remove the stains around my mouth from where I'd licked my paintbrush to gain a fine point.

Granny Emmy is not my grandmother; she is the grandmother of the now-grown-up-and-left-home children of George and Marion. They have another grandparent, called Granny Robinson. The grannies live in homes either side of the large, two-storey farmhouse. So they're both grandmothers, and they're both widows, but otherwise they don't have much in common.

Bruiser and I make our way across some fields to Granny Emmy's bungalow. A few cattle lift their heads and watch us pass by. In the distance, on the far side of the farmhouse, I can see Granny Robinson's stone cottage, low and squat and flanked by fir trees that bite jagged shapes into the sky. They're like Granny Robinson's temperament — sometimes she is sharp, which makes me feel uncomfortable, and sometimes she is peppery, as though she's in pain or something has disappointed her. She keeps rabbits, and has a vegetable garden that under the heat of the sun smells pungently of tomatoes. She also rents out stables to neighbours, including me, and takes a particular interest in my horse. I'm not sure why she gets so involved with Star, and I'm not sure I like it either, especially when it extends to how well or not I ride her.

Granny Robinson has beautiful long charcoal-grey hair, which she ties back with an elastic band that is so twisted up with hair you can't see it. Her face is dirt smudged, and Edith would disapprove of her fingernails, which are bitten short and ragged and ingrained with soil. She smells of the whisky she carries in a silver hip flask in the back pocket of her trousers. The pockets of her man's tweed jacket are usually stuffed with cheroots and with dandelion leaves for her rabbits.

Granny Emmy is a very different character. As we approach her bungalow, I can see her waiting on the wooden veranda. Behind her, the floral curtains at the open windows are billowing clean and fresh in the breeze that sweeps through the house. I open the garden gate and walk along beside the winding herbaceous border. Bruiser speeds up to greet Granny Emmy.

'Come in, come in both of you,' she trills, patting Bruiser's head before giving me a light, warm hug.

Granny Robinson doesn't greet or embrace me like this. She barely acknowledges me when I arrive for my daily visits to Star. But I find her silence preferable to the occasions when she does decide to talk to me, which can be disconcerting. Yesterday, when I was helping feed her rabbits and clean their hutches, she suddenly reached out and caught a flying ant.

'Do you know these are tasty?' She popped the ant in her mouth. I felt my jaw drop, but closed it again quickly in case she caught another one.

On the veranda, Bruiser's nose nudges the table of food. Granny Emmy lifts the edge of the tablecloth and makes a sweeping gesture with her hand. 'Under,' she says to him. 'Go under.' He does as he is told, as always. She then offers me a chair. 'Now, would you like tea, or milk, or freshly squeezed orange juice?'

I hesitate. I don't like tea, but as I was invited for tea, wouldn't Granny Emmy expect me to choose this? And the thought of sipping tea does make me feel grown up. 'Tea, please,' I say.

'Sugar?'

'Two, please.' That should make it more palatable.

A white jug filled with straggles of fresh flowers sits on the pale blue tablecloth, which is patterned with delicate blooms of mauve, white and lavender flowers – an echo of the garden, Granny Emmy's dress and the curtains. There is another jug on the table too, containing water and ice, the rivulets of condensation on the clear glass making it look extra refreshing. Cucumber and egg and cress sandwiches, with their crusts cut off, are arranged neatly on plates graced with doilies. A glass dish of red jelly embedded with raspberries is luminous in a slant of sunshine, and a bone china tea set and Madeira cake complete the tableau.

Granny Emmy loves gardening but always wears gloves, so her fingernails stay clean, her hands white and smooth. She is dainty and wears fine cotton dresses. Many of these dresses have a pocket over the breast, into which she neatly tucks a clean handkerchief sprinkled with lemon cologne. Her hair is as beautiful as Granny Robinson's but short, soft and snowy, and when she stands against a blue sky and moves her head, it drifts like a cloud on a breath of wind. The tomboy in me should prefer Granny Robinson because of her love of rabbits, disregard of dirt, and wildness – and I certainly admire how she washes down sausages eaten straight from the frying pan with a swig of Tusker beer – but Granny Emmy likes me, and that counts for a lot.

As we drink our tea, Granny Emmy tells me that this area reminds her of the green countryside of Surrey, with emerald fields of soft grass and gentle rain. But I love the dramatic rain we have here and the way the earth smells warm and fresh afterwards, and how the rivers are full of brown trout and their banks are draped with weeping willows, trailing tendril leaves across the running water.

Bruiser emerges from under the table with his ears cocked towards the main house. He runs to the gate, but finding it closed runs back and wags his tail and huffs at Granny Emmy.

'He's obviously heard himself being called for food,' she says, getting to her feet. 'Marion must be back from the fields.'

'I'll open the gate,' I say, scraping back my chair and running down the veranda steps. As soon as it's opened, Bruiser surges through and stretches out in a long body shape for home.

Granny Emmy fetches the tapestry that we usually work on in the afternoons. The design on hers is flowery, of course, and mine is from my own drawing of Bruiser sniffing one of Granny Robinson's rabbits. The cotton has a more satisfactory range of colours to describe a chocolate gun dog than my watercolours. I can choose coppery, gingery browns for highlights and bluish brown hues to express shadow and shade.

We are quiet and absorbed for a while until, from the direction of Granny Robinson's house, we feel darkness coming in. We turn and see clouds banking up over the group of pine trees flanking the fields. The breeze carries such a chill that I shiver and let my teeth chatter, enjoying the feeling and the sound. Granny Emmy puts on the cardigan from the back of her chair and hurries to fetch a plaid rug to drape round my shoulders. We settle back to our embroidery, but the atmosphere has changed.

Granny Emmy puts down her tapestry. She clears her throat with a soft scratchy sound. 'My dear,' she says, 'I have something to tell you.' There is something in her voice that sounds nervous rather than just old. But then she resumes her needlework, dipping the needle in and out of her cloth. Although she keeps her eyes down, she can't seem to stop them flickering and skidding over me.

I can't sew anymore. When Granny Emmy's eyes next skitter in my direction, she halts with surprise that I am so concentrated on her. She clears her throat again, and my anxiety swings to irritation. Suddenly, I want to shake her. But I'm paralysed, staring at her mouth, waiting for words.

'Marion had a long-distance phone call last night,' she says.

An ache builds in my chest. I try to focus on the flower prints on the tablecloth. I don't want to hear her; I don't want her voice to reach me. My ears hum with a strange insulating sound. I try and hold my face still as an aeroplane screams into a dive.

An aeroplane screams into a dive and explodes into a mountain and a massive fireball swells into a darkening sky and burns the moon and my mother to ashes.

'Your mother is not returning for another fortnight.' She takes a deep breath, stitches another dip or two, then lays down her sewing and gets to her feet uncertainly, leaning towards me.

I don't speak. The relief is dizzying.

The weakness in my body makes me lean forward onto the table, my tapestry cushioning my forehead. At least now I'll be able to finish it in time to give Edith as a gift. This reminds me of the handkerchief. I raise my head and reach for my pocket, but Granny Emmy catches me in her arms and presses my face against her bony chest. Lemon cologne fills my nostrils. She gathers the rug around us both and rocks me, crooning soft noises in my ear. I start to weep, not just with relief that Edith has not been burned up in a fireball but also because I think Granny Emmy expects me to.

'There, there,' she says.

Her words fill my heart with grief and joy; they are words my mother often says to me. Edith, though, doesn't use them to soothe me when I'm upset – she doesn't tolerate crying – rather she employs them to try and coax me out of a temper, patting my knee rhythmically at the same time. As I calm down I feel how old and skinny Granny Emmy is, and how flowery, kind and large her spirit.

The sky has darkened, making me worried about going back to the main house. I pull away from Granny Emmy. She's just an old woman and can't help me with my anxiety about night time. I look towards the glimmer of lights puncturing the darkness at the farmhouse and the echoing low glow from the cottage by the fir trees – their distance is enormous. Granny Emmy goes inside to put on a light, and instantly the night is more deeply black and the tiny pinprick stars far too high in space. I'm frozen with indecision. Are insects clamouring or is my head chanting with fear? As I bring my hands up to cover my ears, I hear a short sharp bark, full of demand.

I laugh. 'It's Bruiser!' I jump down the veranda steps and rush to the gate. Bruiser runs down the path to greet Granny Emmy before returning to bounce around me. He's still wearing the blue ribbon. I hurry back to the veranda. The rug has fallen to the floor so

I pick it up and fold it neatly. 'Thank you for having me,' I say to Granny Emmy. 'Thank you for tea and for the lovely, lovely jelly.'

I can hear Bruiser ahead of me as I run and stumble through the night towards the lights.

Years later, at the convent boarding school in Shropshire, I am waiting with a group of girls for a prefect to distribute the day's post. We are gathered near the portico at the front of the Palladian-style building. It's a highlight of the school day. As if in recognition of this, when the prefect comes through the main door, a pale yellow light filters through the thin cloud and reflects off the windows. It makes the expectant faces look rather jaundiced.

There is a letter from Edith, and the familiarity of her large loose handwriting makes me feel, just for a moment, as though she has stroked my cheek and pushed my hair back off my forehead. She has enclosed a cutting from the *East African Standard*. It shows a grainy print of Granny Emmy, looking less groomed than I remember her, and even thinner, posing on the deck of a Trimaran yacht. She has a mop in her hands and the reader is supposed to believe she is swabbing the deck. The article describes how Granny Emmy Cole, 92, and her family have sailed 6,700 miles to Australia in her son's homemade forty-foot boat. Lieutenant Commander George Cole said, 'We didn't have one decent wind. We had to tack all the way.'

Was it fear of being alone in Africa that made Granny Emmy choose to emigrate with her family? And was it fear of emigrating that made Granny Robinson choose to stay? I imagine her taking a swig from her hip flask and offering Bruiser a flying ant to taste.

I sellotape the cutting to the underneath of my desk lid. Much later, I transfer it to the shoebox in which I keep precious letters and keepsakes – snippets of memories. As I do this, a fragment of handkerchief is visible at the bottom of the box, so I unearth it. Examining the embroidered 'E', I think with surprise how much I used to enjoy needlecraft. A faint smell of lemon cologne tugs at my memory. Lavender, mauve and lilac colours swim around me, before a vision of an aeroplane spilling out of the sky and burning up the moon explodes in my head.

Rosette for a War Horse

Star casts white-edged and malevolent eyes towards me as she munches the grass, while I stand holding her reins and kicking clumps off the top of molehills. This is how we are, isolated from the rest of the gymkhana – Star mutinous, me morose.

The tournament is drawing to an end.

'Older children – ten to thirteens – for the potato ring event,' Jane Dawson orders through the megaphone. 'No exceptions!'

I don't want to play this stupid game. Maybe I can get Star to hide with me under the pine trees? As I'm thinking about how to escape, Granny Robinson's Holden estate draws up alongside the other cars. I watch her get out and search the field, her hand shading her eyes. When she sees us, she waves briefly and climbs onto the bonnet, delving into her jacket pocket for cheroots. She then settles down to smoke and spectate.

Embarrassment and bad temper deepen within me. I snatch at Star's reins and haul her forwards; she follows reluctantly. Tears mix with sweat on my lips, stinging a cut where I had bitten off dried skin. I loop the reins under my arm and ram on my riding hat. When we are near the ring of stakes with potatoes skewered on the top, I turn, put my foot in the stirrup and swing onto Star's back. Usually, my effort to mount is dramatic. Usually, I am swung out in an arc away from the saddle like some fairground ride as Star whirls, trying to rid herself of me. But this time I am on her back with a different energy, taut and light with fury. I am like a feather caught by static. She won't find any substance in me to resist, no weight to dislodge. I ride her towards the event, remembering it like musical chairs at childhood parties. There is one stake with potato on top fewer than the number of competitors, so when Jane Dawson blows the whistle, one horse and rider will not be able to claim a potato.

As we circle the outside of the ring of stakes, I suddenly become heavy again – leaden and hopeless. Horses steer clear of Star, who is showing her teeth and rump to any that come close. Jane Dawson blows the whistle and my ears are filled with the noise of hooves thudding into soft earth and the rhythm of the horses' laboured breathing. Star throws her head far back and fights against my hold. She starts forward, ambitious to take a lump out of the horse in front, then whirls round in an attempt to bite the one behind. My pubic bone comes down hard on the back of the saddle, and for a second the pain makes the world go black. When I open my eyes again, I see Star is speeding towards a stake, so I slip my left hand from the reins and reach out to snatch the potato.

I look across at Granny Robinson, who is now standing against the fence. I hold up the potato. 'At least I'm not last,' I'll tell her later.

'Replace your potatoes on the stakes!' comes through the megaphone. But because I can't get Star close enough, a marshal has to do mine for me, then moves quickly out of the way. I'm bewildered by the speed of it all. Then noise fills the air again, horses plunge and gallop, and again I have a potato clutched to my chest when the whistle blows. This time, I get Star close enough to replace it. I am churned about as though I am in the middle of a whirlwind, thrown around with a roar of sound in my ears. The noise rises with encouraging shouts from the spectators.

Star responds to my request to stop. Lowering her head, she blows through her nostrils, and my legs move in and out with the expansion of her lungs. She is tired. We rest as somebody puts a potato on a pole in the middle of the ring. My hands are trembling and I'm feeling weak. Dropping the reins, I feel a wetness on my right hand. At first, I think it's sweat, but then I see it's dark – the horsehair has cut into my flesh, the blood drying in patches. Although I feel no pain, I blow on my hand to soothe it anyway. Then my eyes drift to take stock of the field. It's down to the last two competitors – myself and a boy on a large strawberry roan. I ease my feet out of the stirrups and let my legs hang down, wondering if I could pretend to faint, slide sideways and fall to the ground, giving default victory to the boy. Granny Robinson couldn't despise me for coming second, could she? But I have the uncomfortable feeling that she will see through me, instinctively recognising my cowardice. At the same time as I'm thinking about staging an exit, I'm wondering from which side of the stake to approach the potato.

'On your marks!' A fist of fear hits my chest and I jerk up, grabbing the reins and flailing my feet to get them back in the stirrups. The whistle sounds. Star doesn't wait for me; her ears are flat and her nose almost horizontally stretched in front of her as I slip about in the saddle. I manage to clamp my legs round her belly and grip with my thigh and calf muscles, holding the reins in my right hand and leaving the left free. The other horse's hooves are ploughing the ground and I hear its breath snort – or is it Star's? Through half-closed eyes I can see the potato amidst flying clods of earth. The noise of horses and shouting fades as I reach out to it. A screaming neigh comes from Star, and the prize is in my hand. I slump onto Star's neck and wait for the pounding in my ears to subside.

When I look up again, I see Granny Robinson striding towards me. She strokes the white star on Star's forehead then takes the potato from my hand. 'Such a waste of good spuds,' she says. Then she sees the blood, bright and dark, streaking my palm. 'You should go to the first aid tent, get that cleaned up and bandaged.' She shakes the bridle, and Star shakes her head. 'Not a bad effort, Tanzie, considering you weren't really in control of this naughty horse.'

'Should I go back to the stables now?'

'Certainly not! You've won a rosette; you must wait for the prize giving. But just make sure you're back before it's dark.'

As I watch her walk away my spirits rise. Winning a rosette is something I've always envied in others, never believing I could achieve it myself. Although I know we only won this time because the other horses were too busy trying to avoid Star's aggression, I allow my imagination to see us as warriors. Star is a warhorse, smelling the fight from afar, and I have the survival instinct to lean out and gather the fruits of the battle.

'Bloody well done!' The boy from the roan horse is coming towards me. 'Well done, girl,' he says to Star. He looks up into my face. 'You too.'

I know those freckles. 'Duncan?'

He peers at me closely, but there is no recognition.

I'm worried about his horse – untethered, its reins looped over the saddle and the boy's riding hat attached to the stirrups. 'Is your horse alright?'

'Sinbad? Yeah, he's fine.' The way Sinbad is so relaxed, and the way Star is settling under me, makes me aware of the boy's ease and horse sense.

'You used to go to Naivasha kindergarten!'

'Uh huh!'

'Duncan McLeod.'

'Uh huh!'

'We were in the same dormitory. You were in the end bed next to the veranda.'

He doesn't reply. He takes his hand from Star's neck and wipes the back of it across his nose, then squints at me. I remember myself, a frightened-of-the-dark child, climbing into his bed and him moving over in his sleep to make room for me. Then I remember his temper when he woke up in the morning and found me, his freckles becoming half-freckles in the concertina of his red-rage forehead. I wince.

'Where is your school now?' he says.

'Nakuru – you?'

'Prince of Wales.'

The announcement for prize giving comes over the megaphone.

'Let's go to the tent,' says Duncan.

I jump down from the saddle, and lose my balance. Duncan steadies me. I'm embarrassed, but I'm also pleased, quickened.

'We should go to the first aid tent first,' he says, examining my hand.

Duncan is taller than me and has a wide chest. His freckles are darker than I remember, playing over his nose and cheeks and rioting over his forehead before hiding in his thick chestnut hair. He takes Star's reins, and I move to fetch Sinbad but he tells me to leave him. As we join others milling near the tents, I look back. Sinbad snatches a clump of grass and, unhurried, follows us.

I am happy sitting on Star's back. Her mood is quiet, as though she is as content walking alongside Sinbad as I am beside Duncan. A bright blue rosette is attached to her bridle. The sound of hooves rhythmically plodding the earthy road and the smell of horse sweat and linseed oil from the saddle makes me feel different from how I'd felt riding to the gymkhana, when I'd been full of dread. Bright light and blue shade stripe the red soil as the sun moves west of us, dipping slightly below the sparse trees that line the road.

I tell Duncan about Edith being in London and my staying with the Coles. I watch his face. He turns to me frequently, which shows he is listening, and I enjoy the change of shadow and sunlight over his skin as we ride along. We leave the road and take a short cut through some fir trees, where the smell of damp earth and pine needles fills my nostrils and I savour the freshening in my lungs.

Stinkweed and nettles line the narrow lane to Granny Robinson's cottage. We dismount and I lead Star into her stable. Duncan removes her saddle and stands holding it while I take off her bridle. I detach the rosette and pin it to my shirt. While Duncan rubs Star down I put the tack away and then bring a bucket of oats and bran. I love the sound of a horse munching with its nose in a pail and blowing breath through wide nostrils.

Granny Robinson's head appears over the stable door. 'Who's this?'

'Duncan McLeod,' I say. 'Duncan, this is Mrs Robinson.'

'This your horse?'

'Yes – Sinbad.'

'You're the boy she beat. Where are you from?'

'Njoro, but I'm staying with my aunt, Jane Dawson, next farm along.'

'Beer?'

'Do you have lemonade?'

'I have beer, water, and whisky – and I'm not offering whisky.'

'Beer then, thanks.'

Granny Robinson turns to me. 'You?'

'Beer, please.'

'Don't forget to check Star's hay and water. Boy, you can put your horse in the small field over there.'

'He'll be fine waiting in the lane, Mrs Robinson.'

Granny Robinson fetches us a bottle of Tusker beer each from the kitchen and uses the doorjamb to knock off the tops. 'Cheers!' she says, taking her hip flask from her back pocket. 'Let me know when you leave for the main house,' she says to me. 'And don't wait until it's dark.'

As I take a sip of the beer, I remember I don't like the taste, but I try to conceal this from Duncan. We lean against the gate while Sinbad crops some long grass from under the fence. Star watches him with her head over the stable door.

'Will you be my girlfriend?' Duncan says, looking down at his feet.

Usually, I like boys older than Duncan, but his calmness and horse sense make him appear quite mature. Also, I'm as impressed with his freckles now as I was when we were five years old. But I'm still concerned about the practicalities.

'How could that work, with us living nowhere near each other and at different schools?'

'We could write.'

I like letter writing. 'Okay.'

'That's settled then.'

'Okay.' I drink up the beer, wince, and burp loudly.

Lots of Love, Leo

Even though Gerard is two years older than his brother Leo, he's not as strong, and he's not as good looking either. His blue-black hair stands up in tufts round his head, making him appear young and boyish. But his fierce blue eyes and 'strike and retreat' verbal tactics ensure he easily maintains the dominance of an older brother.

Gerard straddles his motorbike and his will glints steely in his eyes. 'Leo, you take the gun while I distract the stag. Track round to the left and I'll approach it from the right.'

The stag views us, alert and focused, from the other side of a large field of wheat.

Leo frowns. 'Why don't I ride the bike? You need some shooting practice…'

'We haven't got bullets to waste and you're the best shot. Make it a single one, and make it clean.'

Gerard hauls me onto the back of the motorbike. I hold my arms around his waist as he manoeuvres very slowly, occasionally making the engine roar to keep the stag's attention on us rather than on Leo.

When the gun goes off I feel the bullet slam into my own chest and lodge like a shard of ice while silence sings a high monotone through my head. One minute the stag is proud against the gold and blue of wheat and sky, the next it is slumped out of sight. I hope the bullet hole is neat, the wound clean. But perhaps it is spilling blood from the still-pumping heart, spreading and glistening in the sun and staining the golden field crimson. Leo begins to move through the wheat, crouching to come upon the deer unseen.

I hate these adolescent boys, hate their practical, unemotional ability to kill. But I am angry and sad too about the uncompromising reality of life: the dogs need to eat. The dogs need to eat…to eat…toweat, toweet, tweet, tweet – my thoughts madden and run into a groove.

I am sitting with my face pressed against Gerard's back as if I can draw comfort from him even while hating him. Leo holds the gun above his head to show us where he is. He is a killer. He is a heck of a good shot.

Gerard waves to Leo to indicate that we have seen him. Leo puts the gun across the back of his neck and hangs his arms on either side of it like a water-carrier. I know what happens next. He will wait for Gerard to pick up the deer and drape its poor body over the seat of the motorbike as though he cherishes it; there'll be no room for me. Leo and I will walk back to the house.

Gerard revs the engine and half turns his head to me. 'I'll slow down when we get near them, and when I shout, jump off.'

The air is rushing by my head, whipping my hair into the dust. The ground is speeding under the wheels, the wheat streaking by like walls of amber light. Leo is watching us careen towards him. We are getting closer and closer. I have to jump off, but Gerard is not slowing down…I'm in a vortex, racing through space…I'm supposed to jump…I have to jump…I can't do it! I can't do it, cantdoit, cantdweet, dweet, dweet, dweet –

I jump. The ground rushes up to meet me as I slam into it, my chest sledgehammered, my teeth shattered. The world is red dust, thick and clotting inside my head, clogging my throat. I hold my face straight down to let the earth and blood and teeth run out of my mouth so that I can breathe. The engine has stopped and Gerard is beside me. He gently pulls my head towards him, strokes my hair back from my face and looks into my mouth. But I shake him off to look for my broken teeth, stirring the dusty ground with my fingers. They must have gone deep into the earth. Then my tongue finds them – numb and bloody, but still securely attached to my gums.

'Tanzie! Why did you jump before I slowed down? How could you be so stupid? You could have broken bones, teeth…you could have broken your neck, you idiot girl. Let's get you up. How are your knees? It looks like you've bitten your lip. Don't get up too fast. Steady! Lean on me…'

But it's Leo I want to have fussing over me. As he strolls towards us, his rifle slung over his shoulder, he looks older than his sixteen years. I have never seen anyone as beautiful, as perfectly formed. Why isn't he hurrying to show he cares about me too?

I know he isn't one to show concern though. He often comes to our farm to shoot deer for the dogs or duck for the table because Edith and Ken, British and with no farming background, are too squeamish to do it themselves. He usually takes his shirt off and leaves it with his Lambretta at the back door, telling the dogs to guard it so they won't follow him. His chest is smooth and bronzed and I long to run my hands over his skin. I always follow in his slipstream on these shoots, struggling to keep up and wanting him to notice me, but he is indifferent to my presence. I try, often, to lengthen my stride to place my feet in his footfall, to stay close and smell the hot dust and sweat on him. Once, I brushed too close to the nettles that edge the dust tracks. 'Ow! Owie, man, I'm stung! Leo, I'm stung!' But even though the thing I longed for most was his hands on my thighs where my flesh was sore and red, he just turned to look at me, shrugged, and continued on his way.

I accept Gerard's arm to get me to my feet and then let him dust me down. Leo's emotional neutrality makes me promise myself that I will no longer follow him like an obedient gun dog. But I won't honour this pledge, on account of his beauty.

Leo went on to work in the North Sea oilfields, then in the Texan oil industry. He wrote to me in a flawless hand; a protractor confirmed what my eyes told me – the upright letters were uniformly at ninety degrees, and my ruler confirmed that the distance between one word and another was the same. Leo told me about wild oceans and southern sands and engineering. He told me that he was sought after for baseball teams in Texas, and I liked to imagine him, hot with exertion after a game, tugging his shirt off and discarding it on the ground. But I searched his letters in vain for a mild endearment or even a personal comment.

I receive Leo's letters in Our Lady of Sion convent in Shropshire. I have been sent here to keep me safe from the danger brewing in Kenya as it wins independence from British rule – well, that's what my mother says but I sometimes think it's just to keep me out of my stepfather's way. The nuns are determined to keep us safe from sin too, which includes monitoring all incoming and outgoing mail. This is Sister Edmund's responsibility. She finds nothing in Leo's letters to disturb her, but once I forgot myself and signed a letter to him with 'lots of love'.

Sister Edmund's lips were pursed as she came towards me, letter in hand. 'Tanzie, this will not do! We only tolerate this man writing to you because you're far from home and because he is completely without sentiment; I suggest you respond to his letters with the same. In other words, keep it formal! And tuck your shirt in – you look like a bag of laundry.'

But I wasn't too disappointed because I knew that nothing would ever make Leo write any endearments anyway; it's obvious that he just wants an audience, and I happen to be the most willing. My cheeks were still hot with embarrassment though and I pulled my hair over my face and hung my head.

'You may not be a Catholic, Tanzie, but you're under our care and you need to know that it is a sin to express affection for a man who is not a member of your family, and to tempt him into error.'

But Sister Edmund cannot monitor my thoughts. When the long days are over and I sink into bed, sin has free rein in my mind. At least the nuns would regard what I think about as sin, but I know it's just a lovely dream. And if imagining being in Leo's arms is wrong, then I'm happy to be sinful.

As soon as the familiar feeling of missing my mother comes into my head and swells under my ribs, bruising my soul, I transfer my thoughts to Leo. I reach under my pillow for the earphone to the tiny Sony transistor radio that Edith bought me from Naivasha. It is encased in soft leather and its size makes it easy to hide from the nuns. Combined with my fantasies about Leo, tuning in to Radio Luxembourg becomes a weapon against backward thoughts of home.

'Telstar' by The Tornados is top of the hit parade during my first year at the convent. I imagine myself sliding through indigo air, looping misty galaxies, my limbs intertwined with Leo's. During my second year, when I am in the long, cubicled dormitory at the top of the school, my favourite song is Carole King's 'It Might as Well Rain Until September'. This is played often, and sometimes when I listen to it under the eaves, rivulets of rain run down the sloping window above as though spilling over my closed eyelids. Listening to the forbidden world of pop music, I am cocooned with a lovely colonial boy who is caring, responsive and warm. I can see Leo looking out over a heat haze, concentrating all of himself to pinpoint a distant shimmering prey.

Leo had a car accident and broke his neck, but fortunately he was not paralysed. I was at college when this happened and Edith phoned me with the news; she had no other details. I sent Leo a card, wishing him a speedy recovery. A few months later, Edith phoned to tell me Leo had been diagnosed with schizophrenia.

I sent him another card, saying I was sorry to hear he was unwell.

Although our letter-writing relationship had lapsed, my second card elicited a response. But this time his handwriting was almost illegible, and his character seemed different too, as if echoing his shattered bones. It was obvious though that he still only needed an audience, so I hardly bothered to read his scrawled letters, and began to respond with just a card or postcard.

'Dear Leo, I'm on holiday here! As you can see, the scenery is spectacular, though the weather is variable. Hope you're well! Lots of love, Tanzie'

'Hope you're well!' – how crass; of course he wasn't well. And 'lots of love'? I was just entertaining myself with imagined defiance of Sister Edmund from my convent days. I didn't know how to communicate with this Leo – I didn't know this Leo – so I didn't try to reach him anymore. My cards to him were frequent, but they were just a habit.

Leo's mother, Dorothy, was a friend of Edith's. Now living in KwaZulu-Natal, she began writing to me, telling me how worried she was about Leo. This was repeated in her phone conversations with Edith, saying how violent and deranged he had become, how hopeless.

I kept on sending cards.

One day, I summoned up the courage to visit him. He had moved into sheltered accommodation in a small town in Buckinghamshire, and Dorothy was trying to sell up and emigrate to England to be close to him. In the meantime, because she knew 'how fond of Leo' I was, she pleaded with me to go and see him, to make sure he was being well cared for.

*

He lets me into his ground-floor flat. He is taller than I remember. Although his beauty has gone, he could still be handsome if he took an interest in his appearance. His dark hair is even darker from grease, his face is unshaven, and his ragged, badly cut beard is flecked with food. He peers at me from drugged, vague eyes. I am surprised, experiencing the unfamiliarity of eye contact from him.

'It's Edith, isn't it? Edith from the Kinangop?' He puts his tongue out to retrieve some dribble from the corner of his mouth.

'No, Leo. I'm Tanzie. Remember?'

'Tanzie sends me cards?'

'Yes. That's me. I send you cards.'

'You do?' He peers and concentrates. 'Tanzie?'

'It's been a hell of a long time – no wonder you don't recognise me!' I cough up an artificial laugh and extend my arm to shake hands. His grasp is strong and dry and brief.

We sit down on high-backed chairs.

'I haven't seen you since before.'

'Since before…?' I hesitate. 'Since before your accident?'

'It wasn't an accident.' He swivels his eyes and drops his chin onto his chest. He takes a deep breath, brings his head up and looks straight at me again. 'Everybody believes it was an accident, and it's best that way – for my mother, you know.'

'You crashed your car deliberately?'

'Yep.'

I shuffle around in my mind, waiting for the shock to subside so that I can find something to say. It's a familiar feeling from my childhood, this awe, submission and voicelessness in his company. I remember when I walked in his wake down the dust tracks as he listened for a rustle of wheat or watched for a darkening in the shimmer of heat haze close to the horizon.

I think for a moment that I catch the smell of salty sweat from his body, but it's only my memory confusing me. When I lean close to confirm my mistake I find he smells of damp wool, and his breath is both sweetish and foetid with creamy vegetable soup.

A thought suddenly breaks into my head, producing a flash of triumph so swift that I only half apprehend it: I don't care very much about Leo's affliction; perhaps it even serves him right. But if this is really how I think and feel, why do I want to enclose him with my strength and protect his sixteen-year-old self from the event that was to smash up his body, from the schizophrenia that was to mess up his mind? I am with him now, and I was with him then, when I was twelve years old, on that wheaten plain with my skin alive to his nearness. We are moving through a soft breeze that has awoken in the mountains, and the land undulates and whispers as the flow caresses the plateau. We tread the sadness in the wind, my feet reaching for the imprint of his, until we hear our own sadness sighing through the eucalyptus wood that stands close by the house.

Leo's letters become madder, but warmer and more interesting too. I sometimes get caught up with his adventures as he describes his duty to save the planet. Voices in his head have told him that aliens are going to land on the roof of his building in a bid to destroy all life. But the voices don't tell him exactly when this attack is going to happen, and he gets stressed out from having to remain constantly alert. An upside to being the one chosen to save mankind though is the sense of importance it brings him, which he can't help expressing in his writing.

He moves to an apartment on the top floor of the same sheltered accommodation. There is a large roof window in the attic and he puts a ladder underneath it, in readiness for the alien invasion. His carers tell me that he had made himself very unpopular with the previous occupant, constantly barging into the flat and surging into the attic to check the roof.

Reading Leo's letters can leave me breathless with the drama of the storytelling. Gone is the aloof, self-possessed, unemotional Leo. He is frenetic, constantly on guard, but still as egocentric as ever. He still just needs an audience, although there is sometimes a question or two, a passing interest in who I might be. 'Are you married?' he writes. 'I've never had a wife. There was a woman once in Mexico who pursued me to South Africa but I managed to lose her – lucky escape, that.'

He calls me Tanzie Panzie and Rafiki, Swahili for 'friend', and sends me several of the same Christmas cards each year. I continue to send him lots of love in my cards.

Whenever I visit his mother, who is now living in a cottage near his flat, he joins us. Even though he knows Edith has died, he still mistakes me for her if his medication isn't quite in tune. When, eventually, I manage to convince him I am Tanzie, he inspects me closely. Then he smiles and turns to Dorothy. 'She's like Edith,' he says. 'She's just like Edith.'

*

When Dorothy dies, I attend her funeral. I gather Leo into my arms for the first time and hold him close. This hug will have to last forever. His body is warm. He relaxes and for a while, at least, the need to stay on guard leaves him.

As I head for my car, I turn to wave. Leo's arms hang down and his shoulders slump. He is probably better off on guard. I keep walking backwards, waving, until he lifts a hand and spreads his fingers wide towards me.

'Lots of love,' I call out. 'Lots of love, Leo.'

Stain

It is the Christmas term and in the music room below me the choir is practising three-part harmonies for the carols they will be singing around Shrewsbury town. There will be a nativity there too, with Jemima in the starring role, as she is every year.

Jemima is a sweet donkey with a healthy soft grey hide and gentle eyes. She is the responsibility of Sister Agnes, a small nun packed with energy. Every year a horsebox is borrowed from a local farmer, furnished with bucket and spade, water and feed, and Jemima and Sister Agnes loaded into it. They're taken to the little town of Bethlehem – outside Timothy Whites the chemists in the high street.

This is my first Christmas term at the convent and I have not made the grade for the choir, nor found a role as a shepherd or wise man in the nativity, so I'm not needed for rehearsals. I'm alone in St. Joseph's classroom, reading *The Life of St. Teresa of Jesus*. I'm not permitted to read anything that isn't devotional, but I don't mind because I enjoy reading and am open to receiving the wisdom of saints – for now, at least.

I'm sitting on the window seat over the radiator and feeling unusually peaceful. Unlike many of the saints, I haven't had any visitations from angels, the thought of which unnerves me, so I've begun to trust being alone. I feel sorry for those chosen to be saints, having their lives changed so much through being favoured by heaven; I wouldn't want to attract that kind of attention from on high.

Last night was my turn on the bath rota, and it feels nice to be warm and clean. We are allowed a bath just once a week. At school in Kenya we used to shower every morning and bath every evening. When I told Alice this, she blinked her long curling eyelashes. 'Yeah? Well, I suppose you need to in such a hot, sweaty country.'

'Kenya is dry, not humid,' I said, shifting uncomfortably in my seat. I was very new to the school then and in awe of Alice, who was clever, popular and full of physical grace.

'So why do you have to wash so much?'

'I smell if I'm not clean,' I said, then added stroppily, 'and so do you.'

Alice tutted and looked at me as if I smelled bad then. 'Oh, be quiet,' she said, turning her back on me and shifting her weight to read her book.

I shut up, but only to stop myself revealing that we also had to share our baths with another boarder. I always shared with my best friend Joy. Joy had a warm, moist, animal smell that wasn't at all offensive and, unlike me, she had already begun menstruating. Alice would have been shocked if I'd revealed our ease with nakedness in Kenya; in the convent it's frowned upon, like many other things, as part of the constant vigilance to prevent sin.

Remembering Joy makes me sad but my present little oasis of peace is too rare and delicious to be disturbed, so I try to return to feeling happy about being clean. But then I become conscious of how fat I am. When I first wore the compulsory suspender belt, only a few months ago, it was too big for me, but now it makes deep weals of red in my flesh. I loathe the stupid thing, and the stockings I have to wear with it. My mood is spoiling.

I need Joy. I'd like to share with her the horror of the suspender belt and having the flesh on my thighs bulge over the top of my stockings and rub together. I'd also like to tell her, now that my periods have started, about having to pad the sanitary towels out with great wads of tissue because we're not given enough of them. The foetid smell of warm menstrual blood hangs around me and all the other girls; Joy would be disgusted.

I remember Joy taking her first period in her stride, having been told how to manage it by her mother. She showed me a sanitary towel and the belt to pin it to, and explained that dragging pains in the back and lower abdomen were common during menstruation. She was matter of fact about it all, but also pleased that she could now have babies.

'But do you even want babies?' I asked, as though she had just turned into somebody I didn't know.

'Of course! I want six – three girls and three boys. I have names for all of them.'

I was stunned. Joy had never told me about these dreams and I hadn't suspected she had such things in her head.

'But your tummy will grow huge and then you'll have to push out an enormous baby through a tiny wee hole. First you'll look disgusting, then you'll hurt like hell. And you could die!'

'It's all just natural,' Joy said calmly, putting the palm of her hand against my cheek. 'And your vagina is separate from your wee hole.'

'Really?'

Joy smiled. 'Yes, really.'

She had moved on from me. She embodied mystery and womanhood. She was an eleven-year-old woman, and I had no way of understanding her. But I'd like to tell her now that our regular mutual nakedness and her touching my face like she did put us in danger of mortal sin. And I'd like to tell her about my first period.

'Joy – you have to imagine a small dormitory, nothing like those at Nakuru. This dorm only holds six beds, all completely curtained off so nobody can see anybody else naked. It smells of wax polish, wet wood, stale blood and soapy flannels. We each have a basin on our lockers, and a jug to fetch water from the tap under the stairs, for washing morning and evening. But we only have one flannel for our face *and* our private bits! *One* flannel!' I fully expect her mouth to drop open.

'One night, I woke up and there was a sticky wetness between my legs. Because there was hardly any light in the room, all I could see was something dark and spread out like a flood. I thought it must be my first period, but then I couldn't remember you mentioning a lot of blood – you only talked about some staining, a brownish smearing, didn't you?'

I move deeper into my memory. Perhaps this isn't a period. Perhaps I'm haemorrhaging, bleeding to death.

I leap out of bed, open my cubicle curtain and turn on the main light. My nightdress is heavy with blood.

On the right side of the room is a cubicle where Sister Consuelo sleeps. We rarely see her as she only goes to bed after we are curtained off in our worlds of private sinlessness. She works in the kitchen and is often made fun of by the other girls. It's difficult to communicate with her as she speaks a strange mixture of pidgin English, explosive Spanish and dismembered French.

'Sister!' My voice obliterates the hum of the fluorescent light. 'Sister, wake up!' As there are only curtains around the cubicle, I kneel down and knock on the wooden floor, smearing blood.

Alice's bed creaks in the cubicle next to mine and her face appears round her curtain. 'What's wrong? Oh Lord – is that blood?'

Our calling and knocking eventually wakens Sister Consuela, and then we have to wait for her to put on her habit. As she emerges, she looks at me and quickly backs away, her cheeks reddening and wobbling with embarrassment.

'Sister! I am bleeding! Que pasa? Can you call a doctor? Get me an ambulance. Please hurry. Je suis bleeding badly.'

Sister Consuela rushes off – a black mass of fluttering, floundering fabric, like a bird with disordered feathers – and returns with Sister Joan, a no-nonsense martinet whose temper is obviously not improved by being woken in the night.

'Alice, will you please fetch a sanitary towel and a clean sheet from the store cupboard. Oh, and a clean nightdress. A large one. And then strip the bed. Tanzie, go and fetch water and clean yourself up. Be quick about it.'

'But how can I wipe off the blood, Sister?' I ask.

'You've got a flannel, use that.'

I grimace. Then I start panicking again. 'One sanitary towel won't be enough, Sister. I'm bleeding like a stuck pig. I think I'm haemorrhaging!'

'Don't be ridiculous, and don't be crude. Say ten Hail Marys.'

When I am back in bed, I am restless. The thick stickiness between my legs worries me; the sanitary towel definitely won't last till the morning, and I'll have to plead for more. I wonder how Alice manages. 'Alice! Are you awake?' Although she doesn't answer, I'm sure she's not sleeping. Why is she ignoring me? When she handed me the sanitary towel and the clean nightwear, she avoided eye contact. No doubt the commotion I caused must have woken the other girls too, and she would have been mortified at being involved in such a floor show. I pull my pillow over my head and screw up my eyes; my face just won't relax. Despite the wax polish, the floor outside my cubicle will stain with my blood. It will be there forever, a permanent reminder to everybody of the need to despise me.

'Hail Mary, full of grace, blessed art though among women, and blessed is the fruit of thy womb, Jesus.' How Mary can be full of grace and blessed as a menstruating woman is beyond me. My soul is darkening, congealing along with my thickening blood.

Reliving all this, on top of feeling fat, dissipates my contentment entirely. I look out of the window at the ruined castle nearby. In a field alongside it, Jemima and a local farmer's horse are grazing together. A sudden, intense yearning to be with them engulfs me. I can't read *The Life of St. Teresa of Jesus* anymore.

There are to be no lessons for a whole week as the choir, nuns and nativity group are busy collecting for charity in the town. I will spend the week alone and unsupervised on the window seat in the wood-panelled library. Books that are by no means devotional – by Dickens, Thackeray, Walter Scott and the Brontës – line the shelves, and there is even a copy of *The Canterbury Tales*. I wonder why the nuns allow these books in the convent, then decide they've obviously never read them and just assume that because they're classics, they must be acceptable. I'm particularly looking forward to re-reading *Jane Eyre*.

The door opens and Sister Joan comes in.

'Tanzie, you grew up on a farm – you are comfortable around animals?'

'Yes, Sister.'

'Sister Agnes has been taken ill and won't be able to look after Jemima tomorrow. Go to Sister Francesca and get a shepherd's outfit. And tomorrow fetch Jemima to load into the horsebox; Sister Agnes doesn't like her getting upset and wants you to travel with her.'

'What about the bucket and spade and food and water?'

'See Tom about that.'

'By myself?' I couldn't believe she was expecting me to be alone in the presence of a man, even though it was only Tom, who carried out maintenance at the convent.

'Take Alice with you. Have the donkey round the front straight after breakfast, sharp.'

I wait outside the music room. When the choir comes out I catch Alice's arm. She steps back, startled, lifting her arm up and away. She looks annoyed.

Am I so disgusting? The thought of my menstrual blood all over the floor confirms that I am. I shrink inside myself. But then I can't help adding anger to the sin of being disgusting. 'It was only bloody blood, for bloody God's sake!'

Alice looks at me with distaste and fear. 'What are you talking about?'

'Sister Agnes is ill, so I have to be in charge of Jemima tomorrow and I need to find Tom and get a bucket and spade and stuff and a halter.' I'm breathless with the speed at which the words are spilling from my mouth in an attempt to stop Alice thinking of my night of shame.

She waits, frowning. Then she sighs and rolls her eyes. 'So?'

'So someone has to come with me as we're not supposed to be alone with a man.'

'You'll have to find someone else.'

'But Sister Joan said to ask you.'

Alice remains still but drops her eyes to the floor. I wait an eternity before I turn away. 'It's alright. I'll find somebody else.'

'Wait,' she says. 'I'll come.'

I freeze. She can't mean it; she's planning to make me look foolish.

'I'll come with you. We'd better go now, before Benediction.'

I try to unscramble her change of mind. Perhaps she is afraid of Sister Joan – who wouldn't be? Or maybe she's just pleased to miss Benediction?

Alice moves ahead of me, her feet quick and light, and my breathing soon becomes laboured as I strain to keep up with her. 'Slow down, can't you! What's the big fat hurry?'

She doesn't pause or turn to look at me. She wants to get this job done as quickly as possible. I want her to be the same with me as she is with the other girls – accepting and friendly. We have reached the shrubbery and I'm losing sight of her as she follows the winding path leading to the stables and sheds.

'Oh, I don't care,' I say to myself, to the bees, to the sky, to the world. 'I don't bloody care.'

I stop to catch my breath. My chest hurts and I start to cry.

Alice comes back and watches me. Silent and awkward, she warps and glitters through the spangle of my tears. The waxy leaves of the rhododendron shrubs flood with glassy wet reflections as though it has rained. I blink and Alice is clear again. My breathing eases and I stare at her, uncertain how to behave or what to say.

'What's wrong?' She tilts her head slightly and her dark hair swings to frame her face.

I want to go back to a time before the convent. I want to be home with my mother. I need my mother.

'Nothing.' I wipe my nose on my sleeve.

Alice hands me a tissue from her pocket. She watches me clean up my face. 'That's better!' Her mouth lifts at the corners in a suggestion of a smile. 'C'mon,' she says. 'Let's go.'

Sister Gabriel

She's a robed Modigliani, a Middle Eastern Virgin Mary, a saffron mother of God. She sways slightly, flowing like a river along the high polish of the top corridor. The hem of her habit dusts the yellow sheen of electric light reflecting off the dark wood floor and whispers a soft rhythm.

Her gold-brown eyes are streaked with a pale yellow that tones with the skin of her oval face. Short lashes of the same hue line her eyelids, giving her a finely sculpted look, and her mouth, full but well defined, might have been drawn with a magenta pencil.

She is always graceful and serene.

But I once saw her trip over the stone slabs under the portico. It was as though a great bale of black cotton had launched into the air. She landed strung out and splayed. I held my breath, appalled. Then she scrambled up and laughed, and I didn't recognise her. Her laughter delighted me. She amazed me.

She didn't see me witness her fall. I was beneath her notice generally. There didn't seem a way I could flicker the smallest light of interest in her eyes.

Not until I was rude to her. Since then, I have become an obvious irritation. Now she always chastises and curls her lip at me.

I fear her. She is alien, strange and inscrutable. There are things she believes in that are unbelievable – the communion host and altar wine becoming the body and blood of Christ in her mouth; Christ rising from the dead to redeem her sins; miracles and stigmata and absolution. The Confessional cleanses her, the lives of the saints inspire her, and she understands 'the word made flesh'.

I am a Protestant, and I am shallow, unformed, lumpy, slow and bad. It has been a revelation to me, this badness, this terrible sinfulness. I still only half believe it.

I have just slammed the door to St. Raphael's classroom, annoyed that Sister Gabriel kept me behind to tidy myself up. Since I'd found the comforting sweetness of golden syrup at teatime, my clothes no longer fit me. My shirt is only comfortable with the buttons undone under my jumper and dislodged from my skirt. I am walking away from the violence of the slammed door, and my eyes, smarting with shame, swim with a watery jaundiced light. The corridor lengthens and darkens in front of me and I hurry to hide in its shadow. But the door opens behind me, and I hear the familiar swish of hem. 'Come back here, Tanzie.'

I don't want to listen. I want to keep walking. But I am turning to face her. 'Why?' I say belligerently.

Silence hangs in the high ceiling.

What can she do to me? But even as I decide to ignore her, I walk towards her. She steps aside as I go back into the classroom and then follows. She closes the door softly and leans against it, her arms behind her on the handle, her head inclined slightly backwards. She is so graceful, and I hate her.

'Apologise for your rudeness.'

I stare up at the crucifix on the wall. A white alabaster Christ on a wooden cross, a Christ who died to save us from our sins. I hadn't been troubled by the idea of sin before I came to the convent. Christ – please don't die for my sins, don't die because I have offended a nun of the Catholic Church.

But it's not just hatred I feel for Sister Gabriel. I want her to like me.

The air is becoming heavy. How can I breathe, let alone speak?

'I'm sorry.' I spit the words with venom. But I don't mean this aggression, in the same way I don't mean the apology. I want the confrontation to be over. I want the quietness punctured. 'I'm sorry, okay?'

'An apology must be humble and gracious.'

I think about humility and grace, but I don't know how to do either.

'I'm humbly and graciously sorry.'

She lowers her eyelids. She's either closed her eyes or is looking at the floor. Her stillness panics me.

'I'm so sorry. I'm not sorry. I don't care.' I go to my desk and crash into the seat and bury my head in my arms. I can smell chalk and incense on my jumper and nylon sweat in the creases of my body. I raise my head. Even in her frozenness, Sister Gabriel is fluid and graceful. I peer up at the crucifix again. Bloodless and white, drained of its holy and redemptive scarlet, it makes the wall look dirty. To the side of it stands Sister Gabriel, the living flesh – bride of the plaster Christ.

'May I go now?'

She doesn't stir. It would be sacrilege to hit a Sister of the convent of Sion; but she's just a woman really, isn't she? 'Sister, may I go now?'

Still she doesn't move.

'Look, I'm sorry for my rudeness. I am rude, and I hope Jesus will forgive me if I beseech him tonight in my prayers. I'm sorry.' I'm surprised how firm my voice sounds and am tempted to embellish my apology with more of Jesus and the forgiveness of sin.

Sister Gabriel sways, and with one fluid movement swings the door open and glides through it, leaving me with the white Jesus on the wall, and confusion. Perhaps firmness is as potent as humility and grace.

The shock of this encounter makes me careful for a while – until one evening in the refectory after I've just finished my semolina pudding laden with the consoling golden syrup. I put my elbows on the table, lean my chin on my hands and try to make myself listen to the tape recording of the life of St. Bernadette coming at us through the speakers. The girl next to me gives me a nudge. I rouse myself enough to see our form prefect Claire gesturing to me to remove my elbows from the table. I'm sleepy now that my sugar levels are starting to drop, and spiteful too. So I hold my elbows a fraction of an inch above the surface and exaggerate a listening stance. Claire stands up, walks towards me, flaps at my arms and then quickly returns to her seat.

Suddenly the tape recording stops, cutting the reader off in mid-sentence. Sister Gabriel is standing beside the machine, and her eyes are resting on me. I stare back, while my heart hammers a blur of noise in my ears.

Sister Gabriel glides between the rows of tables and leans her head close to Claire's. Claire explains about me and my elbows.

'Tanzie, will you get up, please?' Sister Gabriel's voice is soft, threatening. The eyes of the school are watching me as I stand and grow huge and conspicuous.

'You seem to have little respect for your form prefect, or for the lives of the saints.'

I want to argue with her but can't summon up enough conviction that what she's saying is wrong. I am dull, tamed by the flood of fear in my heartbeat. Once again, this nun has me cowed, but this time I am the centre of attention.

She goes to the sideboard, takes out a packet of digestive biscuits and places three carefully on a plate.

She then hands me the plate. 'Eat those,' she says, 'after you have said grace.'

'For what I am about to receive may the Lord make me truly thankful.' I sit down and pick up a biscuit.

'No, stand up. And remain standing so that everyone can witness how grateful you are.'

My mouth is as dry as Kalahari sand. I'm going to choke as the biscuit fills and clogs my mouth, but I can't swallow. I have no spit and no throat muscles. I don't mind if I suffocate as long as I don't do it publicly. My legs are sagging. My will is collapsing and pouring out of my body so there is nothing to hold me up for everybody to witness my gratitude. I catch Claire's eye and she shakes her head slightly, her hair falling over her face; at least she has the grace to appear uncomfortable at my distress.

I want to reverse time. I want saliva and willpower and legs as strong as the pillars of the portico. I want St. Bernadette to intercede for me in her prayers in the grotto in Lourdes. I'm beginning to know how sinful I must be to find myself here in a convent in Shropshire. Shame and humiliation make me conscious that I will have to submit to the stronger will of others forever and ever, Amen.

I seethe for a long time after this experience, nurturing malice towards Sister Gabriel. But I dread her more than I hate her, so I try to avoid her in spirit even if I can't in reality. I use my imagination and the world of stories, even that of St. Bernadette of Lourdes, to avoid thinking about a nun whose attention I courted but who dislikes me.

Meanwhile, I have my daily dealings with religion. I try to look on the face of God, but to my relief, He doesn't reveal himself. During Mass, when all the Catholics go up to the altar to receive Holy Communion, I examine the Stations of the Cross that line the chapel walls. I focus on the image of Simon of Cyrene, who was made to carry the cross when Jesus fell. It was an imposition. He was just wandering along, when he came upon the crucifixion of a Jew who had offended the Romans by calling himself the Son of God.

I imagine being there, in the crowd. At first, Simon is reluctant to shoulder the cross. He has been singled out because he is large and muscular. He looks at the fallen Jesus and seems to want to carry him rather than the cross, but a vicious jab in the ribs and a blow to the head make him change his mind. Being there in the crowd, jostled and shoved, I feel a liking for Simon, an admiration for his quiet submission. He is peaceable and dignified, his dusty face streaked with sweat, or tears. 'Blessed are the peacemakers, for they shall be called sons of God.' Simon is too powerless to be a peacemaker, but I think he is a son of God, and I want to be like him. Incense and stale bodies mix with the sweat and dust round Simon and Jesus. I want to bellow, 'Hey, Pilate, stop this nonsense! *I* am the sinful one. I am shallow and I am arrogant!' I want to expunge the Crucifixion. *Mea culpa*, I want to deny God the chance to redeem the world of its sin.

The gentler side of Catholicism attracts me too. Mary, full of grace, is beautiful; her maternity is young and sweet, her suffering mature and heart-rending. She is wholesome, and sinless, which is a relief. I think that if Sister Gabriel's robes were blue, she would look like Mary. But she would still have an imperfection.

It's a while before I understand the true nature of her fallibility. I am leaping about in the changing rooms after tennis one afternoon, swiping the air with my tennis racket and pretending to be a Wimbledon champion. Everybody is laughing at my inelegant, hefty display. But a board of clothes hooks has fallen off the wall and I land on one of the rusty nails sticking out of it. The nail skewers my tennis shoe through to my foot. I convulse in sobs. Claire hurries to put her arms around me and supports me to the pharmacy. Here, Sister Gabriel prepares a tetanus injection. She pulls off my shoe, the nail still attached, while Claire holds my head. Close physical contact is a temptation to sin, but Sister Gabriel doesn't seem to care. 'This will also be painful,' she says, picking up the syringe. She pulls down my skirt and knickers. My embarrassment about my flabby blancmange flesh, whiter than my tennis skirt, is intense. There's nothing funny now about my overweight body. I tremble with physical and emotional pain as the injection in my buttocks aches its way into my veins.

'It's alright,' Sister Gabriel says, 'take these painkillers, and rest a while on the couch. I'll make you some hot tea.' She strokes my hair and her gentleness is sweeter than the golden syrup at teatime, sweeter even than Claire's embrace.

Despite this kindness, I still hold my distance from Sister Gabriel, afraid of her humiliating me again. Many of the pupils at the convent adore her. Her magnetism is feline. She is self-contained and she gives and receives affection according to her choice. This is her imperfection. My power to attract her lies in my resistance to her charm. The other girls whisper that I am her most beloved. Whenever I hear this, I try to feel indifferent, but still my heart lurches.

Cologne and Stale Cigarettes

Huge and glamorous, Mrs Kingsley floats in a medium of silk and perfume. She is engaged by the nuns at the Shropshire convent to produce the school plays, which are always Shakespeare and always take place towards the end of summer term.

We give Mrs Kingsley our all. She claims more of our attention than our young and attractive tennis coach Mr Flower does. Mr Flower is popular and we work hard at our groundstrokes and volleys to impress him. We hitch our white tennis skirts a bit higher, undo our blouse buttons to entice, and walk swinging our hips. Our mouths pout suggestively and some of us develop a tendency to feel faint in his presence. Will he notice how wan we are, how laboured our breathing is, and how the rise and fall of our chests quickens when he comes to revive us?

We are enfeebled by our desire to attract him.

But we are thrillingly empowered by Mrs Kingsley. To see a vast middle-aged matriarch transform herself into the beautiful young Viola from *Twelfth Night* impresses us, but to then see this Viola masquerading as a eunuch has us feeling we are in the presence of magic. Or Mrs Kingsley teaches us to be Puck from *A Midsummer Night's Dream* – sometimes a horse, a hound, a hog, a headless bear; swifter than the wind, we can put a girdle around the earth in forty minutes. She shows us that coarseness and comedy are not beyond our range; passion and cool self-sufficiency are a matter of choice. We can encompass magic and miracle, sweetness and sourness, heavenly delight and hellish despair. All things can be created from our own will, without God and without the Pope, and especially without nuns, from whom Mrs Kingsley won't brook any interference.

When we staged *As You Like It*, I was given the role of Phoebe. During rehearsals, I wore my peasant skirt and a corset that was tight enough to encourage a prominent cleavage. I draped myself round the newel post at the bottom of the great staircase and leaned into the imagined audience seated in the hall.

'More passion, Tanzie! Exploit your bosom, dear heart. Don't be modest! You must use all your wiles to attract Ganymede. Give the audience a treat. Come on, girl – live, breathe, wilt, sigh. You're a natural! A peasant to your very soul. A wild seductress. Again now, make love to the newel post.'

Then Sister Joan passed on the way from the music room to the kitchen, and suddenly I was inhibited. If it's a sin to expose your body, or to think of passion, making love to a newel post must surely be close to mortal sin. Sister Joan's eyes were lowered, and if she were in fear for my soul, she didn't stop to save me. So,

I continued to sigh and sway and be louche and suggestive, with relish.

When we put on *A Midsummer Night's Dream*, I was disappointed at first to be given the part of the rough mechanical Snug the Joiner. But it wasn't long into rehearsals before I was enjoying the humour of the role, hanging open my mouth, turning my toes in, picking my nose and scratching my groin. This exaggerated and enthusiastic portrayal of the rude yokel was encouraged by Mrs Kingsley, so much so that I found it very difficult to come out of character after rehearsals, drawing pained expressions from the nuns.

Mrs Kingsley was every inch a dark male beauty as she showed Ursula how to play the fairy king Oberon, striding the world, arrogant and beautiful. 'Use your stature, Ursula! Don't stoop. Be proud of your height. Feel like the king of the whole woodland, use your beauty and your natural Irish temper. Good girl. Head high – no, higher!' She showed Sally how to be Oberon's wife Titania, full of majestic disdain, flashing anger from her eyes like lightning bolts that scorched the sweet musk roses and eglantine. We all watched and listened, and we all learned how to strike fear into the darkness of a woodland, shaking the ground and making the wildlife tremble. Leaves and foliage shredded as we swept by with cosmic anger. We were glittering and silvered in the moonlight, ill met and ill tempered, spreading our fairy charms of shadows.

As with most of the plays, *A Midsummer Night's Dream* was staged in the castle ruins in the school grounds. It was ideally suited to the grandeur and dignity of Theseus and Hippolyta's nuptials, and to the fairy kingdom and the mechanicals and their play-within-a-play, 'Pyramus and Thisbe'.

Sometimes Mrs Kingsley brings her husband along to rehearsals. He is a thin, tiny man with high-octane energy and swift busy movements, and even if he didn't dwell in the mountainous shadow of his wife, he would still have nothing to make us want to attract him. He might corrupt us with radical ideas, but we are safe from what the nuns would call 'impure thoughts' where he is concerned. We enjoy his company though and lock around him, eager to hear his jokes, his praise for us, and his running commentaries on the progress of the rehearsals. We often get in his way as he's trying to adjust a prop here, rearrange a laurel there. 'Make way, girls, make way,' he says, gesturing with fingers yellowed from chain smoking. We don't mind that he smells of a heady mix of cologne and stale cigarettes and are amused whenever Sister Joan discusses a play's music with him, inspecting him down the length of her nose as though he were a dead rat.

At seventeen, I am given the role of Feste the court jester in *Twelfth Night*, and to finally be playing a witty fool rather than a foolish wit delights me. This pleasure obviously finds its way through to my acting. 'That's splendid, Tanzie!' Mrs Kingsley holds her fleshy arms in the air and smiles. 'You understand the wit nicely. Examine your feet by all means when you pretend to think, but hold your head high when you come forward. That's it. Engage the audience. Bravo!'

As the rehearsals are in progress, Mrs Kingsley comes to speak to me. 'Tony Hatch from the BBC has written music for Feste's songs, which Sister Joan will be playing on the piano. So I'll need you to attend rehearsals an hour earlier tomorrow, along with Sister Joan.'

I feel as though the window on my world has blurred over with a dense mist. Sound has dulled and movement has become vague. And then my heart breaks through the haziness and pounds in my ears.

'Mrs Kingsley...um...' I gulp, 'I...I...can't...sing.'

'Oh nonsense, dear heart, you'll be able to sing well enough. You can act, so as long as you are expressive and interpret the songs with energy, nobody will notice if you're not Maria Callas.'

'I *really* can't sing.'

She picks up her bag. 'Don't worry,' she says, walking away, '*really* don't worry!'

For the first time, her confidence in me isn't reassuring. She seems to think that I just don't have a high opinion of my own voice, not that I can't sing a note. I sit in the failing light of a summer evening, under the great Lebanese cedar, stitching my red and green jester's outfit, and I fret. I make up my mind to withdraw from the role.

I tell Mrs Kingsley of my decision. 'Nonsense, you can't give up,' she says. 'We're too far into rehearsals to replace you. You're just nervous, darling. I'll help you to use your voice strongly so that no one will even notice if it isn't sweet. Now listen to the music for 'O Mistress Mine'. She nods to Sister Joan, who is seated at the piano. 'If you please, Sister.'

Sister Joan begins to play, and Mrs Kingsley smiles at me encouragingly. 'Listen how interesting that is, how the notes descend in semitones,' she says. Sister Joan looks as if she'd rather thump the piano keys than play them sensitively.

I am standing on the top step of the raised area that runs from the music room, past the library and towards the refectory. Our performance will be taking place here this year, rather than outside. Sister Joan is behind the second pillar from the left, hidden from what will be the audience in the well of the marbled hall. Mrs Kingsley inclines her head and listens attentively. 'Play it more softly, Sister, please…it's like rain falling down a terraced mountain side.' She raises her right arm above her head and sings the half-notes, *la la*, running her fingers down the air.

I can't differentiate the semitones. I look down at my lyric sheet as though it will yield understanding.

'Have a go with me!' says Mrs Kingsley. 'The first few lines. Ready?'

'*O mistress mine, where are you roaming?*
O stay and hear your true love's coming.
That can sing both high and low.'

I try, but Mrs Kingsley must know by now that she has a Feste who cannot sing – high or low.

'Don't be nervous, Tanzie. Try again.' She sings softly so that she can hear my voice, then with more volume to give me confidence.

She thinks for a moment. 'Sing *do, ray, me* a few times. Up and down a few scales. If you will, please, Sister?'

I have a go. I think I do well but Mrs Kingsley is looking puzzled. She puts a hand up to her forehead then moves it down to hold her chin.

'Sister Joan,' she says, walking forward, putting her heels down deliberately as if examining the toes of her fine Italian shoes. 'Do you teach this child singing?'

Sister Joan's response is instant. 'She has a deficient sense of pitch.'

I'm surprised she even remembers me from singing classes.

Mrs Kingsley waits, as though expecting some helpful suggestions to follow from Sister Joan. Finally she shrugs and says, 'Well, if the worst comes to the worst, she'll have to speak through the music.' She turns to me. 'You have a pleasant speaking voice, Tanzie. Don't worry. It's lovely music and the audience will appreciate that anyway. Speaking through the music will help you stay in character.'

She is determined that everything will be alright. 'Come in on the third bar.' She nods towards Sister Joan and holds her hands ready to count me in. But I don't know what a bar is and tears are stinging my eyes. None of this is fun anymore.

'Never mind, my dear. The music speaks for itself. Sister Joan will make the music tune in with your voice; you just concentrate on the sense of the words and the mood of the refrain. Stay in character.'

But Sister Joan looks confused and disapproving and doesn't follow my voice smoothly. She has large capable hands and is technically skilled and disciplined in her music, but maybe she finds extemporising difficult. Feste's reaching out to a crowd of imaginary lovely girls with arms held wide, inviting them to '*come kiss me, sweet and twenty*', seems to throw her. Maybe she finds passion hard.

The other girls begin to turn up for rehearsal and Sister Joan puts down the piano lid abruptly.

Mrs Kingsley consults with her. 'She has a pretty voice. I don't understand it.'

'She's tone deaf. She can sing very high notes but only if she's in a group singing strongly around her.'

'We have some girls just doing costumes and props, don't we, Sister? Could you perhaps put together a small choir? We could place them behind the library door. Do you think it's possible Tanzie could cope then?'

Either Sister Joan thinks it is possible or she has no other choice at this late stage because she nods, stands up, and strides along the bottom corridor, her habit and veil flapping in the rush to catch up with her.

When performance day arrives, the gravel scrunches under car wheels, and the hall begins to fill up with parents who've driven a long way to show their support. But there will be nobody in the audience for me, and I feel sad. Even if Edith were in the same country as me, she'd probably be too busy to attend a school event. This thought sinks me into self-pity, but then I realise it's actually better that she's not here. As a child, she was a solo performer in her church in Yorkshire – this is about the only fact I remember concerning her childhood. Besides, her constant smoker's cough would be just as embarrassing to me as my inability to sing would be to her. Whenever I hear her run out of breath at the end of a crescendo of coughing, I worry and fight for air myself. Heck, I'm glad she's not here.

I still imagine her in the audience though – well turned out, smiling, assessing the other mothers' clothes and manners. She would be surreptitiously popping humbugs in her mouth, which would compete with the aroma of her Chanel N° 5. She has no interest in Shakespeare and would be fidgeting on the uncomfortable plain wooden chair, aggrieved to be in a situation so beneath her dignity, and desperate for a cigarette.

Now, I'm *delighted* that she is not here, that she is four thousand miles south of me. She'll be enjoying a gin and tonic just before the evening meal, talking about the day's farming and the neighbours she'd met while grocery shopping in Naivasha.

I enjoy being Feste, and I'm sure I'm holding the audience, but I lose confidence when song time approaches. I back up to the library door as closely as I can, and pretend to lean in a casual way, but my nerves are bad.

At the end of the show, the audience claps enthusiastically, and as I take my bow, I'm sure the clapping gets louder. Mrs Kingsley appears from the music room and is presented with flowers. She accepts them graciously then sweeps her hand sideways and backwards to encourage more applause for the actors. Catching my eye, she blows a kiss, then she blows another one for the rest of the cast.

As we spill into the audience, Mr Kingsley thumps me on the back. 'Bravo, girl,' he says, 'you were splendid. Such an intelligent understanding of Feste, and such good delivery.' I catch a strong whiff of his cigarette-smelling jacket and realise that he and Edith would get on well. She'd enjoy his energy, humour and kindness as much as I do. 'I need a smoke, Tanzie.'

'What about under the cedar tree?' I say. 'It's a nice mild night. Moon's out too. I'll come with you. Maybe I could cadge a ciggie?'

'More than my life is worth, young Tanzie! My dearly beloved wife would string me up, never mind what the nuns would do. Can't imperil your immortal soul.' He grins and winks at me. 'Oh, c'mon then, let's take the night air!'

As we thread our way through flushed, exhilarated girls and their proud families, Mr Kingsley pulls out a pack of Gauloises from his jacket pocket. As soon as we reach the cedar, he lights up and takes a couple of grateful drags, then offers me a puff. I inhale deeply, and cough. It's been a while since I've gone with the other girls to the clearing in the shrubbery where we smoke. And this tobacco is stronger than I'm used to.

Mr Kingsley doesn't seem to notice my suffering. 'No doting parents here to watch you, Tanzie? You're from abroad, I think?' He puts his head on one side and looks at me through the grey mist he's blowing out of the corner of his mouth. 'Daddy in the armed forces? Sorry, none of my business, I know. I'm just a nosey old parker. It's a shame though, Tanzie girl, that your M and D weren't here to see you tonight. They would have been proud of you.' He smiles and nods his head. '*I'm* proud of you.'

After we've finished sharing the cigarette, Mr Kingsley puts another two in his mouth, lights them, and hands one to me. I think we're just like Paul Henreid and Bette Davis in *Now, Voyager*, and I smile.

Sunset in a Wristwatch

When her mother and stepfather bought a farm in north Devon, Tanzie was ecstatic. She would soon be leaving school and relished the thought of living there with them, to being with her mother again. But it didn't take long for this delight to wear off. Settled now, they were all miserable. They loved the huge, white cob-walled farmhouse with its thatched roof and lupins and gladioli nodding above the garden walls, but they had forgotten how to love each other.

'What have you done to your eyes?' Ken was standing in front of Tanzie in the yard. 'What's that black stuff? You look like a common tart. Go and take it off.'

Tanzie adjusted her grip on the buckets of pignuts she was taking to feed the gilts in the woodland. 'I've been wearing make-up for years, without your permission. And I'm not going to take it off just to please you.'

'You'll do as you're bloody well told, or you can get off my farm.'

Tanzie threw the buckets to the ground. 'Feed your own bloody pigs then.' She stormed into the house to collect a few things, determined to get away from the constant rowing.

Ken was distinguished looking and proud of his appearance. He saw himself as a gentleman farmer. Every evening he would have a bath, change for dinner and drink a couple of glasses of whisky with a splash of soda water. His temper was far from gentlemanly though and it used to frighten Tanzie. But she'd been a match for him until he ordered her off the property; now, suddenly, she was exhausted and sickened by the whole situation.

Edith and Ken were arguing in the yard when Tanzie marched through, crunching over the pignuts on her way to the village to catch the daily bus. 'You can't do this!' Edith shouted to Ken. 'Where will she go?' Unused to having Edith defend her, Tanzie's heart lifted, but she strode on. She headed over the fields, suitcase in hand.

At the bus stop, Tanzie tried to make herself inconspicuous, not wanting attention from curious villagers. Someone might even stop to offer her a lift, which she didn't want either as they would be sure to ask questions. It would be embarrassing for Ken and Edith if the villagers knew about this falling out. Tanzie didn't really care about Ken's discomfort, but she did care how Edith would feel. She'd become a familiar sight in her Ford Cortina, with the large head of Roley the Airedale sitting in the passenger seat.

Her car pulled up at the bus stop just as Tanzie was trying to hide behind a hawthorn bush. Edith leaned across Roley and opened the passenger window.

'Get in.'

'I don't want to fight with him all summer, Ma.'

'Well, don't then. You don't have to answer back.'

Tanzie looked at her mother's averted face, her jawline taut and her mouth clamped over clenched teeth. Her fingers held tight to the steering wheel. It was obvious that she didn't want to defend her husband but neither did she want to explain anything to Tanzie.

Tanzie got in the back seat then Edith turned the car around and drove home without a word.

After this, Ken and Tanzie agreed that, for Edith's sake, they should try to stop arguing. It wasn't easy, but they soon found peace between them. With renewed enthusiasm, Tanzie launched herself into hedging and ditching, mending fences, and feeding and mucking out animals. She scrubbed pigsties, whitewashed outbuildings, and looked after sows as they farrowed, clearing the airways of the newborn piglets with straw. She collected eggs and gathered fruit from the orchard. She also worked in the house, painting walls and windows, washing and ironing. Having a home, contributing to getting it into shape, being with Edith, was bliss. She was happy.

Family harmony, fresh air, and weight loss resulting from so much activity combined to make Tanzie feel beautiful. Ken was hale, and Edith lively but tranquil too. When they were in hearing distance of each other outdoors they'd shout cheerily or laugh out of sheer pleasure. They were proud of their farm. Tanzie didn't often wear make-up anymore, but when she did Ken would say with exaggerated largesse, 'You look nice. Very attractive indeed! What have you done to your eyes?'

And they'd laugh.

But still. Still Tanzie worried whether this harmony could be maintained. It was this nagging concern that eventually made her decide it would be best to leave the farm now, with these good relations still intact. Her new destination was live-in employment in a private prep school in Plymouth. Ken found a farm labourer and Tanzie suspected that he was pleased to be free of the effort of maintaining goodwill.

It was Christmas and Tanzie was home for the holidays. She gathered holly from the outlying parts of the farm and mistletoe and pinecones. She sprayed the pinecones gold and, along with the holly berries, made table decorations. The fact that they were only together for a short time meant Tanzie, Edith and Ken were happy and relaxed.

On New Year's Eve, Ken and Edith's new friends from the neighbouring village came round for drinks. Fred and Kristin also brought their son Charles, who was on holiday from university in Bristol, where he was studying engineering. Charles had obviously been told that Tanzie was good at art because the first thing he said to her after their introduction was, 'What do you think of Picasso's *Guernica*?'

How should she know? The convent had taught her how to be a good Catholic wife and mother, but nothing about art history and artists. She felt stupid, embarrassed, and resentful.

But there was plenty of good food and alcohol, and Fred's daftness appealed to Tanzie, so she concentrated on him. They all drank too much. Although Fred tried to match Ken, who maintained a swaying dignity even when inebriated, he could not hold his drink and happily let his knees buckle. Finding himself at floor level with the dog, he reached up to fetch some food off the table and then went under it on all fours. He fed Roley prime hand-reared goose. Tanzie enjoyed all this idiocy and sank to the floor too, burbling happily and trying to interest Roley in fine dry sherry. The table was a huge mahogany thing of baronial proportions, plenty of room for Fred and Tanzie to lie stretched out underneath and for Roley to lie on his back with his paws up and head flat to the floor. Sighing deeply and turning her head sideways, Tanzie caught Fred's beatific smile before he closed his eyes and began to snore.

From her ground-level vantage point, Tanzie could see Charles on the big sofa, whisky in hand, looking bored. Edith and Kristin were slumped against each other on the two-seater sofa, chins tucked in, brows crumpled, breathing heavily.

Tanzie crawled from under the table and plonked herself down next to Charles. She felt loose and free, and oddly superior to this person who may be clever but who had very poor social skills. It was time to get her own back on him for making her feel stupid, time to make him squirm with awkwardness. She moved as close as possible, with the aim of just teasing him, but their mouths found each other. Tanzie twisted and stretched the length of the sofa. Charles's mouth was soft. She had worried about how to kiss a boy. What do you do with your nose? How do you breathe? What if there is too much saliva? But it was like tasting sweetness, laced with the whisky. Her body was less fit than when she'd been working on the farm, but it still pleased her; she liked the feel of her hipbone carrying the weight of her flank. She was as taut as stretched canvas, loose as dropped reins, and she loved the way Charles's mouth slackened the sharpness of her perception and made her breathing uneven.

Tanzie was desirable, and she was desirous. She quickly surveyed the scene around her. Ken was asleep in the chair by the fire, his glass still firmly in his hand. Fred and Roley were still belly-up under the table, Edith and Kristin still A-framed on the two-seater. Tanzie guided Charles's hand to her breast. He reached inside her unfashionable maroon V-necked jumper.

Her diary entry for New Year's Eve 1966 said, 'Heaven!'

Tanzie returned to the prep school and Charles returned to being a student. He wrote to her every day. She daydreamed about him. Writing to him, thinking about him every day, she lived intensely. She was in love.

She cooked breakfast for twenty boarders, prepared some evening meals, managed the floor-standing paraffin heaters, and taught a little Tudor history. She also assisted the matron. Conditions were almost Dickensian, and the work was hard, but Tanzie was strong. And she knew it was all a stopgap anyway – her future lay with Charles.

Sometimes Charles drove down to visit her in his old Volkswagen Beetle. They walked on Dartmoor, felt the wildness, imagined themselves romantic. They visited Fred and Kristin. Tanzie and Fred were matey, as they had been from the start, and they laughed a lot together. Kristin though was abrupt and sometimes mildly, sometimes overtly, hostile towards Tanzie, probably jealous of her closeness to her son. 'Get the girl a seat,' she'd say, to which Tanzie would respond, 'The girl is capable of fetching herself a seat, but thank you ever so kindly.' She didn't want to upset Kristin but at the same time felt it was important to hold her own against her.

Tanzie didn't go all the way with Charles. To her, it was normal to wait until marriage. She was also terrified of getting pregnant. In addition, she discovered she was afraid of men.

She and Charles were on the edge of the moor one Sunday evening before his return to Bristol. The atmosphere between them was tense, Charles's silence weighted with malaise. Tanzie felt as though she had failed at something important. The sky was grey and melon streaked as the sun lay low on the horizon. Tanzie watched the colours of the sunset reflected in the glass of Charles's watch. His arm was manly, muscular – not boyish. The shock realisation that she was afraid of manliness, of men, of sex made her struggle to breathe.

But she still had a lot of faith in the future because of their closeness, their declarations of forever love. They would be married one day; it was her destiny. Love like this could not fade as a result of fear, or ignorance, or distance. She would mature, relax, and sex would follow naturally, full blooded and as sweet as honey. So she didn't consult a doctor about birth control, didn't rush to Bristol to be with Charles; instead she applied to a college in Sussex to train as a teacher.

It was a couple of months before she was due to start teacher training that Tanzie received the letter. '*You have given me some of the best times of my life, and some of the most heartbreaking...*' She tried to think how her behaviour could have caused him pain. In the enormous stack of love letters she'd written and received, had there been evidence of heartbreak? Certainly there was the daily recording of how much they missed each other, but wasn't this all the more reason to look forward to being together one day? '*I have decided to bring forward the date of our separation...*' What did he mean? '*I have met somebody else. Admittedly she has an unfair advantage – she lives in Bristol.*'

Tanzie slept badly. At breakfast, she was quiet. The smell of freshly lit paraffin heaters hung in the air and lingered faintly on her fingers.

'This porridge is a bit cold.' John peered into Tanzie's face.

'If you talked less, it would be fine.'

'I had a strange dream last night.' John enjoyed entertaining Tanzie at breakfast time. He liked to wait for her to sit down beside him after serving all the boys.

'Uh, uh…'

'Aren't you interested, Miss?'

'Not really, no. Just eat up, will you?'

'You're cross because I said my porridge was cold. You like my dreams. You were in my dream last night. I was in a spaceship with Jesus and you were –'

'Pass the milk please, John.'

'Here you are!' He put down his spoon to lift the jug with both hands. 'And you were on the planet Jupiter.' He looked at Tanzie, sure that he must have caught her attention now.

'Was I? Well, I would be, wouldn't I? That would be exactly right, wouldn't it? You with Jesus and me sitting around on Jupiter. Pass the toast.'

'Miss, but me and Jesus were looking for you. We were looking all over space. We were trying to rescue you.'

'Yes?' Tanzie looked into his tawny eight-year-old eyes and saw growing confusion and mistrust. 'I'm glad, John, I'm glad. Did you find me?'

'Yes, and we were waving to you, and I told Jesus that there wasn't room for all of us in the spacecraft. And we landed on Jupiter. And I woke up.'

'What did Jesus look like?'

John had his glass of milk half way to his mouth. He paused and knitted his brows. 'I dunno. He was sitting behind me. I was in charge! It was only a small craft, just for two people. Miss, you'll get skinny if you don't eat up.'

Tanzie munched on the toast with a pretended voracious appetite, showing big greedy eyes. She detected a ghost of a smile hovering round John's mouth.

'Are you on bath time duty tonight, Miss?' John exaggerated his toast munching to match Tanzie's, talking with his mouth full. 'Because I like your hands better than Matron's.'

'No, John, my hero of Jupiter and the highways of outer space! I have to go away after breakfast and will be back late. But I'll be around tomorrow night for your bath.'

There was no answer when Tanzie rang the doorbell. She checked her watch – perhaps it was a bit early for him to be back from lectures. What if he doesn't turn up? What if he brings *her* home with him, since she has the advantage of living in Bristol? Maybe he'll go straight from campus to see her?

Tanzie couldn't believe now that she hadn't been here many times before. It wasn't so far from Devon, and she loved train journeys. She could have saved enough money for the fare. Hell, she could have found a job here in Bristol. She could have had the advantage of living in Bristol. As she waited in a state of indecision, Charles appeared behind her.

'It's you!' He smiled and seemed pleased to see her.

'Do you mind? I need to talk to you.'

He had his key in the lock. 'Come in.'

Tanzie followed him upstairs. She knew he shared the flat with another student, who went home at weekends.

'I'm starving.' Charles went into the kitchen and Tanzie followed. 'Do you want some spag bol?'

'No, thanks.'

'You'll get thin if you don't eat.'

'I've eaten, thanks.'

Charles began chopping onions while Tanzie chopped carrots.

Tanzie couldn't hold back the words any longer. 'Do you love me?' She despised herself for her lack of self-respect, but she needed to hear him say that he still loved her. And if he couldn't say it, she needed to hear that too.

'I don't know.'

'Have you slept with her?'

'Not yet.'

He grated Parmesan cheese. It smelt like vomit. Tanzie felt like vomiting. His sleeves were rolled up to his elbows, showing his muscular forearms and exposing his wristwatch, which reflected the gas flame. Tanzie's heart flipped over with fear. Of course he'd slept with her – why wouldn't he? She was here in Bristol, and she obviously wasn't afraid of manliness.

'Shall I go now?'

'No, don't. I thought you wanted to talk.'

'I think it's too late for that.'

'Well, maybe. But stay until I've finished this and I'll run you to the station.'

Tanzie watched him eat, dipping his fork, scooping, twirling, lifting spaghetti into his mouth. He put his fork down and leaned towards her. His mouth was savoury with tomato and garlic. His hands were like sanctuary, his arms a haven. She needed him. They stood up and her hip followed the line of his body. They moved to the bedroom, floating without volition.

Tanzie's slip was silk, dark and forbidden, and as he moved his hands across it, ripples of material slid over her skin. He caressed her with long, slow strokes.

'What if I get pregnant?' Tanzie whispered.

'I'll marry you.'

His voice was in her ear, soft and gruff with desire; his sweat was like a film of satin, smoothing the friction between their bodies. Tanzie felt as though she was rising on wings of ecstasy, soaring on updrafts of intense pleasure. Deep in her womb she felt him thrusting, rhythmical, joining them, welding them and then suddenly a slow explosion released the exhilarating tension, and she fell, softly pulsing, slower and slower through delicious sensation.

She slept, and when she woke it was morning, and he was dressing.

'I'll give you a lift to the station,' he said.

'Toast?' he said.

'You'll get thin if you don't eat,' he said.

The train was on the platform. They clung to each other, their mouths searching again, their bodies straining – for no reason. It was all over.

She was going back to porridge, to John and his dreams, to bath time and paraffin heaters. She was going back to no daily letters. The train was crowded but it felt empty to her, and it lived on in her memory as empty, echoing cavernously to the rhythm of the wheels crashing down the track.

Tanzie didn't sleep with anyone else for years. The women at college talked about sex, and what to do about birth control. They were fascinated about their first time with a man and Tanzie heard how unsatisfactory, how groping and shameful, how embarrassing and disappointing the experience was for them. For some it was painful. Tanzie thought how her first time with a man had not been a fumbling towards experience. It had come, pure and perfect, out of need and loss – the first giving. And for him it was probably the last time he risked having a child.

A year on from that last meeting, Tanzie received a letter. *'After I left you at the station, I drove around in a daze. I don't know how I didn't kill myself.'* This made no sense to her, so she didn't respond.

Later, Tanzie heard from Kristin that Charles had gone to Canada, had letters after his name, and was married to the girl who'd had the advantage of living in Bristol. Kristin said, 'She's like water to your gin! Clever, though, reads about nuclear physics for pleasure.' They had big careers, the two of them, and made money. Kristin also said that they didn't want children. She said this emphatically, and Tanzie could tell that it bothered her.

Charles and his wife must love the huge landscapes and snows of Canada. They must be happy ever after. 'It's fortunate for him that I didn't get pregnant,' thought Tanzie.

She remembered Charles telling her that Kristin said he was born lucky.

'Why?'

'When she was in Egypt, she met a man with a camel who told her that the child in her womb would be lucky. She didn't know she was pregnant then.'

'And you were that child. But what is luck?'

'Hell, I dunno. I suppose it's about life going smoothly so that you get what you need and what you want.'

He *was* lucky then.

When Fred was old and widowed, Tanzie visited him a few times in his care home in Devon. He had dementia and seemed stuck in an ever-present scene of chatting up the barmaid in his local pub. 'I'll have another of those please, Louise,' he would say, dumping his tea mug firmly on the Formica table. There were lucid days though, when he knew Tanzie. 'How's Roley?' he would say, his eyes twinkling with smiles. But then the shadows would descend and an awareness of loss would make him sad.

When he died, Tanzie wrote to Charles. '*I was fond of Fred. He would always make me laugh and I enjoyed his company. I remember the first day we met, how he ended up under the table with Roley.*' In the letter, Tanzie made the effort to be friendly, telling him about life at home, her family and work. She mentioned her plan to drive across the

Nevada desert sometime soon. Charles responded to her letter, and remarked that crossing Nevada held no appeal for him, that he didn't think it would be very interesting. Tanzie was shocked. How could it not be the most numinous experience possible, to travel to the middle of such emptiness, to feel the vastness of it, to feel the full canopy of space, blue and endless above and around you? How could you not consider infinity and feel awed? Charles now appeared to Tanzie as dreary and colourless. She was sure he never looked up in awe from his garden gate to those great snow-sculpted mountains, and was more concerned with clearing the snow from his path. She was sure now too that his questions about art history when they were first introduced were just an attempt to impress; he had no real interest in Picasso's *Guernica*.

Shoulder to Shoulder

I've been waiting for you all my life. I knew you before I met you. Yours is an answering voice in the wilderness.

It is early morning, and although we only met the evening before, the clichés in my mind are as fresh and exhilarating to me as they are disturbing. I want to stay like this forever, side by side with him, shoulder to shoulder, leaning on the ship's rail. I look down into the water. The propeller churns ocean depths, slewing swathes of cobalt blue and night-black silk to the surface. The turbulence convulsing under the ship vibrates in my heart.

Anthony and I are mirror imaging, book ending, as we lean, shoulder touching shoulder. The thick water shines with a silvery film beyond the wake, where the sea is calm. A memory of leaning like this over a veranda wall and vomiting onto an anthill comes into my mind. I remember emerging in a thin dress from the waves on an incoming tide, clinging to Peter's back.

The icy air of the English Channel makes me gather my flimsy wet dress in freezing fingers, before I realise I am not on the shore of the Indian Ocean and I am not wearing a summer dress. I quickly shake off the queasy memory of sunstroke and ants scurrying in the wetness of lemonade vomit. It is being with Anthony that has reminded me of Peter. They are not similar, and Peter was a child at the time of the beach rescue; it's more how I feel. I like being myself – being more completely myself. Anthony can have no idea of the recognition I am feeling, that I already know I want to be with him until death.

But I am happily married. That's what I told him.

I was only being polite when I spoke to him for the first time.

'What are you reading?' I asked, struggling out of my coat and removing one of my jumpers; the ferry lounge bar was warm after the iciness outdoors. My sixth form students and fellow art teachers had almost taken over the bar, and the only unoccupied seat was next to the new drama teacher who, I was to quickly learn, also had a passion for art. After the walk between galleries in the coldest Paris winter in a decade, the wind blowing straight from Siberia, I was looking forward to warming up.

'*A History of Religious Ideas*, by Mircea Eliade,' he said, half closing the book and placing his finger between the pages to save his place. The jacket was covered in brown parcel paper and had handwriting on the front.

'Oh?'

'What are you reading?' He indicated the book I'd flung on the table.

'Kipling's *Just So* stories.' My book was sitting in beer spills, so I wiped it on my coat.

'My father reads Kipling.'

'Oh?'

'He likes Dickens as well.'

'Yes, so do I.'

'I think he's overrated.'

'Oh!' I wondered if I should get a drink.

'My father,' said Anthony, 'had a thing about Dickens. He bought all of his books and made us read them. My brothers and sister, we all had to read them.'

'But that's perfect. We didn't have books in my house when I was growing up. I'd have given my eye teeth to have some Dickens hanging about.'

'You wouldn't have liked to be forced to read. Especially Dickens. My father selected him as an author who "ought" to be read. He made us concentrate on him, at the expense of other writers.'

'At the expense of Kipling?'

'We had to read Dickens *and* Kipling.'

I was just deciding that I'd been polite enough when he said, 'Do you read much?'

'I don't have a lot of time but I do read more now that my kids are growing up.' I took my purse from my pocket and looked towards the bar.

'So you're married?'

'Yes, but not to the father of my children. I'm on my second marriage.' I realised I had made it sound as though many more might follow.

'Are you happily married?' he said.

I thought about it and decided that I was, at least for the ears of a stranger. 'Yes. You?'

'I've never married.'

'Girlfriend?'

'Nobody special.'

I thought about that too. I knew I was 'nobody special' to my husband, knew I was a disappointment to him. Our marriage was polite, pointless, weighed down with emptiness, with rigorous routine. Outwardly worthy, inwardly joyless.

I am at war with myself all the time, grateful for my comfortable lifestyle, my safe home, the good school for the girls. But I know I am too wild for my husband and suburbia. My being slightly out of step, marginally out of line, is magnified by his strict conventionality. I curb myself and inhibit my personality. Day by day I try to please him. I keep busy – God knows there's enough to do, and I do it from morning to night, to avoid noticing how little my effort to please him is recognised. He wants me to be more like his mother; she is the benchmark beside which I am judged. I hate her. I *truly* hate her. But I wear a pleasant mask and maintain good behaviour. My husband and I are playing at happy families in our larger-than-average box, made of ticky tacky, on the hillside. I am sick as I think about my girls, who are as well behaved and buttoned down as I am; sick as I realise I have settled for this pretence of happiness, this tight domestic schedule of joyless routine. How can this be the meaning of my days?

'What are you drinking?' I said, waving my purse at Anthony's empty glass.

We talked all night. Colleagues drifted off to overnight cabins and students slumped like broken dolls to sleep on chairs. One student settled on the floor, almost under my feet, his hair tracing the pattern of the carpet, which was partly obscured and darkened by spillage. I tucked my jumper under his head.

It's not that we had anything extraordinary to say. Anthony expressed a liking for brown parcel paper. I enjoyed, though I shivered at, his definition of hell. He informed me of the virtues and weaknesses of Newcastle United. I walked in his shoes in Sudan, where he taught English for a year, coming home to the compound drunk at night, catching the yellow eyes of starved dogs in his torchlight. He told me about travelling with his theatre company, playing Macbeth in Hong Kong. Picnicking in Jordan with friends. His love of Irish folktales, of Chekhov, Nabokov, Hemingway and Vonnegut.

I told him how allergic I am to modern white, male, middle-aged, middle-class writers. There was a silence between us while we listened to hear the significance of this blurted revelation. Then we talked on. Our words told of high altitudes, hinterlands, and blasted landscapes. I told him about my hope and despair and he told me about his. Our heads filled with the rain moving like a dark curtain across vast landscapes, slickening the hides and hair of beasts, and we watched wild geese flying in the clean blue air above the storm. They winged over the bright and beautiful cities of the plain. We stood in London galleries – stunned in front of a Rothko, trying not to be seduced by a Pollock, cherishing a Berthe Morisot. We talked of the best and worst of countries, books and paintings. I quoted bits from the film *To Kill a Mocking Bird*, and declared my love for Gregory Peck. We talked about cabbages and kings; we journeyed far.

The most personal thing I shared with Anthony was the strange sensation I had in my head sometimes. It felt as if something stringy, like a ribbon of seaweed, was snagged on the inside roof of my skull. It often made me shake my head. I was shocked that I'd revealed this. It was worse than the shame about my second marriage after he told me he was a Catholic. It was as bad as telling him about my allergy to Hemingway and Nabokov, though I didn't think it was as bad as his weariness with Dickens. But he seemed to take the information about the loose seaweed in his stride.

I realised that it was not too late to be myself. He could show me his wounds; they wouldn't offend me. I might say, 'Look, these are my scars. They're nothing much, but they make me afraid of loose seaweed in my brain. You and me, we can escape gravity just with the words we use. We can be weightless and use our powers of invention, our invention of powers, to cut loose and fly with the wild geese honking above the cities of the plain.'

When dawn silvered the condensation on the windows and penetrated the dank smoky atmosphere, we were still talking.

'We should get breakfast,' Anthony said.

I fetched coffee and a crisp green apple from the canteen display while Anthony opted for a full cooked breakfast. I was acutely awake. My eyes felt wider than the universe and I looked through a lens that sharpened vision to precise edges, crystal light and clear colour. I wondered if this is what it feels like to be tripping. The apple was smooth, its waxy surface reflecting the winter dawn. The light bleached Anthony's face and whitened his stubble. I discovered I had no appetite. Anthony ate energetically, forking too much food into his mouth and chewing noisily, but it didn't irritate me.

*

As we lean on the railing, we are silent. I watch Anthony's face, while he watches the spume in the ship's wake. He tastes the salt air on his lips and then draws his forearm across his eyes. I look down again and my heart tumbles into the darkness where the force of the blades makes the water appear thick and sleek. They draw up deep ocean stillness and power it into wild disorder. The misgivings I am having about my marriage churn through the revolving beat and throb of the propeller. I feel the undertow. But I feel the surge like an uplifting confidence, a dizzying relief, and a homecoming.

I punch Anthony's arm. I run along the deck, and then dance round to see if he is following me. My laughter sounds above the noise as though it is lifting clear of an oppressive storm. I wipe my nose on my sleeve and blink to clear my eyes of water and watch him come towards me as I skip backwards. He settles his shoulders under my gaze and narrows his eyes. His walk is a casual sashay and he plunges his hands into his pockets to adopt an ironic posturing. He approaches me in a glare of spilt white sunlight and, removing a hand from his pocket, holds it in a shallow crescent for me to move into. We dance in the winter dawn, squinting and smiling, and our breath surrounds us like thin mountain mist. Underneath his loose-limbed playfulness, I feel a vital energy, and I tremble for the courage that I hope I will need.

Lilac-Tinted Love Affair

Tanzie reached round his shoulders and stood on his shoes as soon as he came into the kitchen, only giving him time to dump a book and bottle of wine on the table. His face was cold from the outdoors. Their double-decker feet shuffled to the slow music on the tape recorder.

Suddenly Anthony stood still and Tanzie fell off his feet. She stepped back on and looked at him as he, in turn, strained his head backwards to peer into her face, his forehead creased with exaggerated bafflement.

'Leonard Cohen? You listen to *Leonard Cohen?*'

'So?'

'Bit dirgey.'

'It's blood letting!'

'Blood draining, for sure.' He grimaced. 'It's not exactly upbeat.'

'Yeah, well, it's like finding something nasty in the cupboard and keeping it, living with it, getting used to it.'

'Like a dead rat, you mean?'

Tanzie jumped off his feet and gave him a punch. 'Like a broken heart.'

He pretended to hurt, doubling up. He then filled two glasses with wine.

Tanzie picked up the book from the table. *Poems of the Deep Song* by Federico Garcia Lorca. 'Deep song?' She tasted the wine and looked at Anthony through the bowl of her green glass.

'It's about the oldest form of using the voice to sing emotion,' he said, looking at her through his glass in return.

'Sing emotion! Bit like Cohen then? Culturally more potent – but still, a bit like keeping company with a dead rodent.' She tilted her wine at the tape deck as if to toast Cohen's 'Suzanne', now playing.

Anthony turned down the heat under the saucepan of boiling potatoes. Steam misted the window and reflections of candle flames danced in the hazy dimness of the glass. Watching this made Tanzie feel squiffy. She glanced at the wine bottle. No – she wasn't drunk, just in a blur of happiness. She felt happiness a lot lately, as though it existed in the reach of an arm, a shuffle of feet, the distortion of an eye seen through the bottom of a green glass. As though it existed in the opposition of Lorca and Cohen.

One Easter, they were in Granada during Holy Week. It had been a last-minute decision when term ended. They'd hung around the reception desk at Bristol Airport waiting for cancellations, preferably on the same flight, to Malaga. Tanzie wanted to see the Alhambra Palace and Anthony was keen to visit Lorca's childhood home.

They visited the Alhambra first. Spring was exploding in its grounds. Lilac wisteria festooned the filigree and lattice of the architecture, hanging in fronds and filtering sunlight like filmy fabric. Tanzie saw Anthony walk beside her in pale violet air; the Alhambra was fragile, made of lace and net, forming an illusion of columns and arches glimpsed through swathes of flowers. Fountains and pools reflected dazzle and glinted off Anthony's sunglasses. The Alhambra was a glorious citadel above the town, a palace for sultans. It was a backdrop for Holy Week and for Tanzie's lilac-tinted love affair.

She smiled. The subtle amethyst hue of the air made her think of a mauve jacket that Anthony was wearing when she first met him. Then, he had nothing but a thousand books, a bike and some clothes from Oxfam, the jacket included. He was not materialistic – his books weren't just for display – though he did have an interest in fountain pens, and hair products. One day he held up the jacket, wondering whether he should add it to Tanzie's pile of clothes for the local charity shop.

'I dunno…I suppose I have had a lot of wear out of it…' He hesitated a moment more and then dropped it onto the pile.

'Thank God for that,' Tanzie said, forgetting herself.

'What?'

'Oh, it's just that…I…I never liked it, I'm sorry.'

'What's wrong with it?'

'Well, the colour doesn't suit you, it doesn't fit you properly, and apart from that, it's a woman's.'

'Why didn't you tell me before? I had no idea. And how do you know it's a woman's anyway – is it the pretty colour?' He picked it up and searched for labels.

'It does up on the female side.'

'How could you just let me wear it then? Don't you care if I look a fool?'

'You could wear a bin bag and I'd still walk beside you anywhere, so don't get snotty.'

He frowned and shook his head. 'I can't believe you didn't say anything,' he said, getting snotty.

Tanzie thought that the soft, blue-pink sunlight filtering through the lilac wisteria suited him in a way the jacket had not.

Anthony said, 'Time for one of those invigorating coffees with brandy?'

She could already smell the coffee through the screen of fragrant foliage and they wasted no time in walking down the hill to its source – and got unexpectedly caught up in the Semana Santa celebrations. Within minutes, bodies were spilling out of side streets, streaming past them, and then slowing in the crush. Jesus, instead of walking on water, was walking on a sea of people. Behind him was another Jesus, fabulously attired in gold and silver robes. Catholic ritual was feverish in procession and prayer. Huge hand-held floats containing statues of the Virgin, or the Christ figure, rocked through the arteries and veins of streets and alleys. The icons towered above the crowds, lurching in rhythmical madness.

As the throng became denser, Tanzie felt fear prickling inside her. The penitents in their hooded robes were alarming, not seeming holy at all; in fact they reminded her of the Klu Klux Klan. She climbed onto the base of a pillar near the cathedral. Although she could see the floats better from here, she could also see the crowds in every direction – a great press of humanity brought to a standstill, with no empty space to move into. Anthony was hemmed in some distance to the front of her. She shouted for him to stay close, but he was in conversation with a smiling moustachioed Spaniard and didn't hear her. Her arms were aching, trying to keep a grip of the wide pillar. If only she could get Anthony's attention, hold his hand, feel connected.

From a side alley, a float came swaying to join the main stream, and considering the squash of people, seemed to be making headway. It was like an old galleon rolling and righting itself through waves. Tanzie wondered if she could get into the flow and movement of its slipstream. But she needed to be close to Anthony. One of the few things he didn't know about her was that she had a phobia of crowds. So he wouldn't worry about her if they became temporarily separated. But Tanzie knew she was going to be crushed, trampled to a sticky pulp under a zillion feet.

She shouted again to attract Anthony's attention, gesturing wildly. But her arms flailed and she tipped into the crowd. A burly Spaniard steadied her, placing her on her feet. He smelt of garlic and grease, and his strength made her want to ride on his shoulders.

Then Anthony's hand reached through the crowd and grabbed her T-shirt. 'What's the matter?'

'I can't breathe.'

'Hang onto me.'

She hung onto him. They weaved and threaded, squeezed under armpits and around stomachs, pressing through flesh that was hot, sweaty and smelly, until they reached the main river of floats. The crowds were still thick but areas opened up for a moment. People were moving, almost milling, although the movement was one way, like a river.

The place where they were staying was in the opposite direction from the flow of the procession, but at least they could move a little now. Tanzie began to calm down and loosened her grip on Anthony. Then they had to pause to let another float go by, pressing backwards into the crowd again. A tall, silvered and crowned Virgin towered over them, losing its rhythm for a moment and swinging wildly before it slung side to side, side to side, to the slap and thump of many pairs of feet.

Tanzie saw a man disappear under the apron of a float with a lit cigarette, and then emerge without it. Clutching hold of Anthony again, she put her lips near his ear. 'Watch out for a holy conflagration!' They then saw other smokers doing the same and wondered how many float carriers could fit under the Virgin Mary. This shared amusement helped Tanzie calm down further.

But as soon as she realised she had relaxed, fear crashed back through her body. She caught Anthony again. 'I can't breathe.' They concentrated on moving forward and out of the throng, and when the crowd thinned out they swung their arms and made steady progress back to their rented room.

It was cheap, nylon-carpeted accommodation. At night a naked light bulb with a low wattage made the corners murky with shadow, and the building echoed with footfall and plumbing from the two bathrooms that served eight rooms. Because their room was not the most pleasant place to be, they climbed up to the flat rooftop, which had fine views over the city. After the procession, they were hot and drained of energy. They spread their towels, Anthony took off his T-shirt, and they lay entwined in the sun in a delicious drowse of relaxation. They could still hear the crowds moving, shouting and laughing. Anthony's hand-washed socks, hanging from a string across the vista of the Alhambra, cast a shadow across his chest. Tanzie kissed his sock-shadowed nipple.

'That was a bonus,' he murmured. She thought briefly that he was referring to her kissing his chest, but he was still thinking of the spectacle in the street. 'Should have guessed how it would be in Holy Week.' He opened one eye and inspected Tanzie satirically. 'Worth being part of, don't you think?'

'Right!' Tanzie smiled. Escaping from this experience unscathed, she knew that from now on her fear of crowds wouldn't be so great. More importantly, she knew she could relax an almost constant tension within her, which had made her careful to protect Anthony from a deep, unhinged part of herself.

The next day they set out by bus for the village of Fuente Vaqueros, Lorca's birthplace, which lay on the Vega outside Granada. Through the windows, the flat country was burnished gold as though, in Cohen's words, the sun poured down like honey. They arrived at the village in the drowse and hush of midday siesta. Between the houses the horizon shimmered, and the sparse trees and distant donkey looked quixotic.

Lorca's childhood home was now a museum. Tanzie took a photo of Anthony posing in the courtyard beside a bust of his idol, looking in the same direction. Anthony was handsome in his flat cap, and he knew it. He pretended that he didn't like his photo being taken, but he was often snapped amongst a hubbub of friends. Whenever she had photos developed and was looking through them, he always feigned indifference. 'Here's a good one of you!' she'd say, but he would just respond with, 'Yeah, yeah', and carry on with whatever it was he was doing, usually cooking or reading. She'd leave the photos on the kitchen table, and when he thought nobody was looking, he would flip through them, focussing closely on the ones of him. So he was vain, despite pretending not to be, but he was transparent too and it made her smile.

They looked around the museum with interest, at the paintings, artefacts and furniture. Anthony was particularly taken with Lorca's first bed, a wooden crib, walking around it a few times and inspecting it closely. After a while, he decided he would like to buy a poster, and knowing he wouldn't be quick choosing, Tanzie went to check out a cabinet displaying letters, images and books.

'Look! Look!' She was excited, beckoning to Anthony. She gestured towards a picture of a man crouching near the crib that Anthony had been paying homage to. The man was touching, as though rocking, the cradle. He was smiling. Tanzie pointed to the typewritten caption underneath the image. Anthony read it, clapped his hands and laughed. 'So, Cohen was a fan of Lorca too!'

Later, they sat on a low wall under a fig tree at the edge of the village. Tanzie handed Anthony an orange from her shoulder bag and began peeling one for herself. She thought again of Cohen, of 'Suzanne', the girl who fed her lover tea and oranges that came all the way from China. But these oranges were from a local market in

Granada, probably grown on the Vega, maybe even here in the fields around Fuente Vaqueros. She thought, 'If nothing else ever happens in my life, this did.' She realised she was feeling the experience with such bliss because she was feeling it consciously. She felt the sun pour down like honey, the sweet tang of the orange on her tongue, and the energetic sound of Anthony slurping his fruit; even the donkey wedged into the small shade at the side of a building made her sure the world was perfect. She tried to click a shutter in her mind to capture the moment, so she could draw on it forever.

Part of the Eagle

Peterson's black skin looks as though it has been buttered where the yellow light falls across his face. He sits with his elbows on the Formica tabletop and the tips of his fingers touch each other in an arch in front of his face. His eyes glisten like melted tar. We drink Tusker beer and are tired – we have been talking for hours. Peterson says my name softly, like a mantra, 'Tanzie…Tanzie….Tanzie…' It's as if he's distracted by a memory of long ago, but I expect he's just weary and doesn't want to appear rude, so he murmurs my name to keep us both in a loop of connection.

The prostitutes have fallen across the tables, cushioning their heads on their arms. Their sleep is drugged by sex or substances or despair, or all of these. Some of the women stay because they have nowhere else to go. But it's safe for no one out in the broken city at night. The barman slumps on his stool behind the iron grate that protects him from violence and theft.

My drinking has slowed, almost stalled. I can't face peeing. The back of The Modern Green bar is unlit, and the toilet is a cubicle without a door. The walls are dark with excrement and there's a caked and soiled hole in the floor.

A man carrying a bucket in each hand materialises from the dimness of the back of the room and calls for everybody to lift their feet. The wristwatch I extract from my sock under cover of the table shows it is almost 4.00 a.m. Three hours before dawn – what a strange time to be disinfecting the floor.

Peterson nudges those around him to wake up. They stir and lift their feet onto adjacent chairs or tables. The man sloshes strong cleaning fluid across the broken linoleum. It swirls and lies in white pools on the uneven floor. It smells powerfully astringent and makes the atmosphere, already heavy with cigarette smoke and body odour, thick as though it has replaced the oxygen. I pull my T-shirt up over my nose while I get used to it. When I take a sip of beer, hoping to reduce the impact of the smell, my tongue feels as pitted and unpleasant as the linoleum. I imagine the beer swirling around my mouth as white and as full of bits of dirt as the fluid underneath my chair.

My eyelids are drooping, and I feel travel weary and alone, but too vulnerable to sleep. I jerk my eyes open, and Peterson smiles. We look around us as everyone settles down to sleep again. I notice how ghostly pale my white skin is next to the much richer, more opaque reflections of light on the dark skins. I am fifty-two, and I am travelling alone in Kenya, looking for my roots. I'm back in the country of my childhood, after forty years, trying to retrieve a sense of belonging to the land. But it's not simply that I wanted to return to

Kenya, rather I wanted it to have always been home. I wanted to feel that I have always been anchored.

I did feel anchored, until a few months ago. A ship weighted with the right ballast, attached to the sea bed but free to drift and swing with the movement of the water, I was able to relax in the harbour of Anthony's love.

The Hickman line was still pumping into his chest when his head fell sideways and went still on my shoulder. As I remember this, I knead the muscles in my upper arm. I remember the sound of the pump, the waxy feel of his skin, and the clear, fixed glassiness of his open eyes that surprised me so much I watched his chest to see him breathe – to see him stop breathing. My shoulder froze that day and stayed that way until recently, unbalancing me. It made me list badly to one side so that I drifted round in circles. My anchor had come completely loose, and I couldn't stabilise.

Whenever I went outside, I couldn't breathe. A quick trip to the supermarket would cause panic to surge in my chest, which combined with the rigidity of my frozen shoulder to hold me like a vice. I was half paralysed, horrified by memories of the plastic body bag taking Anthony away in a white van, of the plastic container holding his ashes. The doctor said I was having panic attacks and that my shoulder was indicative of hysteria. He said I needed therapy. But how could therapy stop me from terrifying myself? How could it stop this fear of my body and mind, of collapse, of aloneness, of dying?

I wanted to feel afraid of something real, outside of me, threatening, raw and primitive. A childhood memory of watching what appeared to be a big log floating towards me on a wide river came into my mind. The log was a good distance away and drifting so slowly that when I looked away at a herd of elephants across the other side and then looked back, it had hardly moved at all. I intended to keep an eye on it. Then a baby elephant playing among the acacia trees drew my attention. When I remembered to look back at the log, it wasn't there. Fear shot through me, lifting me from the water's edge and up the steep bank as though I was a feather caught in a hurricane. When I stopped to look back at the river, there was a crocodile next to where I'd been sitting, its head above the waterline, full of intent. Just remembering the scene made me want to look behind me. I would pack my bag and go in search of that fear.

Peterson is the nearest I've come so far on this trip to relating to anyone from my childhood. He feels familiar because he is from the Kikuyu tribe, the same as Mzee. Unlike Mzee though, he has clear eyes and clean white teeth and he is educated. He tells me that President Moi's men murdered his father and that he is a political activist. I met him this morning.

I'd crossed the road from the cheap hotel I'd booked into for a couple of nights, to be in the open air and drink coffee. In my hand I carried a notebook and biro; in my pocket I had a paper bag with some of Anthony's ashes, and a few loose Kenyan shillings; and in my sock, as well as my wristwatch, I'd stuffed a few banknotes. I sat down in the Thorn Tree Café at the New Stanley Hotel on Kamathi Street. The old tree after which the café was named had been cut down, and its replacement was not much more than a sapling still, so offered very little shelter from the sun. A waiter in a white kanzu and maroon waistcoat, very clean and smart, came and took my order, which was a coffee, please, and make it strong, *asante sana*.

A young man was leaning against the wall of the New Stanley, watching me. His clothes were shabby and dirty. Hurriedly, I opened my notebook, trying to appear busy. But what should I write about? Looking around for inspiration, I found myself meeting his eyes. He smiled, shrugged, and took a few steps towards me.

'I am hungry, Madam.' He had a nice face and a gentle manner.

'I'm just having a coffee,' I said, 'but would you like to join me?'

'The management would not allow it, Memsahib.'

The waiter returned, holding my coffee in one hand and flapping the young man away with the other. But there was something so unthreatening about him that, on impulse, I told the waiter, '*Lete kahawa na maziwa kidogo asante*' then turned and said, 'Or would you prefer *chai*?' I then asked the waiter to bring a fried-egg sandwich too.

I had time to learn little more than the man's name before his tea and sandwich arrived.

When we'd finished and I went to pay the bill, along with the loose coins I mistakenly pulled out the small bag containing Anthony's ashes. Some of the ashes spilled out, and Peterson noticed. So, I explained about Anthony and that I was going to look for a place in the city to scatter his remains.

'That is very strange, Tanzie. Why must you throw your beloved one's ashes around Nairobi?'

'It's not just Nairobi. I'm going to scatter him everywhere.'

'This is very upsetting. He will be far from his ancestors and far from other bits of himself.'

'But he will be part of *everywhere*. He was pleased with the idea of being all over the world.'

'How do you know this?'

My mind went back to a drunken conversation, where Anthony and I had been choosing our top ten *Desert Island Discs*. 'And what three songs would you choose for your funeral service?' he asked, holding his almost empty wine glass to his mouth. Then he put up a hand to stop me answering. 'No – tell me, instead, what would you do with my ashes if I die before you?'

'I'd tie you to the back of an eagle and you would be scattered to the four winds.'

I did my best to tell Peterson about this, the only time Anthony and I had ever discussed his dying. But I found it hard to explain that Anthony was at home anywhere in the world and could relate to anyone. He didn't even need language to communicate. And I found it even harder to convey that Anthony wasn't mine in the sense that he could be reduced to part of my hoard of things. He was always someone I let free. 'He was everyman, Peterson.'

I shrugged, and my shoulder complained, a reminder that it could still threaten me with pain and imbalance.

Peterson regarded me with his head on one side. 'You are the eagle, Tanzie?'

I swallowed. 'I'm part of the eagle. His friends and family are part of it. They all brought empty matchboxes or tobacco pouches to put portions of his ashes in.' I paused, hoping Peterson understood, but his expression was concentrated. 'Then they sent me postcards or photos showing where they had left the ashes, which I stuck next to a world map on the kitchen wall and glued pieces of red string connecting them to the relevant places on the map. The last one was from his brother, from Machu Picchu.' I found myself smiling. 'My favourite is a photo taken in the Sierra Nevada. It shows Anthony's nephew almost disappeared in a mist of ashes, on the side of a mountain.'

'And you have some of Anthony in a paper bag to scatter in Nairobi?'

'Yes, and in Naivasha and Nakuru and the Masai Mara, then I'll go south and throw some in the Knysna River, on the farm in South Africa where one of my brothers lives.'

I was holding the bag in my hand. Peterson leaned forward, took it off me and placed it carefully on the table. 'I salute you, Mr Anthony, Sir,' he said, bringing his hand up to his forehead and looking at the ashes sombrely.

I think Anthony would have enjoyed that small formal gesture.

I returned to the hotel to get some more money, then Peterson and I went to Uhuru Park for me to sprinkle some of the ashes. Peterson said he was going up country tomorrow to visit his brother, who mends bicycles for a living. We walked into the slum of Kibera, where we were a source of interest to children of all ages, who followed us. I felt uncomfortable because it was obvious they were following me, not Peterson, because I was white and they thought I might have money to give them. Miserable in my impotence, I stopped talking. By the time we emerged from the slum, it was too late for me to return to my hotel, and so we ended up in The Modern Green bar.

Peterson's hands have fallen in front of him on the table, his fingernails ragged and dirty. His head has slumped slightly sideways onto his chest, and the movement echoes Anthony's head falling onto my shoulder when he died, making my ears hum with shock. I feel vulnerable. I reach across and place my fingers in the spillage of beer in the spaces between Peterson's fingers. As I drift into sleep, a torn print of Van Gogh's *Sunflowers* hovers in the periphery of my vision. How strange that it should be there, askew and faded on the smeared and grubby mint-green walls of The Modern Green.

A mix of stale beer, smoke, excrement and sweat is heavy in the room. The toxic air feels as though it has penetrated and stiffened my limbs. My tongue is glutinous as it sticks to the roof of my mouth. My waking is like the slow emergence of a tortoise from its shell, stupefied, blinking with sore eyes. The barman opens the metal shutters that secure the entrance, and the morning spills onto the linoleum, white and clean, ballooning sweet air into our faces. I straighten myself painfully and make for the door, my overfull bladder counteracting the delicious feeling of refreshed lungs. I hope I can squat behind a bush, rather than have to use the toilet. Peterson moves slightly but seems reluctant to surface from his sleep. I don't want to leave him. Some of my soul already belongs to him; some of his memory is already mine. I want him to know that I am home in the land of our birth, in the land of his homelessness.

Let's go, I'll say. We'll find a river and sit high on a bank out of reach of crocodiles, and we'll eat bananas and tree tomatoes that we have stolen on our way out of the city, and we'll sleep star shaped alongside each other, with the river at our feet. The river, seen from the air, will be like a thick pencilled line, a rusty copper snake. We will look like splayed frogs to the vultures, like laboratory specimens pinned out for examination. Contrast is our stock-in-trade – male and female – yin and yang – young and old – black and white. But we'll blend ourselves. We'll plaster ourselves in river mud and be the same colour as the elephants and as each other. The mud full of elephant and hippo dung will dry on us like powder in the sun. I will be your mother, or the mud might mask the looseness of my flesh and make me your sister, or your lover, or your brother.

Or we could be one flesh. We could fold into each other like a sacred text closing. We could be one rusted-earth African.

I have to hurry, my bladder hurts. It's so distended I don't think it will be able to release its fluid. I'm going to die, and the pee is going to seep from my body like thin puss from a lanced boil. I can barely walk. I lunge and crash into the undergrowth, struggle with clothing, squat. The pee streams from my body, a yellow transparency edged with froth. Then the earth absorbs it. The relief from pain gives me a strong sense of wellbeing.

I look back at The Modern Green, a dilapidated, crumbling building, square and grey. Behind it is a bank of dry grass, with birds flying above it. I think again of Van Gogh and of crows over cornfields. Some of the women are struggling out of the entrance. I wonder if Peterson has dropped his head on his chest again? I want to go back and drag him out. But I know it's too late.

Running Dreams

The basin is white – shiny, glossy and sacramental white. It stands on a pedestal before the window. It's like an altarpiece. I'm drying my face on the towel, but I can see you through the glass. Today is your wedding day. I have been weaving in and out of the guests on the lawn, smiling, my dress floating about me like a bridal gown. Your guests do not see me, but I'm feeling the strain of being pleasant, so I've come into the cloakroom.

You are on the brow of a slight hill outside the window. Star scattered, daisy showered, you stand with your smile as white as her dress, the stars, the daisies, her happiness. The stars are reflected spangles from the tears that fringe my eyelashes. Who is your bride? Tall, white, sparkling, cleaving to you, she is happy like a trembling marionette. Her hip curves into your side as though the rib she is made of is leaning close to its origins. Her hair falls like a curtain to close you away, hiding you from my bitterness. Does she catch my eye and lift an eyebrow in disdain before she lets the hair swing over you?

I lean my head over the basin. My tears are crystal beads sliding down a rosary string, flashing prisms as they fall into the sink. I retch, but my stomach yields only saliva. Threads of silvered slime spiral out of my mouth. I'm crying and vomiting diamonds along with slivers of sorrow.

The world swims white as I lift my head from the pillow. Because I sleep on my stomach, the world is an enclosed vision of milky cotton when I wake; I must change the colour of my bedding. My face is wet and my heart is wrenched. This is the first dream I've had where you've got married.

You've left me before, in earlier dreams. Everyone knows where you've gone, except me. Our friends have been loyal to you, side-stepping my pleading enquiries, muttering that you are in London, or somewhere else. Finally they've been forced to be brutal, to tell me you don't want to be found.

In my dreams, I have searched for you. I have peered into hearts, probed minds, scanned faces, and stared down cul-de-sacs so banal I could hear a lawn mower purr in a square back garden. Might I have found you planting pansies beside a neat nail-scissored lawn, talking politely to Mrs Brown? I've hunted at high altitudes, tracing the peaks of the Urals, sifted like a comb through the rain forests of the Amazon, searching for a scent of you. My arms have felt the smoothness of slithering through the belly of tropical waters on the back of an anaconda. My hope has been to reach out and touch your smooth nakedness, undulating like a pale underwater plant, as I pass in the swirl of rushing water. I've been a huntress like Diana, crashing down the valleys, following the rivers to the sea with my toes splayed wide. My arrow has been drawn to splinter your heart on the crest of a wave, as you splintered mine in the trough of your dying moment.

I have clung to the folds of the curtains in the theatre and waited for 'curtain up' to reveal you as you strut your hour upon the stage. Are you there, in the Hope Chapel Community Centre, bowing ironically, holding your arm in a crescent shape to receive my body against your heart? Shall we dance? Shall we dance to the music your friend the trombonist dedicated to you? We'll see our reflection in the bottle of cheap red wine on a table somewhere, in the shadow of dreams. Are you there?

Are you shape-shifting in the clouds? Can I see you amongst the stars? Is there a trace of you under my fingernails? Can I feel your presence in the ink of your fountain pen, or in the flow of your handwriting? In dreams, I have flowed down the slide of the ink that told me you loved me, and jerked abruptly when the letters end. Your inky kisses have been one or two. I have traced them slowly, applied my mouth to feel them. They are faint shadows now. They've transferred to my lips, blue black, as if I have a failing heart.

I have squeezed between books, flattened myself wafer thin between the pages of Chekhov, searching for the tone of you. In the stitching of your fifties' brown leather car coat, is there a skin flake of you, trapped for me to find? I have tried to conjure you up, to hear your applause. I have landed a teabag, thrown backwards across the kitchen, into the bin. What a smooth and beautiful arc it made as it sailed past the evidence of failed launches – stains splattered and splayed across the ceiling. Surely now you'll be generous with delight – 'Bull's eye!'

In my dreams, I have searched for you. And finally I have found you, on the slight rise of a hill, amongst daisies, on your wedding day. And I have striven to be jubilant, to celebrate. But I have cried crystals and diamonds into the pedestal basin, and vomited strings of pearls and shards of broken heart.

I must change the colour of my bedding. No more wedding-day white. A wholesome tomato red would be nice.

Outside of my dreams, I have not looked for you. Lion hearted, you called me, and so I have been. Since you left me, I have moved on, with my lion's heart. I sold the house with the tea stains on the kitchen ceiling. I threw salt over my left shoulder, for luck. But still my health got ruined; my looks became distorted with illness, sadness, and age. If you saw me now, you wouldn't find me physically attractive. Do you remember walking between here and there, between now and then, between twilight and sunrise, between dreams and waking? Do you remember that time you took off down Park Street like John Mills in *Ryan's Daughter*? You limped and you lurched and you rolled. You called back to me, 'Would you love me if I walked like this?' And people stared. And I loved you more than ever. But would you love me, now that I am really unsteady on my feet?

I am running. They have told me I must run, or I will die. My captives have given me a choice. Run or die. You are there – on their side. You are challenging me to run or die. If I die, will I be with you? If I run, will you run with me? In my dream, there is a vast green in front of the castle, a flat expanse of land following up to a bank that hides an earth road. I am aiming for the bank. My heels are splintered with gunfire, and I feel its heat. I am running and running, or I will die. I feel you watching from an attic room. I don't understand how you can do that – even if you don't love me anymore. Even if you don't love me anymore, you know that when hearts have been true, they have a way of calling. I know you! I run, with my heart giving out. The gunfire is at my heels, thudding into this floating, swimming silky whiteness, this leg-wrapping wedding dress. I scrape at the dress with my hands and feel it float free. My limbs are released, and I run like a wild wind streaming through the pages of the books, straightening the folds in the curtain, uprooting the daisies, and scattering the teardrop stars. The weight of my hair is snatched backwards and whirls into the maelstrom behind me. And suddenly you are flying beside me. You are running alongside, and we make it to the bank and we collapse on the other side, and the gunfire sounds far over our heads, and you are there. You are at my side. I breathe your air. Your breath is my breath.

I wake up wildly hopeful, but you are not there. I bury my head in my tomato-red pillow.

Well, you are not there. But since that dream when you ran with me, I hear your intake of breath when a teabag drops into the bin. I hear your laughter when I turn to see you, and my lips smile blue with the ink of your kisses.

Alice in Gold and Light

Alice ordered sunshine for her funeral.

The Anglican church was brilliant with sunlight streaming through the stained glass windows. It did not look memorable on the outside; nestled in the centre of the Devon village, it was humble, ordinary and slightly squat. But inside it was luminous. We breathed lemon gold. A tapestry of light, shot through with threads of emerald, spangled with sapphire and spun with streaks of ruby, glimmered all around us. Or did it just seem that way through the magnifying prism of our tears? Watery eyes, whether from emotion or dazzle, made spikes and spirals and rainbows an additional wonder.

Alice requested colourful clothing.

We responded with red, purple and gold. Jewellery flashed at our wrists and throats, hair gleamed, and even baldness shone with patches of colour like an artist's palette under a skylight. People struggled to find even a place to stand, so we shuffled and edged around and tried to make ourselves smaller.

The sudden emotion weeping from a lone bagpipe that heralded Alice's coffin made our breath snag. A rush of icy Highland air, laden with damp earth, swept through our hearts as the piper preceded the coffin.

Alice requested music.

A musician played a sitar to acknowledge her love of India, and colourful saris weaved through tartan in our minds. A Gregorian chant made us feel calmer for a while, then Elgar's 'Nimrod' stirred us again to heightened emotion.

Alice wanted candles lit.

We all lit candles, one flame from another, until hundreds glowed, but they could not compete with the brilliance of the sun's dazzle.

The vicar stepped forward. 'Alice kept an open mind on the afterlife,' he said.

I knew what a big statement that was – Alice was born into a Catholic family, and the cliché 'once a Catholic, always a Catholic' came into my mind. I couldn't help hoping that there was an afterlife, one that would be flooded with the light, colour and music that Alice adored.

Although when Alice and I met at the convent in Shropshire we did not become instant friends, I grew to love her. Her devout Catholicism at the time made her a favourite of the nuns. I would have been beneath her notice were it not for the fact that I was belligerently unhappy and liable to challenge authority and resist Catholic values and doctrine, which led her to take a dim view of me.

After the vicar spoke about Alice's life, of how cultured and refined she was, of how much she loved entertaining despite the fact that she was shy, he said, 'In this present life, Alice would now like you all to come to her party over at the village hall.'

Alice always loved parties. Once she was invited to the Oxford May Ball, and we were all so envious. She received the invite from a student she knew there, whom we imagined to be beautiful, with dark eyes and curls. We would watch her face as she read the small monastic script of his letters, her smile shy and secretive.

When she returned from the ball, we were so dizzy with excitement that our voices spilled around her like falling raindrops.

'How much did you dance…what kind of music did they play…who did you meet…what did you eat…did you sit in a punt, spread your dress beautifully and get oared along the river…were your eyes filled with stars and fairy lights…what happened with the student…did you kiss him lingeringly, or passionately…did somebody else fall in love with you?'

She just laughed.

I swear that for all of us, there was nobody so magical, so lovely, and so charming as the girl who went to the Oxford May Ball.

Alice played tennis. In the late summer evening light, she was like a white swallow, swooping on the ball, flying backwards with wings stretched to parry a baseline ground stroke, reaching up, arching backwards, pulling the racket through the air to retrieve a lob, glancing for the lethal spot to place a smash, a slice, a volley. She was a bird in flight feeding on unseen insects in the twilight. It was mesmerising to watch, to hear the light rush of her feet as she approached the net to block a ball. It was a summer evening ballet.

She was quicksilver. Because we received very little formal education at the convent, where learning to be good Catholics was the most important subject, we tried to gain knowledge from as many other sources as possible. Alice's mind was quick, drinking in poetry, absorbing history, appreciating music and art and culture. She read twice as fast as the rest of us, and understood more swiftly.

Sometimes she was deep water. There was a still quality in her listening, her head slightly forward, her hair falling in front of her cheek to frame, sometimes to hide, her face. Still, like a gazelle, she was more beautiful than ever, listening beyond the wind, hearing through the storm, sifting, interpreting – she might be hearing you beyond your words.

She was funny. She had a hilarious sense of the ridiculous. She loved The Goons, and Pete 'n' Dud, and would imitate them all, with perhaps her best rendition being a deadpan portrayal of deadpan Pete. She could entertain us with all the characters from *The Flowerpot Men*, her favourite being Weed. Any public figure too pompous, any poetry reading too florid, anything too overblown, and Alice was quick to mimic and to puncture.

She was a lovely Viola in *Twelfth Night*, wandering up the beach, lantern in hand, looking about her. Lightly and swiftly she crossed the Illyrian foreshore, on the marble floor of the school hall. Her hair swung back as she delivered Shakespeare's words, thrilling us all. Her performance didn't come easily though due to her shyness, and she would have to be reminded to speak up. But her audience was carried, delighted by her love of character, story and, especially, language.

I won't again hear the thwack of a tennis racket, the rush of light feet, certain music, poems, jokes, references to the Oxford Ball, or see gold light in a window, without remembering Alice. When I look at the moon, I remember a lantern held aloft, revealing a daft and funny face. And I smile.

Casting Away

We are standing by the stream on the floor of the narrow valley, under the trees. Dinah has dressed up, making an effort for the occasion. I am wearing jeans and a jumper.

We have come to scatter my mother's ashes. I can't explain why I haven't done this before now; it's been years since she died. I haven't cherished her ashes either, just left them in a plastic container in the cupboard under the stairs. I have been indifferent to them, elaborately careless of them.

Dinah visited me one day. 'Mama, why don't we go to the old farm in Devon? I'll take a day off work, and we can scatter Edith's ashes.'

'I don't know, Di. It's a long way. Perhaps I might just throw them around the garden when the weather is fine.'

Dinah didn't reply.

I began to notice her silence. 'How's your tea?' I said brightly. 'Do you want some more? I'll go and put the kettle on. I won't be long.'

'Mum!'

Dinah's voice caught me as I rose from the settee, and threw me back to her childhood. It was the voice of anguish, of a girl who didn't want me to rock the boat. Who didn't want me to divorce her father, to move house, to cry.

I sat again, pushed down by her pain.

Dinah had been close to her grandmother. We would have to scatter her ashes. So I began to tell Dinah this, nodding and smiling like an out of control marionette, and I couldn't seem to bring it to an end.

Dinah's voice became adult again, and she spoke softly. 'It's okay, Mama. We'll go to Devon, but if when we get there you feel the time still isn't right, we'll have a lovely day anyway.'

We are deep in the woodland of the property that Edith used to farm. There is a strong breeze making Dinah's flaxen hair fly round her head, and her skirt flows and darkens as the rain begins to slant and drift. She is struggling to stand upright as her heels sink into the rich mud. I see some bluebells further into the wood. When Dinah was small, Edith would often be with her for her birthday. They would share a picnic in Cotswold woods blue in May. I realise that tomorrow would be Edith's birthday.

A buzzard swoops down, following the direction of the narrow dirt road over the humped bridge, both startling and pleasing us.

Dinah tries her sister's mobile, but there is no signal. We wanted Sophie to be with us today but she was unable to get the time off work. 'We'll phone her when we get back up the hill,' Dinah says.

I start to remove the lid of the ashes container. It's jammed. My knuckles turn white as I try to twist it off. Dinah watches. A loud snort escapes from me and stutters into laughter.

'Oh, Dinah,' I say, weak and gasping, unable to stop laughing. Dinah is leaning against a tree, at an odd angle. Her arms are holding her waist and her hair is hanging down, whipping and lashing in the wind. Her shoulders are shaking.

Suddenly the lid gives. Dinah looks up and our eyes lock, hers blue and wide and expectant, and I hold her gaze. Then I swing my arm sideways in a great sweep of calligraphy, and the grey ash pours out into the wind. Some of it blows against a tree, like an artist's highlight describing light to define the trunk; some settles on the bottom of the stream like aquarium gravel; some arches away over the trees.

I'm reeling. I throw down the container as a pain expands in my chest and lodges like a lid that won't come loose. I can't breathe. Dinah moves behind me and wraps her arms around me.

Then a sob wrenches clear, and my weeping begins, flowing with the stream and the wind and the turning of the world. Dinah's arms loosen and I turn to hug her, gathering her in as though she is a hurt child. When she returns my embrace, I lose definition. Am I her mother or her child? It doesn't matter! I laugh, even though my lungs are spongy with crying. When we eventually release one another, we look for some gift of nature to mark this throwing off, casting away, letting go. We find a few flowers, mostly bluebells, and scatter them on the water, where they straggle and bob in remembrance of Edith.

We watch them drift.

'I used to come here with my boyfriends when I was young,' I say after a while.

'Boyfriends?'

'Well, one boyfriend.'

'What did you do?'

'Tickle trout.'

'What?'

'Trout seem to like being tickled. They go all daft and languid.'

'I believe you, Ma. I mean, you would, wouldn't you, come down to the stream with your boyfriend and tickle trout?'

'It sounds silly, I know.'

'Just a bit! Did you love him?'

'Just a bit.'

We struggle up the hill, and as we emerge into the clearing where we left the car, we are breathing heavily. Dinah tries her mobile again. She has a signal. When Sophie answers, she is already crying.

We form a bedraggled huddle – Dinah, me, and the weeping Sophie at the end of the line.

Dappled Things

My trainers squeak against dew-frosted grass as I cross the field to the estuary shore, which is mud coloured, rock strewn and dull. A pony stands with its feet at the water's edge, as though watching the lap of waves in the receding tide and wondering about the green hills on the opposite shore. Below the hills, the dunes are clean and golden, and the water is striated with sand banks. I stop walking and look away from the estuary up to the slope behind me. A row of trees lines its brow, all bent landward and downward away from Channel storms, like misers hunched over their hoards, mean, dark and sinister even on a sunlit morning.

At my feet, I see a head of dandelion seeds, soft and round and perfect, waiting for a puff of wind to keep it local or a storm to snatch it away to distant climes. I'm amazed by its perfection. Then the dog sends it scattering as he barges towards me. *What are we doing? Why are we standing?* Louis looks at the ground. *Is there a mouse, or a frog? Is it my ball? What are you looking at?*

My trance is broken. I clamber down to the shore and throw pebbles and fragments of rock into the water for Louis to fetch. The pony watches him. Birds are noisy in the hedgerows. The water laps gently. What shall I do today? I feel forsaken.

I might drive inland. It's not far to where Edith and Ken used to farm. Perhaps I'll go to The King's Arms for lunch. They've got a garden, so I can take the dog. Will it upset me? Well, it might, but I want to feel connected. But what if I feel nothing at all? That would be even worse.

The road follows the river through dense trees. The light is dappled. Didn't Gerard Manley Hopkins write about dappled things? I feel glad for Hopkins and for the flicker and gentle strobe effect of passing beneath the trees under the sun.

I wonder if Ted Tyler still goes to The King's Arms at lunchtime. It has to be unlikely. When I was young and at home for the summer holidays, Ted used to work as a labourer on the local farms, and he was hired by my stepfather Ken to bring in the wheat harvest. Ted wasn't much older than me. On Sunday lunchtimes we'd take a break, dress up, and go to the village for a drink. Ken would exercise generosity, like landed gentry, and buy selected locals a drink or two…or three. Ted, vigorous, tall and spare, would grin as wide as the Torridge Estuary and raise his pint. 'Cheers, sir,' he'd say. 'Good 'ealth.' He'd drink deep, satisfaction seeping through every parched part of him. Then, blushing deeply, he'd raise his glass to me, and I'd return the gesture, holding up my pint of bitter. I hated bitter but drank it for silly reasons – for Ken and the local men to think I was tough, and to distance myself from the local women, who sipped Babycham from little glasses, and from my mother, who drank gin and tonic.

But I never really knew Ted Tyler. To me, he was little more than a name, a shape, a sound and a few mannerisms thrown together. There can hardly have been more than a few dozen words passed between us. He seemed more respectful than the other labourers though; his wolf whistles were humorous and friendly rather than leery like theirs. He remained a labourer and a bachelor, just adding a sheep or cow to his smallholding every now and then.

About ten years before, I'd also found myself back in Devon, back in the village. I called in at The King's Arms, hoping I might see someone I knew, but no luck. I was just about to leave when I asked at the bar if Ted Tyler was still in the village.

'Yes,' the barman replied. 'And he's in here most lunchtimes – should be here any minute actually.'

But I didn't wait, just left a drink behind the bar for him, 'on behalf of Ken – for old times' sake.' Thinking about it now, driving through familiar country that nevertheless felt strange, this was a patronising thing to do. But all I'd wanted was to reach out. If Ted ever thought about me all those years ago, I must have seemed very alien to him; he certainly was to me.

I pull up at the entrance to a field to let Louis out for a pee. I open the gate, keeping an eye out for the farmer. There are more dandelions. Louis runs about, distributing the seeds. Fluffy white fairies flood the air – dog shaken, spun off to the next moment, the future, the process of regeneration. Louis barrels out of a cloud of seed, creating a dandelion storm. I just want him to empty his bladder so we can leave, but he cocks his leg over and over again, leaving messages for other dogs that may pass this way. My mind fills with thoughts of an irate farmer with several collie dogs weaving in front and behind him, waiting on his bidding. A collie picks up one of Louis' messages and is soon joined by the other dogs, sniffing around, knowing there is a trespasser on their property.

I call Louis and retire to the safety of the car. 'Phew!' I say to him. 'That was close.'

He wags his tail, unruffled by the madness of my imagination.

We arrive at the pub. I put Louis in the garden and go into the bar. I find myself ordering a pint of bitter, and wonder at my choice. I then order a baguette, and while it's being made up, I take my drink outside. A wasp bothers me. Then two. Then more. They are buzzing angrily, and Louis is getting agitated. So, I take him inside and sit by the unlit wood stove.

Although the fireplace is sooty and cold, I imagine there is a fire there, glowing like molten gold and sending warm tongues of flame that light the faces of the drinkers. I picture red and amber flickering in the dog's eyes, and I could swear I hear my mother's laughter above the bar conversation. I catch a glimpse of Ken holding his pint at chest level, listening to a farmer talking about his sheep being maggoty even though they've been dipped. It's not real, of course – Edith and Ken are dead and gone, but I turn my head, just to make sure. A foot rocks rhythmically to and fro in the corner of the snug leading off the main bar. Then a face pops around and gives the room a quick scan. It is unmistakably Ted Tyler. But he didn't recognise me.

When I have finished eating, I return my empty glass to the bar and go into the snug.

'Ted Tyler?'

'Who wants to know?'

'Tanzie Kent.'

His face lights up. He puts down his pint and rises to his feet, unfolding his great height. He beams, spreads his arms like curved wings and steps towards me. 'My word,' he says. Awkwardly, he bends his knees and puts his arms round me, like a crab pulling its claws into itself.

'My word, Tanzie Kent. It's been a time. I know you bought me a drink once, thank you.' He sits down. 'My word, it's been a time,' he says again, obviously noticing how I have aged. In contrast, he wears his years lightly, still with a full head of hair and full set of white teeth, and only faint lines etched around his mouth and eyes. Is it my changed appearance that prompted him to hug me, or is it increased confidence of his own?

'You're looking good,' I say, smiling.

'Yeah, I'm doin' alright. Got asthma though.'

'Have you?'

'Yeah, since my favourite calf got stuck in a ditch. I tried to get her out but the mother, the silly cow, didn't know as how I was trying to help her and butted me full in the chest. I tried again, and she butted me again. Broke some ribs. Had breathing trouble ever since. I'm sixty-eight, you know? I rattle from all the pills I take.'

'I'm sixty-four.'

He regards me carefully. He cannot say that I don't look my age.

'We've got old,' I say, weaving us together.

'Yeah,' he says. 'Things get harder and harder.' He then looks down at Louis. 'There's an 'andsome dog!'

'Yes, he is, isn't he?'

There's a pause between us. I'm thinking with surprise that he has a favourite calf – am I guilty of regarding farm labourers as having blunted sensibilities? I truly hope not, but then why am I feeling surprised? This makes me humble and irritated at the same time.

'Is your calf alright?'

'That was a time ago. 'Tis a cow now. Got 'er out of the ditch alright.'

'Is she still a favourite?'

'Yeah, she is. Don't appreciate the breathing problems she caused me though. I haven't bred any more since her.'

There is another pause between us. I am satisfied. I feel connected, albeit briefly, through the acquaintance of Ted Tyler. Through someone who has always been part of the village, always gone to the pub at lunchtime, always been connected. He is a seed that has fallen close to home.

'Well, nice to see you,' I say.

'Likewise.'

'Until next time, Ted.'

'Yeah, but don't leave it too long – we might run out of time!'

He laughs. He takes a long haul on his pint, swallows hard, and explodes with more laughter. I reciprocate, infected by his sound and enjoying – almost – the joke.

Acknowledgements

I'm so glad Clare Pugh is my editor. She is uncompromising and assured in her work and a generous supporter and friend. She is empowering and inspirational.

My thanks to Marina McArthur, who is so generous with praise and support that I can't begin to do justice to her grace and goodwill. I'm so touched and in need of this quality in the world.

Very many thanks to John Miller for sharp and steady advice, Sarah Scholefield for warmth in which to flourish, and Jo Scriven Derrick for laughter, tea and cake, and for setting an example of hard work and focus.

Thank you Samantha Harvey for quiet and greatly appreciated guidance.

Many thanks to Lesley Gillilan and to Kathryn Hind.

Thanks also to Nick Stanley for kind and sometimes inspiring standing ovations.

Not least, thanks to Louise Gethin, Tessa Hadley and Jan Smith, who made me feel in good company.

Printed in Great Britain
by Amazon